2·50

PENGUIN BOOKS

NUMBER TEN

'She has unrivalled claim to be this country's foremost practicing comic novelist' *Mail on Sunday*

'She has held a mirror up to the nation and made us happy to laugh at what we see in it' *Sunday Telegraph*

'This is a clever book. Satirical, witty, observant, readable' *Observer*

'As ever with Townsend, her brilliance lies in her simplicity . . . It's a great comic novel this tale of two Britains, and should be on the bedside tables of Downing Street' *The Independent*

'Townsend is one of our finest living comic writers . . . This is a wickedly entertaining and passionate swipe at new Labour' *The Times*

'No Townsend novel can fail to entertain . . . fans will find a smile on every page' *The Sunday Times*

'Brilliant satire. Very contemporary, a bit controversial and loads of fun' *The Mirror*

'Few writers have the wit and powers of observation to write a humourous political satire but Townsend's story of PM Edward Clare is spot on' *Sunday Mirror*

'Politicians beware' *Daily Mail*

'Convincing and amusing' *Express*

D1080830

Sue Townsend, with *The Secret Diary of Adrian Mole Aged 13¾* (1982) and *The Growing Pains of Adrian Mole* (1984), was Britain's bestselling author of the 1980s. Her hugely successful novels are *Rebuilding Coventry* (1988), *True Confessions of Adrian Albert Mole, Margaret Hilda Roberts and Susan Lilian Townsend* (1989), *Adrian Mole: From Minor to Major* (1991), *The Queen and I* (1992), *Adrian Mole: The Wilderness Years* (1993), *Ghost Children* (1997), *Adrian Mole: The Cappuccino Years* (1999), *The Public Confessions of a Middle-aged Woman* (2001) and *Number Ten* (2002). Most of her books are published by Penguin. She is also well known as a playwright. She lives in Leicester.

Number Ten

Sue Townsend

PENGUIN BOOKS

PENGUIN BOOKS

Published by the Penguin Group
Penguin Books Ltd, 80 Strand, London WC2R ORL, England
Penguin Putnam Inc., 375 Hudson Street, New York, New York 10014, USA
Penguin Books Australia Ltd, 250 Camberwell Road,
Camberwell, Victoria 3124, Australia
Penguin Books Canada Ltd, 10 Alcorn Avenue, Toronto, Ontario, Canada M4V 3B2
Penguin Books India (P) Ltd, 11 Community Centre,
Panchsheel Park, New Delhi – 110 017, India
Penguin Books (NZ) Ltd, Cnr Rosedale and Airborne Roads,
Albany, Auckland, New Zealand
Penguin Books (South Africa) (Pty) Ltd, 24 Sturdee Avenue,
Rosebank 2196, South Africa

Penguin Books Ltd, Registered Offices: 80 Strand, London WC2R ORL, England

www.penguin.com

First published by Michael Joseph 2003

1

Extract from 'Cargoes' by John Masefield © by kind permission of The Society of
Authors as the Literary Representative of the Estate of John Masefield.

The moral right of the author has been asserted

Set in Monotype Dante
Typeset by Rowland Phototypesetting Ltd, Bury St Edmunds, Suffolk
Printed in England by Clays Ltd, St Ives plc

To Colin, with my love and thanks

Jack Sprat could eat no fat,
His wife could eat no lean,
And so between them both, you see,
They licked the platter clean.

John Clarke
Paroemiologia Anglo-Latina (1639)

Prologue

Edward Clare was cleaning his teeth in the cavernous bathroom in Number Five Ann Street, Edinburgh. He was counting the brushstrokes in his head, as his mother had instructed; never less than 200. He was almost there when he remembered that he had stopped at 150 last night because he had been impatient to get on with his book – one of Mrs Blyton's, concerning the Famous Five and an evil lighthouse-keeper.

When he reached the 200-brushstroke mark he left the washbasin and the comfort of the rubber mat at its base and walked about in his bare feet on the cold linoleum until he had completed 50 more. He knew that God would be looking down on him, and that He would be pleased when He saw that Edward Clare had made up the deficit.

After rinsing his mouth clean of toothpaste, he wiped the washbasin with the ragged cloth that Mummy had hung on the S-bend. He went to the lavatory and carefully lifted the mahogany seat. He dropped his bri-nylon pyjama trousers then took a square of Bronco toilet paper from the dispenser on the wall and wrapped it carefully around his tiny pink penis.

He was still urinating when he heard the telephone ring in the hall downstairs. It rang for a worryingly long time. Mummy was in hospital and couldn't answer, but where was Daddy?

Then he heard the door to the garden slam shut and his father's footsteps running across the parquet floor in the hall, and the ringing stopped. Edward heard his father's voice boom out: 'Percy Clare here.'

Edward shook the last few drops of urine into the lavatory bowl, unwrapped his penis and pulled up his pyjamas. He gave the lavatory chain two short tugs and watched the Bronco paper swirl around the pan before disappearing. When the water in the pan was still he put down the seat. The garden door banged shut and after quickly washing his hands Edward went to the bedroom window and looked out. His father was walking away from him down the crazy-paving path; his shoulders were shaking as they did when he laughed. Edward smiled, anticipating the joke or the humorous anecdote his father would share with him at breakfast later.

Mummy had been in hospital for seven weeks and three days – since Pamela, Edward's sister, was born – and Daddy now talked to him at the breakfast table instead of reading letters or the *Morning Star*.

Yesterday morning his father had asked Edward if he would 'care to learn a musical instrument'. Edward was anxious to eat his Weetabix before they became unpleasantly soggy, so he said quickly, 'Yes, Daddy.' Then named the first instrument to come into his head. 'The guitar.'

His father had laughed. 'The guitar! I think Mum was thinking of something in keeping with . . . I think Mum saw you joining her and her Thursday group, y'know, as part of the string quartet.'

Edward thought about Mummy's Thursday friends. How dull they all were as they took off their coats and hats in the hall. Just ordinary men and women in heavy clothing with sensible shoes and good-natured, plain faces. How happy they looked once they were playing their instruments.

Edward watched his father sit down on the slimy green garden seat that nobody sat on. At first Edward thought that his father was still laughing – his face was set in a wide-mouthed grin. Edward smiled at the sight. Daddy had been gloomy lately, since Mummy had gone to the hospital. Perhaps the phone call had been from the doctor with the black moustache and red lipstick. Perhaps Mummy would be coming home.

Edward was pleased that his prayers had been answered. He glanced at the vividly coloured picture of Jesus that hung above his bed. Jesus was carrying a lamb under his left arm; in his right hand he carried a shepherd's crook. Other lambs milled around Jesus's bare feet. Edward's father had sometimes grumbled about the picture, saying, 'Eddy, your bloody Jesus looks like Errol Flynn in drag.' But Mummy must have liked Edward's Jesus picture, because once a week she cleaned the picture glass with pink Windowlene and made it sparkle.

Edward struggled to open the sash window. Eventually it rose high enough for him to get his head between the gap. He smelled the rot of autumn air and heard a noise so terrible coming from his father that he was almost sick with fear. His father was wailing like those foreign women on the television news.

Edward pulled his head back inside his bedroom and ducked down under the window. He sat with his back to the wall. With luck his father hadn't seen him. He felt inside his pyjamas and held his little penis in his hand. Mummy had told him not to touch himself down there, but Edward knew that – as of this morning – his mummy would never find out.

Edward didn't go to school that day. He sat quietly in his room and read two chapters of his book.

People began to come to the house. The musicians, his father's friends the communists, the neighbours, the congregation of the Anglican church where Heather played the organ at weddings, christenings and funerals.

Nobody actually told Edward that his mother was dead. Tearful relations grabbed him and wept over his head.

His favourite aunt, Jean, said to him, 'Oh, Eddy, what will we do without her?'

But everybody thought that somebody else had told him, so nobody ever did. In the days before the funeral Edward turned into a spy. He listened at doors; he read every scrap of paper.

He was trying to detach a fossil from a rock face on a school trip to Bamburgh at the precise moment that Mummy was being burned to bits and turned into ashes. The adults around him had decided that it would be too distressing for such a little boy as he to attend a funeral. He had overheard Auntie Jean say to his father, 'He can't go, Percy. The poor kid was unnaturally close to his mother.'

He gleaned from this conversation that Pamela, the sister he had never seen, was to be taken to a country called England where she would live with Auntie Jean and Uncle Ernest.

At eleven o'clock on 1 October 1959 he stopped chipping away at the rock face and took out the piece of paper that was headed 'The Funeral Service of Heather Mary Clare'.

He imagined his mother inside a coffin. What was she wearing? Had somebody combed her hair? Was she properly dead? What if the doctor with the red lipstick and black moustache had made a mistake and his mother was not dead – just sleeping? Hadn't his father said to one of his communist friends that the doctor was a disgrace to the fucking National Health Service?

Edward clutched the funeral-service paper and knelt on the sand. Shards of rock pressed painfully into his bare knees but Edward ignored the pain. He tried to pray to Jesus, but his head was filled with a picture of his mother waking up inside her coffin and shouting to him to set her free. But how could he? He was more than 100 miles away. If he set off now and caught a fast train he would still be too late.

Mr Little, the geology teacher, shouted, 'Clare, get a move on. We've only got half an hour before the tide turns.' The other little boys tapping at the rock looked up briefly, relieved that it wasn't them being admonished by the fierce Mr Little; it was Clare, the boy who wept for no reason at all at various times of the school day.

Jack Sprat first realised that he was poor, dirty and from a disreputable family when he was sent by his mother to a neighbour's house to borrow a saucepan. He was six years old and was wearing plimsolls in the snow. It was his older brother Stuart's turn to wear the Wellingtons. Stuart had been sent to the shop with a note begging for credit, a white sliced loaf, two tins of beans and ten Woodbines.

Jack looked at the red carpet and felt the warmth of the radiator on the wall near the front door. He could see into the kitchen at the end of the passageway. Four saucepans were standing on the hob of the cooker. Steam was rising from under the lids and there was a smell that made his mouth leak.

Graham's mother came into view and said, 'Jack, where's your coat?'

He replied, 'I don't know.'

She said, 'You can't walk around in your shirtsleeves in this weather. Does your mum know you're out?'

He told her that his mum had sent him to ask if she could borrow us a saucepan; theirs had burned out 'cause Mum had fell asleep and let the potatoes burn.

Mrs Worth stared at him and said incredulously, 'You've only got one saucepan?'

'Yes,' Jack said.

Graham Worth looked at his mother and laughed. The lovely smell from their kitchen was like a luscious brown thing shimmering in the air between them all.

'Shut the door and come in,' she said irritably.

Jack closed the front door and walked down the passageway. Graham Worth went into the front room, lay belly-down on a blue fluffy rug in front of the gas fire and resumed watching *Blue Peter*. There was a waste bin next to the fireplace with a piece of orange peel caught on the rim. As Jack watched, Graham reached his hand out and when he brought it back he was holding the orange he'd been peeling before he had got up and answered the door.

Graham's mother was bending down and rummaging around in a noisy cupboard full of metal things. Eventually she straightened up and Jack saw that she had a saucepan and lid in her hands. She wiped the interior of the saucepan with a red-and-white checked teatowel then placed the lid on top and handed the saucepan to Jack.

'You should be wearing a coat,' she said angrily to him.

'Stuart's got it,' answered the boy in his peculiar deep voice.

She watched Jack walk away down her neat path, swept free of snow, and cross the frozen car tracks in the road and make his way towards his own house at Number Ten. The broken toys, rubbish and old car tyres that littered the Sprats' small front garden were hidden by a merciful covering of snow. For once the house looked as neat and respectable as the others in the street.

Chapter One

It was 30 March and Constable Jack Sprat was standing on the doorstep of Number Ten Downing Street, sweating inside his bulletproof jacket and talking to the Prime Minister. The sun was shining through the Prime Minister's thinning hair. A car had just brought him back from the Angolan embassy.

'How's your mother, Jack?'

'She's getting over it slowly; I'm going up to Leicester to see her tonight, thank you, sir.'

'Mugging's a very real problem,' said the Prime Minister.

Jack, who had last seen his mother with her face covered in black bruises like storm clouds, agreed with him.

The Prime Minister squeezed the top of Jack's arm and whispered, 'Tell her I'll pray for her, Jack. God listens.'

Jack was not comforted. He watched as the Prime Minister gave his shy smile to the cameras opposite before unbuttoning the jacket of his navy-blue suit and waving to the photographers. An unseen hand opened the door and the Prime Minister disappeared inside.

Jack spoke into the tiny microphone pinned to his lapel and confirmed that the PM had arrived safely. Jack doubted if the Prime Minister's prayers would make much of a difference to his mother. She was an avowed atheist who had stopped believing in God when Jack's brother, Stuart, had died in a squalid room in Bristol from an injection of adulterated heroin.

A voice in Jack's ear told him that Ms Amelia Badstock and a group of teenage supporters were on their way to Number Ten to present a petition demanding recreational facilities for the youth of Newtown Linford.

He muttered 'OK' and prepared for the first of five petitions that were expected that day.

It was an ordinary day at Number Ten. The shiny black door opened and closed hundreds of times, admitting trades people, florists, dictators, an oil sheik, a pensioners' group, civil servants, a manicurist, spin doctors, Poppy's nanny, Su Lo, cabinet ministers, secretaries and MI5 operatives posing as telephone engineers.

Visitors were so used to seeing a policeman standing in the vicinity of the door that they tended to forget that behind the uniform and under the helmet was a sentient being with ears and a brain. Jack heard bits of conversation and pieces of dialogue and he stored them in his memory.

Inside, the Prime Minister was talking about saving Africa to his closest political friend and colleague, his press officer, Alexander McPherson.

McPherson had enjoyed notoriety at an early age. He was

the youngest of six children, five of them girls, and throughout his childhood was petted and indulged by his elder
sisters to such an extent that unless he got his own way he
would fly into a rage and stage spectacular tantrums in the
shopping street of the commuter village where they lived.

His first memory was of being wheeled around the garden
in a doll's pram while his sisters bickered over whose turn
it was to push him next. He took female attention for
granted and had lost his virginity by the age of thirteen. His
sisters had a taste for novels that featured strong heroines –
Wuthering Heights, *What Katy Did*, *Lolita* – and they would
read to him at bedtime.

After leaving Balliol College, Oxford, he drifted into
publishing and became the letters-page editor of an erotic
magazine called *Fetish*; with *Krafft-Ebing* at his elbow he
composed scurrilous answers to the mostly sad and sometimes boastful letters he received from readers.

There was an ugly rumour doing the rounds at one time
that McPherson's first contact with Edward Clare was via
such a letter, but the truth was that their first meeting
had been at Cambridge when McPherson had taken several
of his girlfriends to see an amateur rock band called Vile
Insinuations. The future Prime Minister was playing bass
guitar and wore his hair in shoulder-length ringlets.
However, McPherson had left in disgust, taking his girls
with him, when Clare announced the band's next number
by saying, 'I hope you enjoy this one, it's called "Rockin'

Round the Cross" and was inspired by Almighty God.'

Their paths next crossed at a fund-raising reception at the House of Commons, where publishers were invited to contribute to Labour Party funds. McPherson stumped up fifty pounds and told Edward Clare, then still in opposition, what needed to be done if Labour were to win an election.

'You've gotta bland everything out, you've gotta duck and dive, you've gotta be all things to all men and you've gotta appeal to the women and so long as you're never pictured in the press kicking a dog to death or something like that, and so long as you smile nicely and remember your manners, and so long as you let me manage the media, you'll get in.'

The pair were now in the private sitting room of Number Ten. A GCSE geography coursework folder lay on the coffee table.

'We can save Africa, Alex.' The Prime Minister's voice shook with emotion.

Alexander swung his big-framed fleshy body up from the arm of the cream sofa where he had been perching and began to roam around. 'Africa?' he said. 'You are, of course, joking?'

It was not a rhetorical question. In Alexander's opinion, not only was Africa the white man's graveyard, but also wanting to *save* Africa was a sign of serious mental derangement. Nothing and nobody could save Africa apart from the Africans themselves.

Alex said, 'Tell you what, Ed, it's perhaps not a good idea to talk about Africa at the moment, not when we're still trying to get the trains to run on time.'

But Edward was ready for him. 'Africa is a dark stain on the conscience of the world. Somebody must lead the people out of the darkness of dying economies and into a sense of fiscal responsibility.'

Alex said impatiently, 'Ed, we've gotta sort out fox hunting before we can start arsing about with the African subcontinent.'

Edward said quietly, 'I do wish you wouldn't swear, Alex. Adele's in the next room feeding Poppy.'

Alex said, 'Excuse me if I larf, but isn't Adele the one who wrote a book called *Arseholes in History*?'

Edward's smile slipped for a moment, then he said, 'That was a book of serious scholarship. Henry Kissinger told me he has it on his bedside table.'

Adele shouted from the next room, 'And it was at the top of *The New York Times* bestseller list for twelve consecutive weeks.'

'Anyroadup,' said Alexander, 'can we sort out a few things, Ed? We've got an arse of a week. There are half a dozen reports out, crime's up, and, according to the Rowntree Trust, five outta ten of the population are outta their minds on drink or drugs at any given time. Oh, and the mortuary workers are striking on Monday unless they get a ten per cent pay rise and a thirty-five-hour week.'

Edward said, 'In Africa a little kid dies every ten seconds from a water-borne disease.'

Alex replied, 'Yeah, my heart bleeds at the thought, but we'll be knee-deep in fuckin' corpses if we don't sort the body-washers out, and the hot weather's on the way, according to Michael Fish-face, so can I steer you back to *this* dark continent, Ed?'

David Samuelson came into the room preceded by the smell of Eau Sauvage. He had been uncharacteristically ham-fisted with the nozzle of the bottle that morning but hadn't had time to change his shirt or jacket, which were now permeated with the stuff.

Samuelson was a grandee of the labour movement. His grandfather, Hector Samuelson, had organised the very first Ideal Home Exhibition at Earl's Court, which had broken all attendance records when the average number of visitors exceeded 300,000 a day.

This exhibition, with its revolutionary steam irons, non-stick frying pans and sputnik-influenced coffee tables, was credited with awakening the British public's desire for consumer durables and kick-starting a manufacturing boom.

Hector Samuelson's grandson, David, had been described by a contemporary at Oxford as 'fiendishly clever'; another contemporary, to whom he still owed a large sum of money, had described him as 'a fiend'.

His homosexuality was the least interesting thing about him. His taste in Portuguese waiters was well known and he had settled in a vast stuccoed house in Ladbroke Grove so as to be near a lot of them. The press occasionally photographed him with one of his waiter friends, but there is a limit to how long the public's interest can be maintained – after all, one handsome Portuguese youth in a waiter's uniform looks very much like another.

Samuelson's vice was money, and he had a love of luxury. He had grown up visiting the mines and factories of the industrial north where his grandfather and father had been Labour MPs. Even as a little boy he had recoiled from the smells and textures of working-class life and the breath and living spaces of working-class people. Even the food on their plates was crowded together and spilling over the edge.

At grammar school he had excelled in history and shown a mature and sympathetic understanding of the development of the labour movement in Britain. He had occasionally been moved to tears by archive accounts of the bedraggled, half-starved child mill-workers who had fallen asleep on their barefoot journeys from the factory to their overcrowded hovels.

He much preferred the working classes of the textbook to their reality, which he abhorred, shuddering when he heard their coarse voices raised in the street. He did not hate them as an entity – some of them came to his parties – but he longed for a time when there was a Parmeggiano grater in every cutlery drawer in the land.

Samuelson said with his usual dramatic delivery, 'I simply *have* to talk to you, Eddy.'

Alexander said, 'We're in the middle of a meeting, Dave.'

Edward looked at David, who said, 'No, you should hear this, Alex, it's important. I've studied the focus-group feedback. I haven't slept, but it doesn't matter,' he added in a martyred tone. 'It's time to change the party's image completely and for good, starting with the name. I've been putting out feelers and I think the time is now.'

Edward and Alexander sat for a full two minutes without interrupting while David outlined his plans. 'We take "Labour" out of the party's name. The word Labour has totally negative connotations; it's associated with sweat and hard work, trade unionism and protracted and painful childbirth. Think about it: most of us don't even break into a sweat at work and most aspirational mothers are opting for Caesareans by appointment – like Adele.'

Alexander said dryly, 'If we drop the "Labour" from "New Labour" we're left with one word: "New". Sorry, but it doesn't set my bollocks on fire.'

Edward asked, 'You got some suggestions, David?'

David scraped his hair back from his forehead with long pale fingers. 'No, I've just identified the problem. I want your go-ahead before I focus on a solution.'

Edward said, 'Are you suggesting we keep "New"?'

Alexander said, 'How can we keep "New"?' "New" was only new in 1997; it's bollocking old now.'

Edward said, 'You'd better go ahead and focus on the solution, David. Otherwise we're left with nothing. Nothing at all.' He stared down at a security report on Bob Marshall Andrews MP, QC, that lay on his desk and required his signature, but he saw nothing. His party had no name. He felt himself begin to disintegrate and dislocate. He excused himself and went into his private bathroom, where he locked the door then sat on the side of the bath before taking two sheets of Bronco toilet paper from a packet he kept in a cupboard under the washbasin and wrapping them expertly around his penis. After a few moments of stillness he flushed the paper away, washed his hands and smiled into the convex shaving mirror, which hugely magnified his face and reassured him that he was still there.

He came back into the sitting room to find Alex and David arguing about the fox-hunting bill. David was looking into the viability of using holograms of foxes beamed from satellites in outer space on to the hunting shires across Britain. Alexander was saying, 'They can crucify the furry red bastards for all I care. I'm sick to death of the whole fucking debate.'

After they had gone Edward sat at his desk and signed the paper that permitted MI5 to bug the house, car and office of Bob Marshall Andrews, MP, QC.

Adele came in and said, 'Ed baby, stay and be charming to a journalist for me will you? Give her your smile and stroke my hair in front of her. Her name is Suzanne Nicholson, she's the women's editor of *Joy*. It's a new mag and I'm going to be on the front cover.'

Adele's nose was extraordinarily large. Her father, Guy Floret, had remarked on seeing her for the first time, only moments after she had been born, '*Mon dieu, ma pauvre enfant. Elle est Pinocchio.*'

Edward nuzzled between her milky-smelling breasts and said huskily, 'You should be the centrefold, Adele baby.'

'He's so *sweet*,' whispered Suzanne Nicholson after the Prime Minister had kissed his wife, stroked her hair and left the room, closing the door quietly, almost apologetically, behind him.

Adele pulled her long thin legs under her and took a sip of her camomile tea. 'He is sweet but he's not *saccharine*.'

Suzanne thought about her own husband, who had slammed out of the house at seven a.m. after shouting at the bedroom door, 'You're a fucking stupid bitch.'

He was angry because she had confessed to him that she had left his three bespoke suits in one of the 315 dry cleaners in central London. The ticket had mysteriously disappeared from each of her many handbags – was not in any pocket of any garment owned, could not be found in either car or in any drawer or cupboard at home or at work.

After a week of prevarication she had burst into tears and told him the horrible truth. She had blamed the incident on the stress of having to prepare for the Adele Floret-Clare interview. 'She's the cleverest woman in the world,' she'd wailed. 'What am I going to ask her? She'll eat me alive!'

Suzanne watched as Adele lifted a telephone and said in a nasal drawl, 'Wendy love, we'd love some more of that *fantastic* tea.'

Suzanne scribbled in rapid shorthand: 'The nose is awesome. Flawless skin, professional make-up, teeth whitened (recently), shoes Prada, check price at Bond Street store. Pleb accent more pronounced when on phone.'

Adele was making small sympathetic sounds down the phone to an obviously distressed Wendy. She then looked at her watch, mouthed 'One minute' to Suzanne and said briskly into the handset, 'Amputation is the only sensible option.' She went to put the phone down but Wendy was obviously trying to have a conversation.

'Not now, Wendy, I'm in the middle of something . . .'

She put down the telephone and smiled at Suzanne. 'I dunno, you ring for a cup of tea and get drawn into somebody else's psycho-drama. Poor Wendy, our housekeeper. Her son Barry – a complete yob, between you and me – mangled his leg in a motorbike accident. The leg won't heal, he's loitering about in a hospital bed on very expensive antibiotics . . . Of course, this is totally off the record . . .'

Suzanne put on her serious face. 'It goes without saying, you've got copy approval . . .'

'I shouldn't have told you about poor Wendy, but I can't help empathising with the staff and their little problems . . .

Sorry, I'll try and stop worrying about Wendy and Barry now. Go on, fire away.'

Suzanne glanced down at her list of questions. 'OK. What's it like to be named by *People* magazine as the cleverest woman in the world?'

Adele laughed. 'Oh, it wasn't the world,' she said, lowering her eyes modestly. 'It was only Europe.'

Suzanne moved on to question two. 'What's a typical day in Adele Floret-Clare's life?'

Adele laughed. 'There's no such thing as a typical day; and, speaking as a philosopher, there's actually no such thing as "life" or "day". I mean, what do you mean by "life" and "day"?'

Suzanne felt her temples begin to throb. 'OK. What did you do yesterday, then?'

Adele appeared to be puzzled. 'Yesterday, as in the previous twenty-four hours?'

Suzanne wanted to shout at the cleverest woman in Europe but then the door opened and a gaunt-faced woman with red puffy eyes came in carrying a tray on which sat a glass teapot and a plate of Scottish shortbread fingers arranged in a fan pattern.

When the tray had been set down, Adele gave a little laugh and said to the woman, 'Wendy love, are you trying to kill us? *Shortbread?* My God, the *fat*, the *sugar*!'

Wendy said, 'I was told by central supplies to buy British.'

'But what about those oatcake thingies we used to have?'

'They're made under licence in Poland now,' said Wendy.

Adele stirred the sachets of tea inside the pot and at the same time she checked her watch. She said, quite sharply, to Wendy, 'About Barry's leg. He'll still be able to get about. Last week Edward and I presented a Children of Courage Award to a boy who had both of his legs amputated by a heritage steam train. He plays wheelchair basketball now . . .'

Suzanne glanced at Wendy and was pleased to see a look of pure venom directed at Adele's back before she closed the door.

'So, back to your fascinating question. The alarm goes at five-thirty but we're usually up by then. It's a precious time, before the world crashes in on us. But it's *yesterday* you want to know about . . . Yeah, so it was up at five, Ed made tea, and we talked. We have a rule: no politics, no family. It was a good conversation.'

'About?' Suzanne asked, though she didn't expect to be told.

'Oh, it was about transubstantiation.'

'Transubstantiation,' said Suzanne, hesitantly. 'That's nothing to do with transport?'

Adele laughed. 'I see you're no theologian, Suzanne.' She leaned back and put her hands behind her head. 'Transubstantiation is to do with the conversion of the Eucharist . . . Is the bread and wine wholly subsumed into the body of Christ?' she said earnestly.

'Fascinating,' murmured Suzanne, who had only a vague idea of what the Eucharist was.

Adele took a sip of tea and pulled a face. 'This is not camomile, it's Lapsang souchong. Honestly. The sooner Barry's leg comes off the better it'll be for us all.' She continued with the previous day's engagements. 'At six, after prayers for Ed and meditation for me, Ed switched on the *Today* programme, he bathed, I showered then Wendy came in with a continental breakfast, then it was feed Poppy, whom I'm still breast-feeding, hair, manicure, kiss children off to school, ten minutes with the papers. Talk to Wendy about the food for the Manchester United Wives and Girl-friends Association reception here at Number Ten. Car to LSE, give lecture on the Feminisation of Western Man. Car back here. Write eight hundred words for *Spectator* on e-mail overload, and then lunch with Camilla P. B., who's promised to teach me to ride when we go to Highgrove next week. Then what? Yes, I fed the baby, did some shoe shopping with Gail Rebuck, met a delegation of nuns from Rwanda, came upstairs, had a sandwich with the older children, Morgan and Estelle. He's doing GCSEs and she's just started at Camden School for Girls. Car to tennis lesson with Andre, back here, shower, hair, make-up. Made phone calls, wrote letters, sent emails, fed baby again, reception with Man-U Wives. Ed came – he adores football. Then, oh yes, went upstairs to kids, helped Morgan with *King Lear* essay. Hair, make-up, changed clothes, dined at French embassy with Charlotte Rampling and Eddie Izzard. Agreed to . . .'

Suzanne, who was a fan of Eddie Izzard, said, 'What's Eddie like?'

Adele said, 'He was wearing black tights with red shoes and he seemed to be laughing at a private joke. I didn't warm to him.'

After Wendy had shown Suzanne out Adele sat alone and replayed the interview in her head. She knew that Suzanne had disliked her. She had known since she was a little girl that cleverness was something that should be kept hidden. Her grandmother had warned her, 'Nobody likes a smart-arse, Adele.' She sometimes envied those thick people who were Ed's constituents, with their banal small talk and their trivial preoccupations. She touched the side of her nose and wondered if she should have it fixed. Ed constantly told her he loved her nose, and he would kiss the length and breadth of it. But she was tired of carrying it in front of her like a warning flag.

As soon as Suzanne was outside the door of Number Ten, she switched on her mobile phone. Jack Sprat, who was admiring Suzanne's legs, heard her say, 'She's an absolute cow,' as she walked away.

He smiled to himself, knowing exactly the cow she was talking about.

Chapter Two

Adele Floret-Clare was born in Paris, the illegitimate child of an English Folies Bergère mother and French accountant father. She was brought up in Hoxton by a grandmother who rose at four a.m. and cleaned offices so as to be able to send Adele to a private school where she felt the other schoolgirls would not tease Adele about her nose. She was wrong: her granddaughter's nickname at school was Le Nez. Adele was the author of four books of popular philosophy. Her first was published when she was nineteen and had become an international bestseller. Its provocative title, *God is a Lesbian*, ensured massive press, radio and television coverage. Adele was asked many times if she herself was a lesbian. She was always careful to give an ambiguous answer, thereby titillating the questioner and ensuring that her name and photograph regularly appeared not only on the book pages but also on the gossip and news pages.

By the time she was twenty-one Adele was a visiting professor at the Sorbonne and had published two more books: *Philosophers' Wives* and *Wittgenstein: The moron behind the myth*.

She had a small flat in St Martin's Lane, London, and a permanent hotel room at the Hôtel Rivoli in Paris.

She had been happy: she was young, healthy, elegant, clever, successful, respected and famous. Unfortunately, Adele heard voices inside her head. Voices that spoke to her using words that were vile and obscene. She saw psychiatrists in London and in Paris, but in neither language did she gain relief. Psychotropic drugs had no effect. The voices continued to jabber and accuse her of heinous crimes. Once, when she was being interviewed by Melvyn Bragg on *The South Bank Show*, the voices charged her with being implicated in the disappearance of Shergar, the racehorse. She had responded out loud: 'Don't be bloody absurd.' This had startled Melvyn, who had actually asked her if Plato had intentionally influenced Alexander the Great into extending the Greek Empire. Her angry reply had not been edited from the tape as it was considered to be good television.

When Adele Floret met Edward Clare he was the newly elected MP for Flitwick East. It was at a reception for Gore Vidal and it was a cataclysmic experience for them both. After a few minutes of intense small talk – about the proliferation of weapons in the Gulf States – it became obvious to them both that they would fall in love. Edward could not take his eyes off her magnificent nose.

When Gore himself was brought over to talk to them they were indifferent to his drawled revelations about a screen goddess, the head of the CIA and an Afghan hound.

After Edward had expressed concern for the dog, they excused themselves and left shortly afterwards in a black cab.

Once the cab had turned the corner they had thrown themselves into each other's arms. Edward had shouted to the driver to drive around the city until told to stop. The driver was unimpressed by this romantic gesture and had said that he was on his way home to Golders Green where his dinner was waiting. Edward had said, 'OK, take us to Golders Green.'

By a massive stroke of luck a young man had jumped from the flyover on the Edgware Road and fallen under the wheels of their cab.

Adele was impressed by the way that Edward had taken charge – he had calmed the hysterical cab driver and removed his own suit jacket and covered the dead man's head.

Edward had not wanted the night to end. Adele was a fabulous woman – she had such *style*, such *control*. Seconds after the young man had fallen in front of the windscreen she had remarked through the squeal of brakes, 'An Achilles in the Edgware Road.' This unpleasant incident quickly led them down pathways that they might have taken months to tread in the normal course of things.

They had known each other for less than two hours when Edward confessed to Adele his political ambitions. Indeed, until he met Adele he hadn't quite realised what these ambitions were himself. But with her in his arms he felt like Superman; and, like Superman, he would save the world if given the chance.

When the statements had been made to the police and the blood had been washed off the road, they went back to Edward's tiny *pied-à-terre* in Westminster. Adele explored the floor-to-ceiling bookshelves which lined the walls while he made bitter-tasting coffee in the kitchenette.

When he brought the cups and saucers through into the sitting room he saw her applying a spray of Yves Saint Laurent's Paris between her breasts. She was not in the least embarrassed. She had re-buttoned her cream silk shirt and said, 'I'm feeling incredibly aroused. I can't decide whether it's the proximity to violent death or to you!'

She noticed a guitar propped in a corner and asked if he could play. He had just picked it up, by way of reply, and played the opening chords of 'Brown Sugar'. In a Pavlovian response she had leaped to her feet and strutted Jagger-like around the small room – one arm in the air. They were made for each other. Such was her euphoria that she took a chance and told him about the voices in her head. He gave her the name of a pal of his at Cambridge who was now a cutting-edge psychiatrist. He assured her that when a Labour government came to power mental-health services would be a top priority.

Each had found their other half. Adele was going to be married to the future Prime Minister.

A month or so later they attended the coroners' court together and found out that the young suicide was called Mohammed Karzai and that he had killed himself because his A-level grades were not good enough to get him into Sheffield University, where his parents were keen for him to study pharmacy.

As Edward and Adele left the court arm in arm, Adele had remarked, 'How horribly ironic: poor dumb Mohammed topped himself in front of two of the cleverest people in Britain.'

Police Constable Jack Sprat often wondered why he had been accepted into the police force at all; if there was a rigorous vetting procedure then Jack had somehow wriggled through it, and had landed what he thought was the best job in policing – that of guarding the door of Number Ten Downing Street.

He was the black sheep of a large extended family. None of whom had ever bought a video recorder from a shop.

When, at thirteen, he had announced to his family that he intended to study for eight GCSEs and would require 'somewhere quiet to revise' they were mystified. Neither his brother nor his sister had shown the slightest interest in examinations; both had left school at the earliest legal opportunity.

Trevor, his last stepfather, was a mildly successful career criminal. They now had a full set of saucepans. He made inquiries among his criminal friends as to where he could lay his hands on a desk, but after waiting a few weeks with no result he generously ordered a corner study centre, comprising a desk and bookshelves, from the furniture section of Littlewoods catalogue. It arrived by Parcel Force three weeks later in seventeen parts with an Allen key and seventy-five screws, wooden dowels and a tube of glue Sellotaped to one of the drawer fronts. As he watched his stepfather swear and fumble over the desk's assembly, Jack had felt his heart beating with excitement. He couldn't wait to place his books on the shelves and arrange his school folders in the pigeon-holes.

There was no room for the desk in the bedroom Jack shared with his acquisitive brother, Stuart, so the furniture in the small living room was moved around to accommodate his ambitions. The television was shifted from one corner, which necessitated rewiring and changing the aerial socket, and the three-piece suite was reconfigured, which meant that the dog's basket had to be moved and placed under the kitchen table, where it stayed inconveniently for seven years until the dog died.

With the money he earned from his newspaper round, Jack bought himself a desk lamp from Boots and night after night, to the accompaniment of *Coronation Street* and other TV programmes, sat enclosed in a pool of yellow light.

Occasionally, during the advertisements, his mother would turn her head and look at Jack stooped over his desk and mutter to Trevor, 'It's not healthy for a lad of his age to be in at night.'

Occasionally, when Jack was at school in the day, Norma would surreptitiously pick up a folder, open it and read a few pages, moving her lips slightly as she did so. 'The blood on Lady Macbeth's hands is a symbol of the guilt she feels for murdering . . .' She would close the folder, feeling proud but wondering where she had gone wrong. Her other children seemed happy enough, so why was Jack concerning himself with blood and murder?

Once, at Sunday dinner, seated at the kitchen table with his feet on the dog's back, Jack had tried to explain to his family that with exams he would be able to get ahead in the world and get a good job.

'Such as what?' said his stepfather, hacking at a piece of Yorkshire pudding.

Jack hesitated. The dog shifted beneath his feet. He pronged a few peas and lifted the fork to his lips. 'I want to be a policeman,' he mumbled before swallowing.

There was silence, and then a huge burst of laughter. His sister, Yvonne, spluttered on a half-chewed piece of lamb and mint sauce.

His brother Stuart said, 'You gotta be jokin'!'

Stuart had recently served five months in a young offenders' centre, having been caught by security guards in a warehouse with a carrier bag full of Head & Shoulders shampoo.

Jack's entire extended family were petty criminals. It was the family business. Almost every object in the house and most of the clothes on their backs had either been stolen or bought fraudulently with forged cheques. Jack's shoes, the ones the dog was licking, had been thieved by a loving uncle from the back of a lorry parked in a motorway car park.

Even Jack's first clothes – a layette consisting of vest, nappy, plastic pants, Babygro, cardigan and shawl – had been stolen in one daring expedition from a Mothercare shop by his auntie Marilyn.

Most nights Jack sat at his desk, with his back to the television, doing his homework. Occasionally, perhaps when the laughter of a studio audience became hysterical, he would turn round and look at the screen. His mother enjoyed these brief moments and tried to persuade him to put his pen down and join her on the sofa – sometimes she moved the ashtray and patted the seat next to her invitingly – but Jack knew that if he abandoned his studies he would be lost for ever and would become an invisible and expendable person like most of the people he knew.

On Friday nights a gloomy woman called Joan came to the house to style his mother's hair into the platinum beehive she had worn since she was a precocious schoolgirl. Norma didn't seem to notice that her face had suffered a flesh landslide, or that the blue eye-shadow and pale-pink lipstick were now inappropriate for a woman whose tired womb had long been replaced with oestrogen supplements. And her clothes! They were the stuff of nightmares.

It was partly due to his mother's clothes that Jack had become a policeman. He remembered the annual parents' day at the comprehensive school that he attended without fail every day. He had tried to prevent his mother from coming – telling her that she would get fed up waiting in a queue to talk to his boring teachers – but she had insisted, saying, 'It'll make a change to hear 'em saying nice things about one of my kids.'

The elder Sprats had disgraced the Sprat name and Yvonne Sprat had accidentally set fire to the store room of the domestic-science unit by leaving a cigarette burning on the edge of a shelf.

Jack watched anxiously from the landing as Norma hovered in front of her crammed wardrobe.

He stopped breathing when she dragged a mock-ocelot jacket from a wire hanger, then breathed again when she threw it on to the bed saying, 'I can't get it buttoned since me tits got bigger.'

Eventually, after much trying on and discarding and consultation with his sister, she settled on a white plastic bomber jacket and matching short skirt, thus realising Jack's worst fears.

They left the house together but Jack quickly outpaced her. At first she shouted at him to wait for her, but he couldn't bring himself to walk alongside her. He was ashamed of her varicose veins stuffed into white stilettos, and the creak of the white plastic suit.

He burned with shame when they entered the school and were greeted by the headmaster. 'Mrs Sprat, is it? You've got a good lad there, we've got great hopes for Jack.'

Jack could see the amused look in the headmaster's eyes as the pompous git took in his mother's appearance. The hanging flamingo earrings, the globs of mascara on the ends of her stubby eyelashes, the orange make-up, which stopped at her jawline, the tired breasts wobbling above the tie-dyed vest. When they walked into the assembly hall where the teachers sat behind tables talking to parents, Jack was convinced that every head in the hall turned to stare and laugh at his mother. He longed for respectability and he wanted it for her too.

When he saw a fat man who was waiting in a queue say, 'Christ, look at that!' to a woman next to him, Jack felt a surge of anger sweep over him, and he put an arm across his mother's white plastic shoulders. Why shouldn't she wear flamingo earrings – they were beautiful birds.

Chapter Three

It took Jack more than five hours to complete a journey that normally took two and a half. A lorry and trailer carrying potatoes from Hungary to Milton Keynes had jack-knifed and spilled its load, gridlocking two motorway systems, the M1 going north and the M25 both east- and westbound.

Jack phoned his mother from the car but there was no reply. She'd grown nervous of answering the telephone since a series of desperate sales people had rung her day and night begging her to buy her electricity from the gas board and pay for her phone calls through the water board. She had thought they were playing a cruel joke on her.

It was one minute to midnight when Jack drew up outside his mother's house, but he saw that every window blazed with light. His mother went in for 100-watt bulbs – it was no wonder, thought Jack, that she was always in debt to Powergen. Norma was still sitting up waiting for him. As he walked down the garden path he could see her silhouette through the thin curtains; she was sitting on the sofa watching *Late Night Line-Up*. She was an indiscriminate viewer. Tom Paulin's big head filled the screen.

Jack knocked on the door and shouted through the letter-box. Eventually he heard her telling Peter, her old budgerigar, that, 'Our Jack's come to see us, Pete.'

When the door opened Jack didn't recognise his mother at first. He had never in his life seen her without make-up. Even in hospital, after the mugging, she had managed to put on lipstick. (Though only one eye had been beautified with blue eye-shadow and mascara, the other eye being swollen and closed.) Now, a week since being discharged, she didn't have her teeth in and her hair had lost its colour and its bouffant height and hung like sad white string around her bruised and sunken face. This was not his mother; it was the skeleton of his mother. She was like a page torn from *Gray's Anatomy*. The young man who stole her pension had taken her flesh and blood with him when he ran away with her shopping bag and purse.

'Hello, Mam. You're looking good,' Jack said. It was automatic; she set great store by her appearance.

She said, 'I've kept you some dinner,' and led the way down the narrow hall to the kitchen.

The Sprat family did not go in for kissing or any other affectionate gestures.

Peter was standing disconsolately on the floor of his cage, ankle-deep in seed husks and his own droppings. His blue feathers looked dull and frayed.

Jack put his finger through the bars and said, 'Cheer up, Pete, your mam's on the mend, all she needs to do is get

35

her hair done.' Pete was often the conduit by which Jack communicated with his mother.

Norma said, 'I'm too frightened to go out the hair-dresser's, Pete.'

Peter hopped on to his little trapeze and stared gloomily into the small mirror that dangled in front of it.

'He's a mardy bugger lately,' she said to Jack, then she opened the oven door and took out a plate covered by another, inverted, plate. Steam rose when she removed the top plate and revealed his dinner. 'Your favourite,' she said.

Jack looked at the bluish strips of breast of lamb, the dried-up carrots, peas and mashed potatoes that were stuck to the bottom plate. Jack said to the bird, 'If I could find the cruel bastard that hurt our mam I think I'd kill him, Pete.'

He forced himself to eat most of his vile dinner. He knew that she hated cooking and had never been any good at it. And he forgave her for forgetting that he had been veg-etarian for more than thirty years, and that it was Stuart, his dead brother, who had been particularly fond of the fat on breast of lamb.

Norma sat and watched Jack eat. She noticed the lines around his eyes and the two deep ridges that now connected his nose to his mouth . . .

As a prelude to going to bed, Norma covered Peter's cage with a piece of fabric made of polyester cotton and printed in a sunflower pattern. Peter continued to move around inside his darkened cage. Jack spoke sternly to the unseen bird. 'Settle down!' he ordered.

He switched off the kitchen light and as he climbed the stairs towards the box room where he would sleep the night he wondered why he had spoken so harshly to the little bird.

He slept badly in the cheap pine bed with the bargain-price mattress; a slight callus on his foot kept catching on the non-iron nylon sheets that his mother preferred.

At some time during the long night he stretched out a hand to check his travelling alarm clock and knocked a pottery donkey off the bedside table. He heard it fall and shatter on the uncarpeted floor next to the bed.

When he next woke it was morning and he lay for a while looking at the miniature donkeys surrounding him. They were decorated in every conceivable pattern, some floral, some realistic, some with panniers, others pulling little carts. Many wore hats, two sported ponchos, one carried the message 'A present from the Lavender Fields of Norfolk' and still had a few dried-up stalks sticking up from a hole in its back.

It had made buying Christmas and birthday presents for his mother easy; there was always donkey stuff in the shops at a price kids could afford.

When he got up he dressed quickly, putting on the Marks & Spencer casuals that lately he never felt quite himself in.

He could not get over the feeling that he was an impostor – only pretending to be like other men.

Before he left the room he picked up the pieces of broken donkey and saw that it was one that Stuart had made in a pottery class at one young offenders' prison he'd been sent to for possession of marijuana. Jack wrapped the pieces in his handkerchief and went downstairs to look for glue. He would have to mend it – the prison donkey was the only present Stuart had ever given Norma, and she often said that in a fire all she'd rescue would be Peter and our Stuart's donkey.

Jack cleaned the kitchen sink with a rusty Brillo pad while he waited for the skyscraper-shaped kettle to boil. He heard Peter moving around on the floor of the darkened cage as he made tea, which he took through into the front room overlooking the street. The house opposite, where he had once been sent to borrow a saucepan, had been boarded up and a smashed-up caravan had come to rest in its front garden. Schoolchildren walked by shouting affectionate obscenities to each other. They were bent under the weight of huge rucksacks; they looked like foot soldiers walking through the ruins of a fallen city.

The lavatory flushed upstairs but this was not followed by the reassuring sound of water running in the washbasin – his mother thought that germs were good for you, and said that there was more illness around since people had started taking daily baths and showers. She laughed in Jack's face when he found food in her fridge long past its sell-by date and told awful stories about cheese heaving with maggots.

Once the children had turned the corner the street was deserted. A few cars passed but to Jack's mind it seemed unnaturally quiet.

Years ago, in the same street on the day that he had left home to go to Hendon Police College, he had stood on the doorstep for ten minutes waiting for a taxi to take him to the railway station and had been surprised by how many people had passed by and wished him well. Small children had been playing in their front gardens and cars were being mended at the kerbside. In those days, Jack remembered, old women wrapped themselves in overalls and leaned on their gates to give and receive news.

When his mother came into the room Jack asked her where everybody was.

'Nobody goes out these days,' she said, coming to stand next to him at the window. 'I don't even nip next door now and I've stopped putting me washing out on the line. One of those bad lads come over the fence last week and stole that garden chair you brought me.'

Jack said, 'I'll build you a higher fence and get you another chair.'

'No, don't bother with the chair,' Norma said irritably. 'They'd only pinch it again, and anyway the sun never shines in England nowadays.'

They went through into the kitchen and Norma tutted when she saw that Peter's cage was still shrouded in the sunflower cloth.

There was no food in the house that Jack could bring himself to eat. And unpaid bills had been stuffed behind the tea caddy on the end of the draining board. The whole house needed cleaning, airing and restocking with necessities; even Peter's food bowl was devoid of seed and an empty packet of Trill had been put back into the cupboard next to the jars of mouldy jams and pickles. Jack had been hoping to return to London that evening to enjoy his second day of leave – he had planned to go to the Tate Modern, to see for himself what everyone was going on about – but he realised now that he would have to stay another night and sort his mother out. He cleared a space on the kitchen table and began to make a list.

Ring locksmith
Clean cage
Asda – food
Find a cleaner
Post office – collect pension
Bank – arrange Direct Debits
Find Yvonne?

He then took out his chequebook and paid his mother's bills.

Norma said, 'I hate not having any money. Why did Trev have to die?'

Jack said, 'He shouldn't have been on a church roof in the dark.'

Jack had been secretly relieved to hear of his stepfather's death. It was one less criminal in the family. And Trevor's conviction rate had been a source of embarrassment to him. Several times in his career he suspected that the living Trevor had held him back from promotion.

Norma went into a reverie about Trevor's funeral. 'I never seen a church so packed, there were hundreds spilling out into the churchyard. People were pushed up against the gravestones, weren't they, Jack? The vicar said some lovely things about Trev.'

Jack remembered sitting in the church only feet away from his stepfather's ornate coffin, wondering how the trainee vicar would cope with Trevor's notorious criminality and the unfortunate circumstances of his accidental death. But the dog-collared fool had called Trevor 'a colourful character' and had glorified Trevor's lead-thieving activities by referring to him as a pioneer who had been recycling long before it became fashionable.

Norma said, 'I wish Trev had been cremated now. I don't like to think of him lying in the earth, all on his own.'

Jack said, 'You've never told me how much Trev left you, Mam.'

Norma began to search through the pockets of her various coats, which were hanging bunched up together from a single hook on the back of the kitchen door. Jack knew she was looking for cigarettes. The whole of his childhood seemed to have been wreathed in cigarette smoke. Eventually she brought out a crumpled, half-smoked Lambert & Butler, which she held up in triumph before putting it between her lips. Jack felt himself tense as she began to search for a light, opening drawers and rummaging through bags before finding a box of Swan Vesta matches in the filthy cleaning cupboard under the sink.

Norma sat down and blew smoke across the table. 'I don't like talking about money,' she said stubbornly.

Jack said, 'We've got to, Mam. Did you get that money back from Yvonne?'

Norma shook her head.

Jack had warned his mother not to invest in his sister Yvonne's women-empowering Women Get Rich Quick pyramid scheme. But she had invested £3,000, having been mesmerised by Yvonne's dramatic stories of ordinary women walking away from the empowerment meeting carrying £24,000 at a time.

Now Yvonne and his mother were not speaking to each other. There had been no contact between them since Yvonne had empowered herself by leaving her baffled husband of twenty-six years and disappearing. Even the police computer had failed to find her. Jack missed Yvonne acutely. His sister had taken care of Norma and now it seemed that Norma was entirely Jack's responsibility.

Jack worked his way through the list. He took his mother

to the frozen-food cabinets at Asda. A card was put into the post-office window which said 'CLEANER WANTED. TWO HOURS A WEEK'.

While they were unpacking the frozen ready-meals from the Asda bags the phone rang in the hall. Jack answered it and a young man's voice said, 'I'm ringing about the cleaning job.'

Jack hesitated.

'I'm a good cleaner,' the young man said. 'I used to work in the hospital.'

'Why aren't you working there now?' asked Jack suspiciously.

'I'm a student now. I need a part-time job to pay for my books.'

Jack asked the young man, James Hamilton, to come round at five o'clock.

Morgan Clare was writing an essay on the Tolpuddle Martyrs. He wrote effortlessly in a good clean hand: 'The Tolpuddle Martyrs were six farm labourers who joined together in 1833 to form a Friendly Society, when their "master" cut their wages from nine shillings a week to six shillings a week.'

He was uncomfortably aware that his sister Estelle was not doing her homework and that there would be a row later on when Mum and Dad came upstairs to give them half an hour of quality time. Morgan said, 'Estelle, you could at least pretend to do some work, at least start it!'

Estelle said, 'I don't give a toss about when I grow up. I want to be an uneducated person.'

Morgan laughed. 'You're already uneducated. You can't uneducate yourself.'

'I shan't take any exams or tests, then,' said Estelle.

Morgan wrote: 'In my opinion these men, James Brine, Thomas Stanfield, John Stanfield, James Hammett, George Loveless and James Loveless, were pioneers of the labour movement who did not deserve to be treated in such a cruel and heartless manner.' He put down his pen and said, 'So you've got no ambitions?'

'I'm very ambitious,' said Estelle. 'I want to be very beautiful and I want a wardrobe full of expensive clothes and shoes and I want to marry a good-looking man who makes me laugh and have a baby.'

MI5 were listening in to the Prime Minister and his wife making love. A tiny microphone no bigger than a baby's fingernail was secreted in the headboard of their *bateau lit*.

'They sound as though they're halfway up Snowdon,' said Robert Palmer.

'I wish they'd get to the fuckin' summit,' grumbled Alan Clarke.

'It's so embarrassing; thank Christ it's only audio.'

A tone change in the Prime Minister's passionate endearments alerted the two men that he would be finished and reaching for a tissue soon.

Morgan Clare did not expect to find his parents in bed together at six in the afternoon. When Poppy was born, four months ago, he had been forced to admit to himself that his parents, though old, were still doing it. It was gross, really gross, but to do it when it was still light outside was abnormal or something. What were they, animals? OK, so he shouldn't have just barged in without knocking, but he had wanted to tell Dad about the Tolpuddle Martyrs.

'Dad, have you heard of the Tolpuddle Martyrs?'

The listening MI5 agent Clarke chuckled and said, 'Talk about coitus interruptus.'

'Of course I have.'

'What do you think of them?'

'Well, I think they were brave but misguided.'

'Misguided? Like how?' Morgan's voice was aggrieved.

'Well, I think that they would have saved themselves and their families a great deal of distress if they had been prepared to negotiate a wage increase with their master, rather than take to the streets as incendiaries.'

In the Prime Minister's bedroom Morgan's face flushed red; he passionately loved the six Tolpuddle Martyrs and their wives and families, and felt now that he could die for their cause. 'Dad, they weren't incendiaries, they volunteered to guard buildings against rioters and fire-raisers.

45

And, Dad, they weren't asking for a rise in their wages, their wages had been cut from nine shillings a week to six shillings.'

Edward smiled and said, 'Perhaps a good compromise would have been to settle for seven shillings and sixpence.'

'Dad, they couldn't even feed their children properly on nine shillings so . . .'

'They signed an illegal oath, Morgan.'

'They formed a Friendly Society, Dad. That's all! They were a hundred per cent in the right.'

'Nothing is ever black and white, Morgan. They were enemies of the state.'

'They were SO not! They were all-right guys who stood up against a cruel and, like, unjust system and they, like, got sent to Australia as a punishment for seven years! Whose side are you on, Dad?'

Adele, her voice muffled by the quilt, said, 'When you say "side", what exactly do you mean?'

Morgan shouted, 'You know what I fucking mean.'

Adele struggled to the surface and screamed, 'You can forget about those Nike trainers and you're grounded for a week. Now go away, I'd like to get out of bed and I'm naked.'

Morgan asked, 'Dad, is there anything you'd die for?'

The Prime Minister replied, 'Not now, son.'

The agents heard a door close. Then Adele saying, 'You're doing live telly tonight, aren't you? Use plenty of antiperspirant after your shower. You sweat like a pig under the lights, Ed.'

Norma went upstairs shortly before five o'clock. When she came back down Jack saw that she had changed into one of her full-skirted summer dresses and that she had pinned her hair up and applied lipstick.

James Hamilton disarmed them both with his apparent enthusiasm for housework. Jack showed him around the small house, apologising for the state it was in, explaining that his mother had been mugged recently and had let things go. This was only a small lie; Norma had never been much of a housekeeper. But for each apology James had simply smiled and said, 'No problem.'

James had made a great fuss of Peter, saying, 'My dad used to have budgies in his garden at home.'

'In an aviary?' asked Jack.

'No. Flying wild. He lived in Trinidad.'

Jack said, 'I thought budgies only flew wild in Australia?'

'No! No! They're all over Trinidad,' replied James.

'Is your mum from Trinidad?' asked Norma.

'No, me mum was from round here, but she's dead now. When do you want me to start?'

Norma said, without looking at or referring to Jack, 'You can start now and clean that poor little bugger's cage out.'

James, however, looked directly at Jack and said, 'Shall we say seven pounds an hour?'

Jack said, 'No, we'll say six.'

By half past seven James had left the house with twelve pounds in his pocket. In two hours he had transformed the kitchen and had even cleaned and polished the mirror in Peter's cage. He promised to return at ten o'clock the next morning, before he went to college.

When James had gone, Jack put two frozen Quorn shepherd's pies into the newly gleaming oven. Norma said, 'He's a lovely lad. Can you afford for him to come twice a week, Jack?'

Jack said, 'Of course I can, can't I, Pete?'

They took their dinners through into the living room because there was a programme on the television they both wanted to watch. A new series was starting tonight, *Face the Press*, which was going out live in front of a celebrity audience. The Prime Minister had agreed to be the first guest.

Jack wanted to watch because of his increasingly close relationship with the Prime Minister; Norma's interests, however, were centred entirely on the celebrities. She was hoping to spot Sir Cliff Richard and to try and work out from his face whether he was a virgin.

Jack sat down at his old desk to eat. Norma sat in front of him on the sofa with her dinner on her lap.

The Prime Minister sat in the hospitality room watching hungrily as Donna Flak, the producer of *Face the Press*, removed clingfilm from an oval platter of quarter-cut sandwiches. His natural good manners prevented him from getting to his feet and helping himself.

Donna balled the clingfilm in one hand and threw it expertly into a BBC waste bin across the other side of the room.

'Blimey!' said the Prime Minister. 'England could use you on the cricket field.'

His aides and the assembled BBC bigwigs laughed for longer than the slight joke deserved.

Donna said, 'I used to keep wicket for Cambridge Ladies first eleven.'

'And you still got a First?' smiled the PM.

Donna handed him a small plate and a napkin, and offered him the platter. He took two smoked-salmon sandwiches and began to eat. He would have liked to have sat quietly for a few moments while he ate, but people gathered around him.

Alexander handed him the list of questions and some suggested answers. 'There's nothing you need worry about,' he said.

He knew every journalist on the panel apart from one, a woman called Mary Murphy. The briefing notes said she was from the *Northants Voice*. That she was twenty-five, had been married and divorced and had a three-year-old daughter, and voted Socialist Alliance.

In the celebrity audience, Ulrika Jonsson sat on the front row between Stephen Hawking and Gary Lineker. There was a warm round of applause when the Prime Minister walked on to the set. He hoiked himself on to the seat of a high stool and experimented with crossing and uncrossing his legs, before settling for resting one foot on the rung and letting the other hang loosely.

After a quick sound-check, during which the Prime Minister recited what he had for breakfast – 'Egg, orange juice, muesli, wholemeal toast and er . . .' – there were questions on the Euro. 'I've made it quite *clear* that a referendum will be held when . . .'

On Africa. '*Clearly* Africa has huge problems . . .'

And Malcolm Black. 'I think it's *clear* to everyone that Malcolm is a wonderful Chancellor of the Exchequer . . .'

All went well until Mary Murphy asked him if he knew the price of a pint of milk.

He smiled and said, 'We're European, Mary, *clearly* you mean a litre.'

The audience laughed. But Mary Murphy did not. 'How much?' she repeated.

He smiled again and, playing for time, asked, 'Fully pasteurised or semi-skimmed?'

The celebrity audience laughed, more nervously this time. Few of them knew the price of milk.

'Either,' said Mary Murphy implacably.

Graham Norton, who was flanked by Adele and Ben Elton, shouted, 'Never mind milk, how much is a bottle of Bollinger?'

When the laughter had died down a panelist from the *Independent* asked, 'Prime Minister, there has been much comment in the media, and this has been backed up by recent polls, that you have lost touch with the realities of daily life. Can you still call yourself the people's Prime Minister?'

It was three long seconds before the Prime Minister spoke. He smiled and blinked rapidly before saying, 'Look, a couple of days ago I was talking to an ordinary bloke about his elderly mother who had been the victim of a vicious street crime.'

Jack said to Norma, 'He's talking about you, Mam.'

'Don't be daft,' she said. 'I'm not elderly.' And Jack thought to himself, 'And I'm not ordinary.'

At 10.15 the next morning Jack phoned his mother's house from the motorway. James answered the phone. The sound of the vacuum cleaner could be heard in the background. James told Jack cheerfully that he was taking Norma into town to get her hair done.

Jack said, 'What about college?'

'The lecturer's got bronchitis, so . . .' answered James.

Jack could hear his mother in the background talking to Peter in the kitchen, asking the little bird what she should wear for her trip into town.

Chapter Four

Before Jack went on duty on the door at two o'clock he went to the staff room at Number Ten and made himself a cup of filter coffee. Wendy was in there talking to Su Lo, Poppy's nanny, about Barry's leg.

Su Lo said, 'I don't know why you don't try Chinese medicine, Wendy, it cured my genital warts.'

Jack wished that he hadn't heard this reference. Now he wouldn't be able to look Su Lo in the face for a few days without thinking about her genital warts.

Wendy said, 'A wart is a wart, but a gangrenous leg is something else.'

While Jack was washing out his mug at the sink he listened to Wendy telling Su Lo that a doctor had been called for in the night to attend to Adele, who had suffered a severe bout of tinnitus. 'Noises in the head?' said Su Lo.

'Something like that,' said Wendy bitterly.

Jack put on his helmet and fastened the strap under his chin. It was a warm April day; he wouldn't need his overcoat.

As he walked through the corridors towards the front door he felt the tension and excitement in the air. It was always like this in the hour before Prime Minister's Questions.

Before getting in his car the Prime Minister stopped and said to Jack, 'How's your mother?'

Jack settled for saying, 'She's on good form, sir, thank you for asking.'

'That's super,' the Prime Minister replied. Then he asked, 'Jack, what in your opinion is the thing that most concerns the people of this country?'

'It's crime, sir,' answered Jack. 'There should be more policemen on the streets.'

Prime Minister's Questions started badly when the Prime Minister misread his notes and erroneously declared in answer to a query about cod stocks that there were only eighty-nine such fish left in the North Sea.

It was some time before the mocking laughter died down and the Prime Minister recovered enough to correct his mistake and inform the honourable members that, though stocks were depleted, 89,100 tonnes of fish were alive and well and currently swimming in British waters.

The leader of the Opposition, Tim Patrick Jones, rose to his feet and said contemptuously, 'Is the Prime Minister aware that the rail network of the southeast came to a complete standstill yesterday morning, and that literally millions, *millions* of long-suffering commuters failed to get to work, not just on time, *but at all!*'

Edward had watched the television news the previous night and had been shocked at the scenes of near anarchy at Waterloo station as frustrated passengers had damaged automatic ticket machines and stormed into W. H. Smith helping themselves to newspapers and confectionery.

The Prime Minister rose to his feet to a barrage of 'Shame! Shame!' He glanced at his notes. Then he lifted his head defiantly, and noticed that the Chancellor of the Exchequer, Malcolm Black, had shifted his huge bulk slightly to the left, causing others on the front bench to squash up even closer.

As Edward rose to his feet he heard Malcolm mutter, 'Butch up, Eddy,' in his refined lowland accent. For a split second Edward wondered if the political friendship he and Malcolm had apparently enjoyed for fifteen years was coming to an end.

His concentration shifted and his explanation for the chaos on the railways was rambling and unfocused. Sweat began to stream from his forehead. Behind him on the bench he heard Malcolm Black expel a quiet but protracted sigh.

When Tim Patrick Jones sneered, 'Will the Prime Minister tell us when he last travelled on a train?' Edward replied instantly with an answer that he immediately regretted and that was to change the rest of his life.

'I am delighted to be able to tell the right honourable gentleman that I last travelled on a train three days ago, with my wife and my three children.'

The Labour backbenchers roared with pleasure. Edward wanted to snatch at his words and cram them back into his mouth, but the renegade answer was already being recorded in Hansard and scribbled in notebooks by the satirists and mockers who sat in the press gallery.

The sentence 'I last travelled on a train three days ago, with my wife and my three children' was to become as infamous as Neville Chamberlain's 'I hold in my hand a piece of paper . . .'

Meanwhile, in a semi-detached house in a suburb of Coventry, a keen amateur photographer, Derek Fisher, who had been listening to Prime Minister's Questions on Radio Five Live, was busy emailing a photograph of the Prime Minister and his family to the picture desk of the *Daily Mail*. The picture editor immediately sent a text message to the *Mail*'s correspondent in the press gallery, who was listening to the Prime Minister answering a question about a British man found guilty of brewing beer in Saudi Arabia and sentenced to death by stoning.

Even before he had sat down, the leader of the Opposition had received a written message which said, 'Ask the Prime Minister if the train he was travelling in on Sunday arrived and departed on time, and the route it took.'

The leader of the Opposition decided to drop his next planned question, on the latest Air Traffic Control fiasco, and take a chance. He asked the question.

The Prime Minister got to his feet slowly and said,

'I have great pleasure in informing the right honourable gentleman that our train left and arrived on time.'

'I believe that it took a circular route,' said Tim Patrick Jones.

In the press gallery a photograph was being passed from hand to cynical hand. None of them could remember having laughed so hard or for so long as they did at the sight of the Prime Minister in a baseball cap and denim jacket sitting with his knees around his ears on a toy train called the *Choo Choo*.

Adele and Poppy, both in baseball caps, sat behind Edward in the first carriage, and the older Clare children were sitting sulking in the guards' van at the back as the train choo-chooed around its circular track. Adele's nose rivalled the peak of her baseball cap, causing a parliamentary sketch-writer to observe, 'Christ, look at that honker! It's the size of an aircraft carrier; you could land a plane on it and still have room for a five-aside!'

News of the photograph swept from the press gallery to the opposition benches in the chamber.

The laughter became hysterical as the delighted politicians dissected the picture.

Meanwhile, Tim Patrick Jones was pressing the Prime Minister to name the train! Name the train!

The Prime Minister refused to answer, citing 'security reasons'.

The Conservative backbenchers erupted and the Speaker

of the House struggled to be heard above the angry jeering, choo-choo and chuff-chuff impressions swept around the chamber, and the member for Barking Southeast, whose party piece was an impression of the *Royal Scot* leaving Waverley station, almost died of pleasure when he realised that he had a captive and appreciative audience.

There was a terrible silence on the benches behind him when Edward sat down, and Malcolm Black said with awful kindness, 'Don't worry, Ed, you'll recover from this.' As he left the chamber, Edward heard somebody singing, 'The runaway train came down the pass and she blew . . .'

Chapter Five

Adele pulled Poppy irritably away from one of her long nipples and offered her the other. 'For Christ's sake, get a move on,' she said to the sucking child. 'I'm in the middle of chairing a bloody meeting!'

Poppy looked up and met Adele's discontented expression, then continued drawing the milk from the blue-veined breast. Adele had come to loathe the whole messy, uncomfortable procedure, but she was a patron of the Breast Is Best campaign, an organisation backed by the Department of Health and many fashionable paediatricians. So she would just have to soldier on, but she looked forward to the day she got her breasts back and didn't have to share them with a snorting, snuffling, greedy child. Christ, it was barbaric.

And look at the fuss it had caused with the powerful artificial-milk lobby, the main opposition, Bottle Is Best, or BIB for short. They had conducted a vicious rearguard attack on her for showing favouritism, and had been joined by a gaggle of racing drivers' wives and girlfriends who had recently given birth. They had formed themselves into a group called Full Throttle With A Bottle. Ferrari had threatened to withdraw from Silverstone and questions had been asked in the House.

Adele reached out and switched on the radio and heard her husband's faltering voice stammering something about a train before it was drowned out by the most extraordinary noise of more than 200 male voices shouting, 'Choo-choo! Choo-choo!'

Downstairs in a small meeting room, the walls of which were hung with significant pieces of Brit Art, waited three powerful and formidable women. They were hoping to secure Adele's support for an anthology they were producing called *Rumble* in aid of the unfashionable cause Irritable Bowel Syndrome. They already had a short story from Martin Amis and a high-fibre recipe from Jamie Oliver.

Lady Leanne Baker had taken advantage of the breast-feeding break to send a text message to her teenage son, reminding him to take his rugby shirt out of the washing machine and hang it on the Aga rail to dry. Sitting across the table from her indulging in gossip were Rosemary Umbago, the blind editor of the *Daily Voice*, and Baroness Hollyoaks, the dishevelled brain of the Liberal Democrats – she had entered the room only an hour before looking neat and almost presentable, but within minutes her hair was on end and her clothes looked as though they belonged to a woman of a different size altogether.

Baroness Hollyoaks, whose breasts had never given comfort to man, woman or child, finished telling a mildly disreputable anecdote about Roy Hattersley then said, 'I do think it's marvellous how you manage with your visual impairment, Rosemary.'

Rosemary snapped, 'Oh please call it blindness. I really can't bear those weasel words of political correctness. I'm blind, for God's sake. I was born blind. I'm not one of those sensitive *nouveau*-blind people who keep whinging on about their precious sight loss.'

Baroness Hollyoaks, mindful of Rosemary's dislike of politically correct language, said, 'So, Rosemary, I understand you married for the second time, to a South African. Is he a nigger?'

When the Prime Minister's car returned from the Commons, Jack was surprised to see that the Prime Minister looked pale and ill, and that the smile that was almost as permanent a feature as his nose and mouth had gone.

On the orders of Alexander McPherson there were no photographers present outside Number Ten. As the Prime Minister passed him Jack caught his eye and said, 'You all right, sir?'

The Prime Minister waved his glowering private secretary inside.

'I've just had a drubbing in the House, Jack.'

Jack noted with alarm that the Prime Minister's eyes were shining with what looked suspiciously like unshed tears.

'I'm sorry about that, sir,' he said gruffly.

Instead of moving on through the door and into his office, the Prime Minister stayed talking to Jack. He told him about the train farce. Jack folded his arms and listened. When the Prime Minister finally stopped talking, Jack said, 'It's April the first, sir – perhaps your answer to the train question was meant to be a joke.'

Edward shook his head. 'No, I told a stupid lie; the truth is I haven't travelled on public transport, or bought a litre of milk, or waited for treatment in a National Health Hospital, for years. I've completely lost touch with how most people live their lives.'

Jack said, 'Don't your advisors keep you in touch, sir?'

Edward blurted, 'They inhabit the same sterile bubble that I inhabit, Jack. It's years since I ate fish and chips from out of a newspaper.'

'It's years since anybody did,' replied Jack. 'It's a violation of the Public Health Act of 1971.' Though it gave him no pleasure to confirm the Prime Minister's sense of isolation from the people he governed.

A voice whispered in Jack's ear that he was to tell the Prime Minister that Colonel Gaddafi was on the telephone and wished to speak to him urgently. Jack relayed the message but the Prime Minister seemed reluctant to go inside. 'How do you relax, Jack?' he asked.

'I sit down with a packet of cheese and onion crisps and a bottle of Kronenbourg and I watch *High Noon*, sir,' Jack answered.

'*High Noon!*' said the Prime Minister excitedly, and began to sing, 'Do not forsake me, oh my darling . . .'

'That's the one,' said Jack. 'I must have watched it twenty times or more.'

When the Prime Minister went in he spoke to his private secretary. Gaddafi would have to call back later. He cancelled his next scheduled meeting, which was with the NATO chief of staff. Then he rang Wendy and asked her to source the Kronenbourg, the crisps and a videotape of *High Noon* and send them upstairs to his sitting room.

He then called Alexander McPherson and asked him to arrange an interview with Andrew Marr of the BBC about his elaborate April Fool's joke. He considered asking Jack to join him, but realised that it was too late to start messing around with the Metropolitan Police's duty roster. So he watched it alone.

Malcolm Black sat at the desk in his shambolic office eating a poached egg on burned toast. He had cooked this himself in the kitchen of the flat. His wife was out and he didn't like to bother the staff. Alexander McPherson said, 'I dunno how you can work in this shithole, Malc.'

Malcolm looked round as if seeing the mess for the first time and said, 'I seem to work very well indeed and the opinion polls appear to confirm it. It's not me that's heading for a mental breakdown.'

David Samuelson was sitting with his head in his hands.

'*High Noon*,' he said in disgust. 'He's regressing. The story-line is simplistic, the use of the time metaphor is overdone and Gary Cooper's acting looks positively arboreal.'

Alexander said, 'If I wanted advice from a bollocking film critic, I'd have sent for Barry bollocking Norman.'

Malcolm said quietly, 'The FTSE was down by two per cent at the close. The Bank of England are worried about deflation. Poor Eddy's becoming a wee bit of a liability.'

Samuelson said, 'Malcolm, you've got a long streak of egg on your tie.'

Malcolm poked at the thin rivulet of yolk and then licked his finger.

Alexander said, 'Ed's OK. He just needs a break. Christ, if I had to do his job I'd be a candidate for Care in the fucking Community by now.'

Malcolm moved his empty plate on to a teetering pile of fiscal papers and said, 'I think I could do his job quite well.'

Samuelson said, 'We agreed, Malcolm, that you'd wait another five years. Are you reneging on that?'

Malcolm smiled and said, 'Events, David, events.'

'Give him a week,' Alexander said. 'I'll sort the press.'

Samuelson said, 'He can hardly be seen to be lolling about on a sunbed in Tuscany with a Campari in his hand.'

Malcolm laughed. 'We could send him to Africa.'

Alexander said, 'Those press bastards would track him down. We'll have to send him underground.'

★

As Gary Cooper and Grace Kelly left town in the buggy and rode away, Alexander barged in. 'Now that's the way to clean up a town, Ed. Give every bastard a gun and let them shoot it out,' he said.

As the credits rolled, Edward pressed the button on the remote to rewind the tape and said, Gary Cooper-like, 'I want some straight talking from you, Alex. Am I still up to the job?'

Alex said, 'You need a break, Ed.'

'Do you think I'm out of touch?'

'Mori did a telephone poll for us this morning. After last night's *Face the Press* fiasco, your personal rating has taken more of a dive than if you were jumping off a cliff face with a jungle creeper tied round your ankle. Eighty-five per cent of the British public reckon you have no understanding of the life of the average man or woman in Britain today.'

Edward stood by the window, then turned as if he were about to deliver a Shakespearian monologue to an audience of A-level students. 'I've lost touch with the people.' He raised his hands as if examining them for blood, then whispered, 'Eighty-five per cent. So who are the fifteen per cent who think I'm *in* touch?'

Alexander replied, 'That's people like us, Ed. The movers and shakers.'

'But that's *clearly* ridiculous, I am in touch with ordinary people. I talk to Wendy, and Jack-at-the-door,' exclaimed the Prime Minister.

'Who's Jack-at-the-door?' asked Alexander.

'Police Constable Jack Sprat,' said Edward. 'He's watched *High Noon* over twenty times, and the April Fool's joke was his idea, and it was his mother who was mugged.'

An hour later, Jack received a message in his ear telling him to go upstairs to the Prime Minister's sitting room as soon as his replacement arrived. It turned out to be Constable Harris, a young black woman whom he had once met at a small-arms training day.

After a bit of banter about why he'd been sent for, Jack took off his helmet and was shown upstairs.

The Prime Minister came forward to greet him and introduced him to Alexander McPherson, who said, 'Congratulations, Constable Sprat, you've just won a week's holiday.'

'Where?'

'Touring Britain.'

'Am I going on my own?' asked Jack. He wondered if he had any choice.

'No,' said the Prime Minister. 'You're taking me, and we're leaving tonight.'

In the intervening hour, inquiries had been made about Jack's suitability. He seemed to be perfect in all respects: he had no wife, no children and no dependants apart from an old mother living in far away Leicester. Nobody in civilian life would miss him.

Alexander had tossed a copy of the security report to Jack. It was impressively comprehensive.

Jack scanned it and thought, 'It makes me sound like a right sad bastard.'

'Incidentally,' Alexander asked casually, 'do you have any politics?'

Jack said, 'I can start the day a communist, eat my lunch a socialist and go to bed a Tory, sir.'

Edward laughed and said, 'And vice versa?'

'Oh no, sir,' said Jack. 'I could never start the day a Tory.'

Edward said, 'I always envied Jesus his trip into the desert – important decisions were made there.'

Alexander snarled, 'Yeah, well, we can't spare you for forty days and forty nights. You can have a week at the max.'

Jack said, 'We'll be pushing it to see Britain in a week, sir. Especially if we're travelling on public transport.'

'Public transport?' said Edward. 'Wouldn't it be easier to get around in a helicopter?'

'Like the ordinary people whose opinions you're so anxious to canvas?' Alexander asked scathingly.

'What's your objective, sir?' asked Jack. 'What is it you want to achieve?'

Edward blinked. 'I dunno, Jack. I suppose I want to reacquaint myself with the concerns of the majority of British people.'

'Do we have an itinerary?' asked Jack.

When nobody answered, Jack went on. 'Right, I'll need to go home and pack a bag.'

'And *I* need to go to Edinburgh,' said the Prime Minister excitedly.

Since he was a small boy, his life and most of the days so far had been scheduled. Even when he had been most carefree, growing his hair and playing guitar in a rock band, there were arrangements to make, rehearsals to attend; and nowadays, when he wasn't, his so-called leisure time was calibrated to the last minute. He had often made speeches about freedom. Now he had the chance to experience it for himself.

With the help of a senior civil servant, plans were made quickly. The Prime Minister's absence would of course be noticed. His cover story was that he was to lead an exercise in post-nuclear government in a secret bunker hundreds of feet below the Wiltshire countryside.

The Deputy Prime Minister, Ron Phillpot, was recalled from his five-star hotel in Belize, where he was attending a conference on the repayment of the Third World debt.

Alexander volunteered to break the news to Adele and to inform her that Edward loved her more than life itself.

'So what exactly are my duties?' asked Jack. 'And for how long?'

Alexander said, 'You'll be an escort.'

Edward said quickly, 'And you'll be in charge of the money and tickets while I interact with the public.'

Jack almost laughed aloud at the Prime Minister's obvious

childlike enthusiasm. In Jack's opinion the public had deteriorated alarmingly since he had first qualified as a policeman. In those days most couples were married – a partner was somebody who part owned a small business, old men and women walked around the streets without a care in the world, and children didn't shout 'Make way for the filth' when they saw you approaching in your uniform.

The three men, Jack, Edward and Alexander, went through into the master bedroom and opened Adele's drawers and wardrobes. The Prime Minister's face was composed of unremarkable features, but it was instantly recognisable from Huddersfield to Soweto and would have to be disguised.

Edward's transformation into Edwina was surprisingly easy to accomplish. It helped that Adele and he were of very similar height and build, and that both of them wore size-eight shoes. And that occasionally, on bad-hair days, Adele wore a wig.

Adele had often boasted to her feminist friends, 'Eddy is such a girly.'

It took only thirty-five minutes (including a close shave and eyebrow tidy) to transform Edward into Edwina, and it would have taken less had Edward not insisted initially on wearing a suspender belt and stockings. None of the men could decide or remember if the lacy purple and black belt with the hanging rubber suspenders was worn under or over Adele's matching knickers.

It was Jack who persuaded the reluctant Prime Minister out of stockings and high heels and into tights and loafers, pointing out that stockings and high heels were all right for wearing at a St Valentine's candlelight dinner, but were completely unsuitable for traipsing around Britain in.

Jack had to do the same when it came to choosing outerwear, persuading Edward that the pretty sun-dresses Adele had worn at their last Tuscan villa were too revealing of masculine flesh – and, he gently reminded the Prime Minister, it was not unusual to see snow in Britain in April. They settled on a capsule wardrobe consisting of a Nicole Farhi wide-legged suit, a couple of cashmere roll-neck sweaters – one pink, one blue – a pair of DKNY tracksuit trousers, and a long sweater to hide the Prime Minister's crotch.

To Jack's eyes the Prime Minister still looked like a bloke wearing his wife's clothes. The wig, however, was a triumph of black curls and tendrils, and once it was in place, and Edward had applied Pan Stik, lipstick and eye make-up, he could almost have passed his own wife on the stairs and not been recognised by her.

Before they left Number Ten, a few ground rules were established. Only Jack would carry a mobile phone, and except in emergencies there was to be no communication between them and Number Ten. Alexander would take charge of everything – Adele would be told her husband was in the bunker and Ron Phillpot would be prevented from making any important decisions during the Prime Minister's absence.

Police Constable Harris wished Jack Sprat and his female companion goodnight and watched them pass through the gates and walk away through a light drizzle. She couldn't suppress a pang of jealousy. It should have been her on Jack's arm.

As the Prime Minister and Jack walked up the road towards Trafalgar Square the Prime Minister's body felt curiously light, as though the burdens of state were actually falling from his shoulders and rolling back in the direction of Downing Street.

'We'll get the Tube from Charing Cross, sir.'

'Look, Jack, I'm a pretty straightforward sort of a guy, and y'know I'd rather you didn't stand on ceremony, so stop calling me "sir", will you?'

Jack nodded and asked what the Prime Minister wanted to be called.

'My friends call me Ed,' said the Prime Minister.

'So what do I call you?' said Jack.

He realised he'd hurt the Prime Minister's feelings when he loosened the grip on Jack's arm, but Jack didn't apologise. 'I'm not his bloody friend,' thought Jack. 'I didn't even vote for him, and now here I am saddled with carrying the bag of somebody who looks like a poor man's Joan Collins for seven long days.'

'Do you think we're being watched, Jack? Under surveillance?' asked the Prime Minister.

Jack nodded glumly and in a room overlooking the Thames Clarke and Palmer shouted with laughter. Palmer said, 'Too right we're watching!'

Clarke added, 'We'll know when you turn in your bed!'

They had laughed themselves sick when they first saw the Prime Minister leave Number Ten in his woman's rig-out, and Palmer had said, 'I'll give him half an hour before some hawk-eye puts the finger on him.'

Clarke had replied laughing. 'Jack looks proper pissed off.'

Clarke pressed the zoom on the satellite picture showing Jack's turned-down mouth. 'Do you reckon Jack knows we're watching him?' asked Palmer.

They both laughed out loud again when Jack looked up past Nelson standing on his column and into the dark sky beyond, to where the satellites that would track their progress were orbiting the earth, and mouthed silently, 'Hello, boys.'

Chapter Six

Norma and James were sitting side by side on the sofa in front of the gas fire. The discarded vacuum cleaner was still plugged in and only a third of the swirly-patterned carpet had been sucked over. An ashtray, their fags and matches and two mugs of coffee were arranged on the coffee table in front of them, together with a pile of Norma's photo albums.

'That's Stuart a month before he died,' said Norma, poking a nicotine-stained forefinger at a photograph of a thin-faced man with terrible teeth.

'Right,' said James, who couldn't find anything complimentary to say about the stupid smack-head loser who was looking out from the photograph with an expression of pure joy.

'He looks happy there, don't he?' Norma wanted to believe that Stuart's short life had not been totally devoid of the odd moment of happiness.

James thought, 'He's happy 'cause he's just jacked up, that's why.' But he said nothing and Norma turned the page and showed him a photograph of Stuart and Jack in the back garden of Number Ten. Both of them were astride gleaming Raleigh racing bikes. The bicycles were in better condition than the boys, who grinned into the camera with faces that already looked worn out.

'Them bikes caused a lot of trouble. Jack wouldn't ride his again when he found out that Trev, my dead husband, had nicked 'em from the front of Halfords. Trev was very hurt; he'd gone to a lot of trouble – finding the right bolt-cutters, turning the fire alarm on in the shop. People think it's easy being a criminal but it's not. There's a lot of planning goes into it, and worry. I mean, we'd promised them lads bikes for Christmas, but it weren't till Christmas Eve that Trev rang to tell me that he'd got two racing bikes in the back of his van.'

James raised his arms and stretched out happily, feeling his body relax into the cushioned softness of the sofa. He had found a place where he felt safe at last. He was among his own kind.

'Norma,' he said, 'you wouldn't know anybody who wants to rent a room out, would you?'

Norma was stroking Stuart's photographic face. He hadn't liked being touched when he was alive. Many of the fights he'd been involved in had been caused by him being inadvertently touched by strangers.

Norma said, 'Is it you what's looking for a room?'

'Yeah. My mum's got took to an hospice last night.' James pulled his soon-to-be-orphaned face and pretended to wipe away imaginary tears. 'I can't stay in that house on my own, Norma.'

Norma said sharply, 'You told me your mam was dead.'

James did his crying act and thought about the day his dog, Sheba, had been run over by a milk float. He cried hot tears.

Norma was alarmed at such a naked display of emotion. After a minute she put an arm around his shoulders and said, 'So, is your mam dead or alive?'

James sobbed. 'My real mum's dead, my adopted mum's dying.'

'What she got?' said Norma, who was a connoisseur of fatal illnesses.

James took a neatly folded square of paper kitchen towel from his pocket and wiped his eyes. 'Liver cancer,' he said.

Norma noticed that his long black eyelashes were wet and sticking together. 'Has she got secondaries?' she asked.

'Yeah, loads of 'em,' sniffed James. He was an imaginative boy and he could clearly see his non-existent adoptive mother in her white hospital bed. She looked a bit like the dying Evita as played by Madonna.

'You can come and stay with me for a bit, if you like,' said Norma. 'You can stay in the donkey room.'

James said, 'I smoke a bit of dope now and again, Norma; it helps with my arthritis.'

Norma, Trevor and Stuart had often smoked a joint when Jack was out of the house doing one of his boring hobbies – photography or ballroom dancing. Some of her happiest moments had been quietly getting stoned with her husband and eldest son. There had been such a sense of family. It had been exciting, how the three of them had dashed around the house opening windows and spraying air freshener before Jack's estimated return.

Norma turned another page of the album, and James was surprised to see ex-President Bill Clinton's big handsome face grinning at him. In the background was the front door of Number Ten Downing Street and a policeman in shirtsleeves, a bulletproof vest and a helmet.

Norma pointed to the policeman and said in a shamed tone, 'You might as well know the truth: that's our Jack, you met him. He might be a policeman, but I love him just the same.'

When James had got over the shock he said, 'Nobody can help how their kids turn out, Norma.'

The song of the little bird in the kitchen alerted Norma to Peter's feeding time. She got up and shuffled out of the room in her slippers, leaving James exclaiming over the photographs of Jack Sprat with Nelson Mandela, Bobby Charlton, Liam Gallagher, Posh and Becks, and some other old blokes whose faces he vaguely knew but whose names he couldn't remember.

While Norma was pouring Trill into Peter's feeding dish she heard James speaking quickly into his mobile phone. 'We've got a lodger, Pete,' she said. 'He's got young legs, he'll help us out and look after us.'

James shouted through, 'Norma, is it OK if I have a few of my mates round?'

Norma said to Peter, 'What do you think, Pete, shall I let him?'

But Peter didn't appear to be listening, so Norma shouted back, 'Go on, then.'

She went upstairs to change out of her slippers and into her high heels. It was a long time since she'd had company.

Jack's aunt Marilyn had said to him a fortnight before she died in hospital, 'The only thing I know about you, our Jack, is that you like beetroot.' And it was true that beetroot had featured heavily in their conversation and family inter-actions. At Christmas parties Marilyn had cried, 'Lock up the beetroot, our Jack's here!' or, 'I've just got some beetroot in for our Jack, so tell him to come.'

There were other women, among them several police-women, who knew Jack Sprat not as a lover of beetroot but as a lover.

Jack had studied the erotic arts and the psychology of women as thoroughly as he undertook any subject that interested him. He had equipped himself with a map of the female genitalia and explored it until he could find his way around blindfold. He was constantly surprised when he found that he was more conversant with women's genitalia than women themselves were.

He took it for granted that most women did not know how to handle a penis, either treating it like a torpedo that might go off at any minute if handled firmly or as though it were an old-fashioned gearstick that could be bent in any direction without harm.

Most women remembered Jack with pleasure because he liked them and their bodies and he told them the truth: that he was unable to love anybody – it was a genetic malfunction and there was nothing he could do about it unless science came up with something to save him from a life without love of any kind.

Jack and the Prime Minister were in darkness, standing on a stationary Northern Line train. The Prime Minister hated the dark. He had once been shown round a heritage mine by a miner in an immaculate miner's uniform and a gleaming helmet. When they had reached the deepest shaft, and were bent double looking at the coal face through a sheet of protective Perspex, the lights had gone out and the Prime Minister had squealed like a girl in the anonymous blackness. The heritage miner had laughed and said, 'Who's the great big Jessie, who's afraid of the dark?'

The Prime Minister had not been brave enough in that extreme masculine space to confess that it was him, and that he hadn't slept entirely in the dark since the night of Mummy's funeral.

He and the others in the party had crouched waiting for an emergency generator to be brought underground.

Now he was hanging on a handle that was suspended from the ceiling of the train, sweat was running between the push-me-up, squeeze-me-together cups of his wife's brassiere. A madman began to shout about Sir Cliff Richard – accusing him of forcing Hank Marvin to become a Jehovah's Witness.

Further down the carriage a man with a public-school accent said, 'This is the last fucking time I attempt to travel on the arse-bumming, fucking cock-sucking bleeding Northern Line. I'd rather crawl to Camden Town on my arse-fucking, mother-fucking knees.'

A woman's voice, thick with tears, said, 'Please, Roddy, we have to move to the country.'

Slow minutes went by and strangers began hesitant conversation. The madman addressed the carriage and informed everyone that David Beckham was the new Messiah and that Jeremy Paxman was the Antichrist.

The public-address system emitted a high-pitched whistle then a laconic south London accent said, 'Ladies, gentlemen and others, London Transport regret to inform you that due to an incident perpetrated by a member of the public this train will be stationary for about twenty minutes. That is two-zero minutes. Once again, London Transport apologise for any inconvenience suffered.'

Very few people had been inside Jack's flat in Ivor Street, Camden Town. He liked most people, and had even come close to loving a few, but he found it impossible to share his living space with another human being. He cared too much about the minutiae of daily life. It caused him pain if a towel was not hanging in the exact middle of the heated towel rail in the bathroom and anguish if a pickle jar was not lined up in order of height next to its fellows in the preserves and jams cupboard. Every object in the four small rooms of the flat had an exact permanent space, and Jack was at his happiest when every spoon was back in the drawer and every CD was back on the rack in its appropriate alphabetical order.

He had once let chaos into the flat in the form of Gwendolyn Farmer, an extraordinarily pretty but persistent woman whom Jack had taken out for three months in 1998 when he was stationed at New Scotland Yard listening to tapped phone conversations. Gwendolyn had accused him of being married. Why else did he never invite her back to his place? She only lived ten minutes away from him, so why did they always go back to her place to make energetic and imaginative love?

In a weak moment Jack had capitulated and invited her back, but within half an hour of her walking in (dislodging the doormat slightly and moving a sofa cushion a little to the right) the relationship was over.

In Jack's quiet, ordered space Gwendolyn stood out like a rampaging beast. She brought disorder and mayhem with her – planets collided, the sun went round the earth, rivers reversed their flow, dogs mated with cats, the dead came back to life and time ran backwards.

Gwendolyn never knew what she'd done wrong. As far as she was concerned she'd gone into the unnaturally clean and tidy flat, thrown her coat on the sofa, kicked her shoes off, made herself comfortable, lit a cigarette and told Jack about her day in Missing Persons.

As she tearfully confided to a colleague the following day: 'His face went white, he started to shake then he asked me to leave. What did I do?'

Jack nearly asked the Prime Minister to wait outside the front door of the flat, in the street, but the poor sod in his ludicrous get-up would be easy prey for any passing chancer. Jack steeled himself and allowed the Prime Minister to step into the narrow hallway before walking in himself and closing the front door behind him.

'Goodness me, what a lot of books,' said the Prime Minister. 'Have you read them all?'

'No sir, I use them for heat and sound insulation,' Jack said sarcastically.

The Prime Minister was almost relieved. He didn't know why, but he wouldn't have felt comfortable spending a week with a man who had actually read the collected works of Marx, Engels and Winston Churchill.

'They're in some sort of order,' the Prime Minister said as he ran his fingers along the spine of Jack's precious books.

'The Dewey system, sir,' said Jack, wincing when he saw that his guest had pulled out Tom Paine's *The Rights of Man* and replaced it incorrectly between Jeremy Paxman's *The*

English and Jennifer Paterson's *Two Fat Ladies* cookbook. Jack left the Prime Minister examining his CD collection in the living room and hurried through to the bedroom where he packed a small bag. He chose a warm suede jacket from one of three hanging in dry cleaner's bags in the casuals wardrobe and within five minutes was back in the living room steering the Prime Minister towards the door.

'So there is no Mrs Sprat?' said the Prime Minister as they were waiting for a Number 73 bus to take them to King's Cross.

'No, sir,' said Jack.

The Prime Minister nodded towards the nearby queue and whispered, 'You simply have to stop calling me "sir"; it's clearly a bit of a giveaway. Call me Edward. No – perhaps Edwina would be more appropriate in the circumstances.' The Prime Minister laughed his girlish laugh and asked, 'Will it be OK to sit upstairs on the bus when it comes?'

Jack practised saying 'Edwina' to himself.

The concourse at King's Cross station resembled a crowd scene from an early Russian film about the October Revolution; there was a similar sense of confusion and despair. A derailment just outside Peterborough station, combined with a computer failure at Swanwick Air Traffic Control, had resulted in a crush of people all wanting to travel to Edinburgh on the overnight train. Jack held the Prime Minister's hand and pulled him through the crowds.

An onlooker would have seen a solicitous husband caring for his highly strung wife. A closer observer would almost certainly have noticed that the wife had a rather large Adam's apple, bits of which needed a shave.

Jack looked up at the destination boards and saw that the Edinburgh train they had intended to catch had been delayed until further notice; there was nowhere to sit, so they sat on the floor. Several times during the long wait Jack left the Prime Minister to look after the bags and joined the long queues for food and drink. The Prime Minister sometimes forgot he was a woman and sat with his legs wide open and his wig askew until Jack gently reminded him of his new gender.

An old woman who was sitting on her suitcase said to the Prime Minister, 'I paid £130 for my ticket and I'm still sitting here, after five hours, with no announcements, no assistance from the staff. In fact, no staff. At least Mussolini got the trains to run on time. What we need in this country is a dictatorship.'

It was five o'clock in the morning before they finally boarded a train. Jack shouldered both bags and pulled the Prime Minister through the jostling crowds who were racing for seats. They made their way down the aisles looking for two adjacent places and eventually sat diagonally opposite each other at a table for four. Ominously one of the strangers, a morose-looking individual in a camouflage jacket, produced a carrier bag containing six tall tins of

McEwan's extra-strong lager and placed it on the table in front of him. The other stranger, a young woman with a severe geometric haircut, opened her book, *Management Systems in a Globalised World*.

Soon every seat in the carriage was filled but still more people came in heaving their heavy cases, awkward bundles and bags with them.

The Prime Minister's wig was almost knocked off several times, until Jack suggested changing places. It offended the Prime Minister's sense of good manners to see women standing in the aisle; his impulse was to offer them a seat. Then he reminded himself that he was a woman and that anyway women like Adele had fought for years for the right to stand on buses and trains while men remained seated.

He pressed his face against the window and peered out at the grey dawn as they passed the outer environs of north London. He was surprised by the untidiness of the back gardens and yards of the houses they passed and the dilapidated condition of their sheds and outhouses. Why did so many people seem to be collecting old fridges and cookers and other rubbish in their back gardens? Did they imagine that they would come in useful sometime in the future? He asked Jack for his opinion.

The man in the camouflage jacket said, 'It will cost you £150 to hire a focking skip, since the focking government brought in a landfill tax.'

He then introduced himself. His name was Mick and he

was going to his brother's wedding. He asked the Prime Minister why she was going to Edinburgh.

The Prime Minister lowered his eyes and said quietly, 'I'm hoping to find my mother's grave.'

'That's heavy,' said Mick, slurping on the third can. 'Is that your husband, then?' He nodded across to Jack.

'No,' lied the Prime Minister. 'He's my brother.'

'So where's your husband?' pressed Mick.

'I've never been married.' Lies came easily to Edward. It was telling the truth that was so difficult. In his political world a single truthful statement could send the value of the pound rocketing up or down.

'I've not had much luck with women,' said Mick, whose voice was now full of self-pity. 'I don't know what I'm doing wrong. I take them out, I buy them drinks, beer, lager, spirits, even cocktails. I'll even buy them food if they're hungry, so you tell me, lassie, what am I doing wrong?'

The young woman with the severe haircut mouthed 'Jesus' to herself. And cracked the spine of her book.

Mick rambled on. 'My brother shouldn't be marrying this woman, she's a dog from Easterhouse. She's only marrying him for his money, he's a subcontractor.'

'What in?' asked the Prime Minister.

'In anything at all,' laughed Mick. 'He doesn't have to do any work because he subcontracts the work out to another subcontractor, and *he* subcontracts the work out to another subcontractor – do you get it?' Mick laughed long and hard.

Jack closed his eyes and allowed himself to be lulled into a state of semiconsciousness by the rhythm of the train as it lurched over the subcontracted rails. He heard Mick telling the Prime Minister that he would make some man a 'bonnie little wife' and why didn't they meet for a drink after his brother's wedding? In fact, why didn't Edwina attend the brother's wedding? He would be proud to turn up at the church with Edwina on his arm. He would ring his brother now and order an extra carnation.

Jack heard the Prime Minister stuttering his excuses. 'It's hugely kind of you but y'know I'm only in Edinburgh for a short time and, well, me and Jack are going to be busy so, y'know, very kind but don't bother ordering another carnation.'

But Mick reacted badly and chose to take offence.

The Prime Minister asked the woman next to him to excuse him. She got up from her seat with ill grace and stood in the aisle holding her mobile phone. She'd been in the middle of sending a text message, and her dextrous fingers continued to spell out the words as the Prime Minister stumbled by on his way to the toilet at the other end of the carriage. He had to get away to somewhere quiet where he could think, not only about the landfill tax and its ugly repercussions but also about the alarming fact that he felt more comfortable wearing his wife's clothes than he did wearing his own.

He sat down on the toilet-seat cover and looked through

his shoulder bag for his lipstick and Pan Stik. It was at least ten hours since he had last shaved and his beard was starting to come through. He smeared the Pan Stik over his face and rubbed it in until it resembled a biscuit-coloured mask, then carefully drew around his mouth with the lipstick. He practised a few womanly expressions in the mirror.

After adjusting the black curls, which were inclined to shift off his head and go skew-whiff, he decided that he was more of a blonde than a brunette and that when they got to Edinburgh he would get Jack to measure his head and send him out to buy a new wig, something in the Marilyn Monroe style from the film *Some Like it Hot*. It was a film he certainly identified with now. And while Jack was out shopping he may as well pick up some different, more exciting clothes. If he was forced to dress as a woman then he might as well be a sensuous and alluring one. He certainly did not want to spend his week as a woman dressed in apologetic safe clothes. He still resented being talked out of wearing high heels. He was sure that with a bit of practice he could manage them.

During the Prime Minister's absence Jack took the opportunity to talk to Mick. He leaned towards him and in a very quiet, authoritative voice said, 'You say one more word to my sister and I'll tear your head off your shoulders and sell it to the lion house at the zoo.'

One of the few things that Jack knew about Edinburgh, apart from the existence of Arthur's Seat and the annual festival, was that there was a zoo.

Mick slurped on his fifth can and nodded respectfully. He would have done the same had his own sister been invited to a wedding by a stranger on a train.

There was a furious banging on the toilet door and a coarse voice shouted, 'What the fock are you doing in there?'

But the Prime Minister was cleaning his teeth and couldn't stop. He was only up to 122 brushstrokes and had another 78 to go. As he brushed he wondered about Adele, how she would have taken the news that he was in a command bunker and incommunicado for a week. Since their first meeting they had never spent a day – half a day, even – without speaking to each other. He hoped that she would remember to take her medication. Without it she became quite a different person – not the confident, A-list celebrity he knew and loved, a woman who strode the international stage like a colossus, but a pathetic whining creature who lay in bed sobbing that her thighs were too fat. He would ask Jack if it was possible to phone Wendy and ask her to stand over Adele and make sure she swallowed her twenty-five milligrams of lithium twice a day.

Jack lay back with his eyes closed listening to the young woman opposite as she made call after call to offices on her mobile phone. 'Fergus, I'm on the train. Listen, I'll not be in time for that meeting with those beakless, footless chicken guys – the chicken-meat people – so you'll have to cover for me. Listen, they'll try to argue for a death rate of one in

87

five. That's pants. If the chicken have no feet then they'll survive for another forty-eight hours longer, so for a unit rate of . . . Hello, hello, Fergus, You're breaking up . . .'

Mick said, 'I like a bit of chicken for my dinner.'

After a fitful sleep Jack woke to find the train jolting through Northumbria. The floor of the carriage had accrued a layer of packaging materials, polystyrene cups rolled up and down the aisles like tumbleweed passing through a Wild West town. There was a smell of fast food and rancid humanity in the air. Jack would like to have strolled along the train to stretch his legs, but when he turned his head to look along the carriages he could see that he would have to step over the bodies of sleeping passengers and their baggage. He would be glad when they got into Edinburgh – he had never cared much for the countryside. When he was a child his mother had talked about sending him there as a punishment, as in, 'If you don't behave yourself, I'll send you to the country.'

Chapter Seven

Norma had never had much to do with foreigners before. There had been Black Charlie at the working men's club; he was a bit of a character, always making jokes about how he didn't need to sunbathe to get a tan, and he never took offence when people chucked bananas at him. But since Charlie had suddenly gone berserk once and been taken off to The Towers with a police escort Norma had not had much to do with black, brown or yellow people. Now all at once, it seemed, her living room was full of them. There was hardly any room to move. Two of them were sitting on Jack's desk and swinging their legs, laughing at a story James was telling about a Mercedes C-class that he had borrowed when it was parked outside the Freemasons' hall and that turned out to belong to the head of the drug squad.

Norma said, 'You're a bad boy, James!' She knew what 'borrowed' meant.

James got up from the floor where he'd been sitting cross-legged and gave her a kiss on her cheek. 'Sorry, Mother,' he said. Then, while she was laughing, he asked, 'Mother, is it all right if we smoke here?'

Norma was puzzled at first because most of the boys

were already smoking; the room was full of smoke, and Norma had a Lambert & Butler on the go at that very moment.

'You don't mind a bit of weed, do you, Mother?'

Norma had seen something on the television news recently, something about policemen in Brixton smoking marijuana on the streets to help them with the pain of their rheumatism. 'No, go on,' she said. 'Light one up and I'll have a puff myself.'

Several hours later a thick cloud of marijuana smoke enveloped Peter's cage in the kitchen. The little bird, asleep on its wooden perch, had a glorious dream: he was flying free, high above the Blue Mountains in Australia, a country he had never seen but had always longed for.

Jack had hardly ever misbehaved. He had once refused to go to the shop for Norma's cigarettes because he was on the penultimate page of *The Grapes of Wrath*, and there'd been one occasion when he had spent his swimming money on a dictionary. But compared to Stuart, who had fought and screamed through most of his childhood days, Jack had been a saint – clean, tidy, polite and quiet. If he wasn't at his desk he was up in his room reading. He didn't seem to want to have any friends, though sometimes a boy called John Bond called for him and they walked to the pork-pie-shaped library on the estate together. Norma had once stood outside Jack's bedroom and listened to Jack and John's conversation. It was about incomprehensible things; they were using a vocabulary that was foreign to her. It was English they were speaking, but she could not have told you what they were saying to each other if you had shoved bamboo shoots down her fingernails. Sometimes she wondered if Jack was quite right in the head. A teacher at his junior school had once said to her at the Christmas concert that Jack was remarkably precocious. She had reacted angrily, saying, 'He don't know nothing about sex, let alone how to do it!' But the teacher had explained that 'precocious' meant that Jack was very clever for his age and that Norma should be proud.

The train stopped at Newcastle station and weary travellers gathered their belongings together, as requested by the guard over the public-address system, and queued to leave the train. The young woman took down a very small suitcase from the overhead locker then made her final call before leaving the train. 'Piers, I'm just about to get off the bloody train. Listen, before I get there can you look up "chicken eyes" on the Net? Yeah, or it could be under "optical-waste distribution", something like that. What I'm looking for is an outlet. At the moment we're treating chicken eyes as waste, but there may be an untapped market here. The Middle East, it's just a thought, and if there's nothing then we'll have to look at breeding them without eyes; they don't need them, they're not going anywhere – it's not as if they do a bit of embroidery while they wait for the chop. Yeah, I know the quantity would be minute, but we have a surplus of fifty cubic feet of freezer space and it could be utilised. It could be a really profitable niche market.'

Jack thought about the eyeless, beakless, clawless chickens in the young woman's care. He wondered, not for the first time, if such creatures had a god to look after them.

When the young woman was rolling her suitcase along the platform Jack said, 'I'm glad I'm not one of her chickens, Edwina.'

The Prime Minister replied, 'We can't be sentimental about animals, Jack. That young woman has the right entrepreneurial spirit; we need more young business people like her.'

But the next time the Prime Minister fell asleep, somewhere around Berwick-upon-Tweed, he had a three-second nightmare: a blind chicken had taken control of the train and they were hurtling past a red light at 100 miles per hour.

Jack, having swapped places with the Prime Minister, had hoped that the seat next to him would remain vacant, but, as the train gathered speed and swayed around a bend and the McEwan's cans rolled about and made a tinkling musical sound that was not displeasing, a fat man lumbered down the aisle and stood towering over Jack. In a surprisingly light voice he gasped, 'Is this seat free?'

The man put his laptop on the table and rammed himself into the seat. The edge of the table cut into his white-shirted belly. A navy-blue tie with a crossed-golf-clubs design hung from the tight collar of his bullish neck. Jack wondered where he had bought his navy-blue suit. There was enough cloth in it to rig a sail in a tall-ships competition.

The fat man's rapid breathing alarmed Jack. Eventually the man gasped, 'Typical, I wait hours for a seriously delayed train then when it comes in I'm in a queue at the Baguette Bar.'

Jack didn't want to talk, so, after giving a small laugh that recognised the irony of having to hurry for a train that was six hours late, he closed his eyes, which in any culture signified that he did not want to take part in a conversation. But the fat man had been forced into the role of extrovert by his size and he was unable to keep quiet.

The Prime Minister woke up to find Mick dribbling saliva on to the shoulder of Adele's silk suit. He gently pushed Mick's head away but it rolled back like a bowling ball propelled by its own weight.

A business card lay on the table between them. Derek F. M. Baker, Financial Advisor, pensions a speciality. Derek Baker was explaining to Jack that endowment mortgages had had a bad press but were still a viable option for the first-time buyer.

Jack felt as though he was an extra in a cowboy film, gathered around a wagon listening to a travelling salesman in a fancy Stetson selling snake oil.

After failing to interest Jack in re-mortgaging his 'London property', Derek inquired into Jack's financial future. When

Jack said that he was 'sorted, thank you', Derek held up a podgy finger and said, 'Ah, but are you "sorted" for your old age? You could live to be ninety, a hundred, even. Will your pension pay for the nursing home of your choice? Or will you be thrown into a state-run institution and left to rot?'

The Prime Minister could not remain silent. 'Sorry, Mr Baker, but can I correct you on one or two facts. First, the Stakeholder Pension Scheme launched by the government in the last parliament is an extremely tax-efficient vehicle and available to all, no matter what their income. And secondly, and perhaps more importantly, in addition this government has done more than any other to encourage savings for retirement with mini and maxi ISAs as well as stakeholder pensions, not to mention the rigorous overhaul of the rules governing occupational schemes.'

Derek F. M. Baker was not exactly stunned by the weird-looking English woman's grasp of the finer details of pension policy, but was certainly impressed by her knowledge. It was a shame she had a horrid problem with facial hair; still, it was nothing a bit of Immac wouldn't solve.

'Are you in business yourself, er . . . ?' asked Baker.

'Edwina,' volunteered the Prime Minister. 'No. I'm . . .' there was a hesitation, and Jack wondered what the Prime Minister had decided upon. Before leaving Downing Street he had been unable to choose between civil servant, house-wife or lecturer in politics.

'I'm an actress,' said the Prime Minister, and flicked a black curl out of his eye.

Baker said, 'I knew I recognised you from somewhere. So what will I have seen you in?'

By the time the train drew into Waverley station in Edinburgh, the Prime Minister had constructed a complete acting career from an early struggle in rep to dining at the Ivy with Maggie Smith and going to garden centres with Judi Dench.

Jack was impressed with the Prime Minister's ability to throw himself so vigorously into his own fantasy and was only slightly alarmed when the Prime Minister said as they stepped off the train, 'Ah, Edinburgh at last. I won a Perrier Award here in 1982.'

Neither of them were happy about sharing a room. However, that was one of the rules they had agreed on with Alexander McPherson – Jack must be within sight of the Prime Minister at all times, the only exception being visits to the lavatory.

The receptionist at the Caledonian Hotel was used to strange-looking guests booking in. My God, you should see it at festival time! The lobby looked like a mental-hospital outing. So the crazed-looking woman with the tall, unsmiling man were more or less run of the mill as far as guests were concerned. He had once been called to one room to find a man cooking a lobster on a Primus stove. The man had been most indignant when he'd been told that cooking was forbidden in the rooms. 'Have you seen the price of lobster in the dining room?' So when Mr and Mrs Sprat rang down for a tape measure and a list of Edinburgh's crematoriums he was unfazed.

Jack went to Bentley's department store on the Royal Mile looking for a Marilyn Monroe wig. The salesgirl was barely aware of who Marilyn Monroe was and had never seen *Some Like it Hot*, so Jack was left to sort through the wigs himself. He was annoyed to find that one size fits all – he need never have bothered measuring the Prime Minister's head after all, nor waiting an eternity for a tape measure to be found and sent to the room.

When the wig had been wrapped and paid for, Jack looked at the list the Prime Minister had drawn up on hotel stationery at the dressing table.

1. Dress, size 14. Must be cocktaily, shimmery or sparkly. Something actressy.

Jack had pointed out to the Prime Minister after reading item one that actresses hardly wore such stuff in the daytime. He had once seen Juliet Stevenson in Waterstones Trafalgar Square and she had been wearing an old brown coat and carrying a Kwik Save bag. But the Prime Minister was not to be deterred, so Jack suggested buying two dresses. So item number two became:

2. A cinched-waisted afternoon frock with a swirly skirt in something silky that moves when you walk.
3. Shoes: MUST BE high heels with straps or peep toes.
4. Long Coat: Furry? Leather? Animal skin? Snakeskin?
5. Sunglasses.
6. Diamonds.

Jack had pointed out that the Prime Minister would be displaying rather a lot of hairy flesh, so the Prime Minister rang the front desk and asked the receptionist to send a porter to Boots to buy four boxes of Immac.

An hour later, when Jack was smearing the depilatory cream behind the Prime Minister's knees with a little spatula, he thought to himself, 'This is beyond surreal.' When Jack left to go shopping the Prime Minister was showering the white paste away from his now almost totally hairless body.

Jack wasn't a natural shopper – he visited Marks & Spencer twice a year, in April and in November, when he bought clothing appropriate for the season, including extreme cold and extreme heat. His inclination was towards the neutral palette – he steered clear of navy blue, it being a colour he associated with work and duty. In his Marks' clothes he felt that he blended in and became almost invisible. There was nothing particularly striking about him; his features were evenly balanced on his face. He had the kind of eyes, nose, mouth and ears that Marks & Spencer might sell, if such things could be bought.

Jack studied the floor plan at the bottom of the escalator in Bentley's department store and went up to the second floor to ladies' special-occasion wear. There were other men in the department, disconsolate, out-of-place men, who sat on chairs that were provided for them. One was doing the *Daily Telegraph* crossword. As Jack passed their eyes met and the man looked away as if ashamed. Jack began rifling through the racks looking for size 14 dresses that fulfilled the Prime Minister's specification. When they were assembled he quickly chose three, and after studying them for a minute or less he made his one final selection. With the red sequinned sheath dress with the chiffon hem and neck trim over his arm, Jack passed through to women's daywear. Again he collected together all the suitable size 14 afternoon frocks. Jack was in luck: the gypsy look was in fashion. There was a seemingly endless supply of the flouncy and feminine to choose from. He finally chose one that wouldn't look out of place in a graveyard, on a bus or walking round a council estate. Black was a daring choice, but he thought that black would look good with the Prime Minister's new blonde hair.

During Jack's absence the Prime Minister had rung down to reception and asked if there was any Bronco toilet paper in the hotel. 'You'll have to ring housekeeping,' said the receptionist, who now suspected that he was possibly the subject of a series of practical jokes. When he had put the phone down he looked around for hidden cameras, almost convinced that he was unintentionally taking part in a reality-TV programme.

When Jack bustled in with the bags, the Prime Minister could hardly contain his excitement. He was wearing the white towelling bathrobe provided by the hotel management for their guests. A laminated card in the pocket warned guests not to steal the bathrobes, though not in such brutally frank language. It said: 'Should you like to purchase this robe a charge of £55 plus VAT will be added to your room bill.' Beneath the robe the Prime Minister's body glistened. He had ignored the instruction leaflet inside the Immac box, which advised those using the product to desist from using any skincare products immediately afterwards. Excited by the hairlessness of his body, he had raided the complimentary toiletries basket, which he found next to the washbasin in the bathroom. He had rubbed in the body lotion and then followed it with something called rehydrating protein gel. He had used several cottonbuds to clean out his nostrils and his ears. He had applied the contents of the conditioner bottle to his hair and was wearing the shower cap. He had even broken into the tiny sewing kit and had tightened the straps on his wife's bra – he was grateful to a master at his prep school for teaching him to sew many years ago. He had filed his nails with the emery board and polished his wife's loafers with the shoeshine pad provided. When he had finished he gave himself a very close shave using the magnifying mirror, which hugely enlarged every bristle, pore and blemish on his face. He took this opportunity to examine himself carefully. Was he a good man? Was he honest? Did he deserve the trust of the British people? Was President Bush right to call him a friend? He was slightly disheartened to see in the magnifying mirror that there was actually no such thing as a close shave. However hard he scraped and for however long the bristles still showed through.

Jack laid the contents of the shopping bags on the Prime Minister's bed. The diamonds, comprising earrings, necklace and ring – £33.50 in total – flashed expensively under the reading light just above the bed head.

Jack removed his shoes and lay on his own bed with his head propped up with one hand and prepared to watch the Prime Minister transform himself into Edwina St Clare, star of stage and screen.

But the Prime Minister said to him coyly, 'No, don't watch, Jack.'

Jack turned his back and watched the CNN news. An immaculately made-up and coiffed American woman was telling the television audience that, 'Edward Clare, the British Prime Minister, was testing the facilities of a post-nuclear holocaust government control centre. Adele Floret-Clare, the Prime Minister's wife, was reported to be incandescent with rage, a source close to the family said today.'

Jack turned his head to see how the Prime Minister had reacted to this disturbing news, but the Prime Minister was in the bathroom and the door was closed. Jack turned off the television and shut his eyes.

When all the slight adjustments had been made and the primping and grooming were over – when the straps on the high heels had been tightened several times, the make-up applied and the wig tousled and teased into a pleasing Monroe-ish mop – the bathroom door opened and the Prime Minister said, 'You can look now.'

Jack was very disturbed by what he saw. In the low light of the hotel room the Prime Minister looked enchanting in his red sequinned dress, and was very like the woman of Jack's dreams.

Jack said huskily, 'My God, sir, you're beautiful.'

The Prime Minister practised walking in his high heels between the beds, while Jack washed and shaved and changed his shirt. They then made their way arm in arm down to the hotel dining room. The Prime Minister was slightly overdressed.

As they walked in one waiter said to another, 'She's a handsome woman, it's a pity she has nay tits on her.'

They talked politics over dinner. The Prime Minister was impressed with Jack's grasp of economics and social policy.

Over a hideous parcel of filo pastry, anchovies and capers wrapped incomprehensibly in string, Jack said that, in his opinion, giving the pensioners a seventy pence pay rise was a major insult and that it would have been better to have given them nothing.

For the main course, for old times' sake, the Prime Minister had chosen haggis, tatties and neeps. He explained to Jack that haggis, potatoes and turnips had been his favourite food as a small boy living in Edinburgh, and he advised Jack to have the same. The humble dish the Prime Minister had expected, however, had been arranged by Monsieur Souris, the chef, into something resembling the Eiffel Tower, and was surrounded not by gravy, as Edward had hoped it would be, but by a tepid pool of rhubarb coulis.

Jack said, 'Christ, how are we meant to tackle this? From the top down or the bottom up?'

The Prime Minister eased a little haggis away from the centre of the tower and said, 'Try the middle way, Jack.'

Over a lemon sorbet ruined by the inclusion of fresh mint leaves and unripe strawberries, they discussed the police retirement issue. Jack, softened by wine and exhilarated by the company of the glamorous Edwina St Clare, lowered his guard for a moment and confessed that a senior officer of his acquaintance had recently retired on health grounds, with full pay, due to the trauma of witnessing two drunks fighting outside a pub on a Friday night.

By the time the foul coffee came the two of them were laughing easily together. The Prime Minister said, 'You know what, Jack, you'd look great with one of those new very short haircuts.'

Jack sighed inwardly. He hated it when a woman tried to change his appearance.

The waiter who had served them all night, mostly incompetently but good-naturedly, presented them with the bill, saying, 'In my country the cost of your dinner would buy a donkey and a cart.'

Jack said, 'Cheeky bugger.'

But the Prime Minister asked the waiter which country he was from.

'Albania, miss. I come here to work. No Scotsman will do this job for the minimum wage.'

'And how did you get into the country?' asked the Prime Minister solicitously.

'It was not so difficult,' shrugged the waiter as Jack signed the bill. 'It is traditional for the men of my village to travel to Britain hidden inside a turnip truck. Most of the village men are here now living in the Colinton area of Edinburgh; the women and children will be coming next year.'

'Why are we importing turnips from Albania?' asked the Prime Minister.

'These are organic turnips for your middle classes,' laughed the waiter. 'They are badly shaped and full of worms because we cannot afford the pesticides.'

Later, as the two men undressed for bed, they discussed the problems of illegal immigration. The Prime Minister recognised that there was a labour shortage, and wondered aloud to Jack if Albania was a country where they should be recruiting for the next intake of trainee policemen.

★

Adele was searching through one of her three wardrobes for her Nicole Farhi trouser suit. Wendy was pulling drawers open, looking for the two cashmere sweaters. Adele said, 'You're responsible for my wardrobe, Wendy, ergo you're responsible for the disappearance of my clothes.'

'Are you accusing me of stealing?' Wendy was tired and wanted to leave and go to the hospital. Barry's leg was coming off tomorrow and she wanted to reassure him that as soon as he was conscious after the operation there would be someone from an amputee self-help group to see him through his darkest hour. 'Because if you are, I'm leaving. I don't know what I'm doing here anyway. I'm not appreciated. I'm vastly overqualified – may I remind you that I have a degree in food science . . .'

'It was a Third from somewhere nobody's ever heard of,' shouted Adele.

'Everybody's heard of Bradford!' yelled Wendy.

Both women started to cry then moved together to comfort each other. Adele said, 'I'm sorry, I'm being a complete cow. You're far too big to fit into my clothes. It's just that I'm furious with Ed for going off like that without saying goodbye. I can't even phone him and he can't phone me. I really can't live without him, Wendy.'

Wendy said, 'I know you're both very fond of each other –'

'Fond? You obviously don't understand,' Adele shrieked. 'I can't live without him.'

At the age of eleven Adele had been taken out of her private day school and sent away to a residential school for gifted children, paid for by her local education authority. Her precociousness had both delighted and alarmed her grandmother, who had treated her as though she was an alien princess. However, at her new school she was merely one of many clever children and overnight she felt herself turn into an ordinary little girl who was not even attractive and didn't seem very popular with the other children.

Edward was Adele's only true friend. She had never had another. Without him she felt herself falling apart, disintegrating cell by cell. When she looked at herself in the wardrobe mirror she saw that she was already fading away – apart from her nose, which looked bigger than ever. A mocking voice in her head spoke: 'Who's a clever girl, then?'

Two days ago Adele had stopped taking her medication.

Chapter Eight

Jack had taken the precaution of stuffing his pockets with the pastel-coloured tissues provided by the hotel, but he soon realised that he should have brought the whole box. The Prime Minister's tears flowed like a torrent released from a dam. His grief was Mediterranean, open-mouthed and noisy. Other visitors to the graveyard crept past on their way to visit their own dead. This area of the graveyard, watched over by pine trees, was seldom disturbed by the sound of raw grief.

In the florist's earlier that morning the Prime Minister had wept a little when the florist asked him for whom he was buying flowers.

'My mother,' he had replied.

When the florist suggested that elderly ladies preferred quite traditional bouquets rather than the more modern spiky arrangements, the Prime Minister had said, 'But my mother is not elderly, she's only thirty-seven.'

The florist withdrew for a moment to allow the peculiar-looking blonde woman to be comforted by the tall silent man with her, and busied herself arranging pussy willow in a galvanised bucket. She was used to dealing with the public in crisis – sometimes she thought counselling should be taught at floristry school. She'd lost count of the marriages she had probably saved. She always spent longer on the bouquets that carried the little card that said simply 'Sorry'. She had stood in the shop and cried with the recently bereaved. Kiddies' floral tributes were always difficult; it was tricky getting the eyes right on a teddy-bear-shaped wreath. And weddings! The trouble they caused. So many brides cancelled at the last minute these days. Not that she blamed them. Why would a young woman want to saddle herself with one man for life when she could more or less buy a baby from a laboratory if she wanted one?

'Perhaps a spring arrangement, then?' said the florist, after watching the woman in sunglasses smelling a bucketful of blue hyacinths.

Jack suggested that a few stems of the pussy willow would be nice, and between the three of them they constructed a sweet-smelling bouquet.

A man was riding a grass-cutting machine over the grave-stones. Jack wondered to himself if this was why the graves in that area had no headstones – was it to ease the path of the machine, or was it a local custom?

The full skirt of the Prime Minister's black dress lifted in the wind that was blowing from the distant sea. 'I got into Ampleforth, Mum,' he said. 'And I qualified for the Bar, and now I'm the Prime Minister. So thanks for . . . y'know, the good early start. I hugely enjoyed the years you were my mother.'

The man on the small cutting machine was revving the engine and eyeing the long grass around Heather Clare's grave. Jack gently led the Prime Minister away before he could talk to his dead mother again; it was bad enough when people did it in films. As they walked down the slight incline towards the entrance Jack said, 'Well she's in a lovely spot, sir.'

They stopped by a sign that said: 'Complaints and inquiries regarding the upkeep and maintenance of the graves should be addressed directly to mortltd.co.uk'.

The Prime Minister said, 'Dad's ashes were scattered in the Gorbals.'

'Why was that, sir?' Jack asked.

'Poor Dad wrote his only will when he was a communist and expected to die for the cause. The money from his estate went to the Communist Party of Great Britain, which was a shock for everyone, because he was the chairman of the Berkshire Conservative Association at the time of his death. He should have brought his will up to date.'

'Or his principles,' said Jack.

'Principles?' the Prime Minister repeated the word as though he had never heard it before.

'I'm a bit mystified as to how a person can change his principles so completely, that's all, sir,' said Jack. 'I believe he joined the Liberals at one point in his life?'

'He moved down to the West Country,' said the Prime Minister defensively. 'The Liberal Party provided him with a good social life.'

Jack pressed on. It was a mystery to him how a person's view could change. 'Then weren't there a couple of years with the Social Democrats?'

'He came briefly under the spell of Shirley Williams, yes,' conceded the Prime Minister.

Jack wondered how low a man's spirits had to sink in order for him to be mesmerised by Shirley Williams. 'So principles are a moveable feast, are they, sir?'

'Look, Jack, you can't eat principles, neither can you be housed, clothed or educated by them,' said the Prime Minister.

It was their first quarrel. As they sat in the back of the taxi, each man thought his private thoughts about the other. They were often not charitable thoughts.

Clarke and Palmer had no secrets from each other – what was the point? Nothing was secret any more. Clarke used to enjoy walking on the South Downs; on his days off he'd drive out of the city without telling any bugger where he was going and sod off into the hills alone with his thoughts. Sometimes he'd sing the hymns he'd been taught at school; he would leave the well-trodden footpaths to avoid other walkers and would enjoy the feeling that he was an unseen speck on the landscape. One Monday morning he'd gone into work and told Palmer he had walked across the South Downs the day before.

'I know,' said Palmer. 'You were wearing new boots but you found it heavy going over the last few hundred metres to Goosehill Camp on the side of Stoughton Down.'

Clarke asked, 'Where were you?'

Palmer said, 'Here in the office.'

Clarke liked his colleague – even loved him a little – but he hated Palmer invading his privacy and he made him promise not to do it again. Palmer had promised, but Clarke could never be quite sure that Palmer resisted the temptation.

The taxi driver eyed the Prime Minister in his driving mirror and said, 'Excuse me, madam, and don't mind me asking, but why would a person be wearing sunglasses on a day like today? I can see you're no blind: do you have an eye condition, or what? I mean, are you trying to make yourself look mysterious, is that it? Is it a personality defect, you attempting to cover up, or what?'

Behind his sunglasses the Prime Minister blinked back tears.

Jack answered for him: 'Look, just shut the fuck up and drive.'

The rest of the journey to the airport was passed in complete silence.

There was an angry crowd outside the terminal at Edinburgh airport. The air-traffic controllers at Swanwick had walked out because as their leader had said, 'We can no longer guarantee the safety of planes flying over UK air-space. It is only forty-eight hours since our last computer failure and we had only just cleared up the backlog.'

At one-thirty p.m., with ninety-seven planes about to land or take off, the computer system had gone dangerously berserk and had started showing an old episode of *Star Trek*.

In the spirit of adventure the Prime Minister suggested that he and Jack take the first available plane flying to a British destination. The cafeteria had run out of refreshments so the Prime Minister joined the queue for the cold-drinks machine. A middle-aged woman in front of him said angrily to nobody in particular, 'I've lost a half-a-million-pound export contract because of this Swanwick business!'

The Prime Minister, ever mindful of the balance of payments, asked the nature of the woman's business. 'I air-freight haggis burgers to hotels on the Costa del Sol,' she said. 'At least, I try to,' she added bitterly. 'This bloody government don't give a toss.'

'Oh, but that's not true,' said the Prime Minister. 'We care, hugely!'

The queue shuffled forward slowly. At its head a man was banging on the franchised soft-drinks machine. He had inserted a Euro coin by mistake and the machine was withholding a can of Fanta from him by way of protest.

After a few vicious kicks the man went off in search of somebody who would take responsibility for his loss.

Jack was standing in the newspaper queue waiting to pay for a copy of the *Edinburgh Evening News*. He had been attracted by the headline, 'PM's Wife: "A wart is holy".'

There was a confrontation taking place at the cash till. Jack had time to read the whole of the front page:

> In an astonishing interview this morning on Radio Four's *Today* programme, Adele Floret-Clare, the Prime Minister's wife, told John Humphrys that human life was absolutely sacred and that since warts grow on the human body they should be regarded as holy and should be buried with care and respect, and that it was 'clearly wrong' to dispose of them in a hospital incinerator. An astonished Humphrys asked, 'And what about corns? Are they holy too?' To which Mrs Floret-Clare replied, 'Clearly.' A spokesperson for the Society of Chiropodists said later, 'If we had to have a funeral service for every corn we remove our costs would go sky-high and would have to be passed on to our customers, many of whom are elderly.'

Underneath a paparazzo picture of Adele Floret-Clare, which made her look both gormless and mad, Jack read, 'Turn to page 3'. Jack turned. There was another picture of Adele, this time with Sir Paul McCartney. The article went on:

A government spokesman said today, 'Mrs Floret-
Clare's views are her own, and it is not government
policy to legislate for the burial of small body-parts.'
The Archbishop of Canterbury's office issued a short
statement: 'The Archbishop of Canterbury does not
comment on religious matters.' Peter Bowron, a
fashionable London chiropodist, has approached several tabloid newspapers offering to tell his story in
exchange for a six-figure sum.

Jack and the Prime Minister got to the head of their queues
at more or less the same time and with equally frustrating
results. The computerised till was refusing to take cash, and
would open up only for Switch cards. Jack handed his over
and said to the girl as she swiped the card, 'It's a bit of a
palaver for the price of a tabloid, isn't it?'

She said, 'I don't care, I don't like touching cash – you
never know where it's been.'

The soft-drinks machine was behaving like a despot in
a Third World country: granting favours to some and
withholding them from others. The Prime Minister felt that
it simply wasn't fair. He had carefully inserted the correct
amount of money. He had pressed the relevant touch
pad indicating his choice but nothing had rolled down the
internal chute and into the stainless steel cradle.

He'd wept convulsively at his mother's graveside and felt
dehydrated like a dried-up fruit. He needed to slake his thirst

urgently. It was hours since he'd had a drink. He pressed the button for the return of his money, but the machine kept it within its mysterious interior. But then a stroke of luck: a man wearing overalls carrying the embroidered logo of the soft-drink company was approaching the machine with a steadfast expression and a big bunch of keys.

The Prime Minister stepped back and allowed the man to open the machine, then asked the man for a can of sugar-free orange pop. The man said robotically, 'If you need to purchase a can of pop, madam, you'll have to put sixty pence in the machine.'

'But I have,' protested the Prime Minister.

'But how would I know that, madam?'

'Because I've just told you so,' he said, smiling at the man who stared back. The man had similar confrontations several times a day. But it was in his short-term contract that he was not allowed to give refunds to the public. At the one-day training course he had attended it was implied that the public were lying, cheating bastards who would sell their small children for a free can of pop.

The man said, 'Write to the company address on the machine.'

'What, go to all that trouble to find pen and paper and an envelope, queue at the post office for a stamp and write away for sixty pee?'

'You'd be surprised how many cheapskates do it,' said the man as he filled the machine with fresh supplies of tins containing carbonated water, flavourings, sweeteners and colourings.

'They're not cheapskates, they're people who have been cheated by your company.'

'My company doesn't own this machine,' said the man triumphantly. 'The leaseholder does.'

'And who is the leaseholder?' demanded the Prime Minister.

'How would I know that?' said the man, turning his back and finishing the conversation.

Jack and the Prime Minister left the chaos of the airport behind them and headed for the long taxi queue. They were intending to go to the coach station, but after waiting an hour and a half in the taxi queue Jack said to the Prime Minister, 'Let's walk.'

'I can't walk in these shoes,' the Prime Minister replied.

'Just to the main road,' said Jack, encouragingly.

They tried hitching a lift together at first, but nobody stopped. It was uncomfortable and frightening standing on the overgrown grass verge as trucks with speeding tyres hurtled past them, almost sucking them into their slip-stream.

Jack thought that the Prime Minister on his own in his Marilyn Monroe get-up would stand a better chance; he was certainly attractive enough from a distance to stop a truck.

Jack crouched behind a white hawthorn shrub, and after

115

only a few minutes heard the sound of hydraulic brakes and a rough voice shouting over the rumble of traffic. Jack leaped to his feet and had just enough time to clamber up into the cab of the articulated lorry.

The driver's face darkened; what had looked like a nice bit of fresh blonde bimbo at the side of the road had turned out to be well past its sell-by date. And she had a bloke with her, an' all.

He, Craig Blundell, was tempted to throw them both out, but his state-of-the-art in-cab radio had got stuck on Radio Three and he had turned it off angrily a few miles back up the road, tortured beyond belief by Bach's cello suites. At least now he had people to talk to; they would help keep him awake, and you never knew – Blondie might be all right in the dark.

They talked football at first. Blondie seemed to know more than the quiet bloke sitting next to her – though she was well out of order when she defended the government's part in the rebuilding of the Wembley fuck-up.

He told them he was going to Leeds first to drop a load off. 'That'll do us,' said Blondie's friend.

Blondie asked, 'What are you carrying?'

Craig longed to tell Blondie the truth: that he had fourteen Afghan asylum seekers hidden under the tarpaulin in the back of the trailer.

He hoped they were all right. They hadn't looked too good when he picked them up from Perth docks. He had almost felt sorry for the poor bastards; according to the first mate of the trawler it had been a particularly bad crossing, and three of them had been carried on to the truck by the others.

Sometimes when he listened to them jabbering away in their own language he wondered what they were saying and who they were. It made him mad when he read in the papers that he, Craig, was trafficking in human misery. He was doing them a favour, wasn't he? England was easily the best country in the world. OK, so diesel was an outrageous price here, outrageous, but he had travelled as far as Russia in his truck and he could tell you from personal experience that there was a lot of bollocks talked about Europe. He knew from personal experience that French food was crap and Swedish girls were frigid. He also knew he was taking a bit of a risk, but what else could he do? Owner-drivers like him lived from day to day; he was always searching for a load, and he sometimes spent days at return load depots around Europe. It killed him to have to come back to the United Kingdom empty, all that diesel and nothing in the back.

He had to make a minimum of £10,000 a month profit: the mortgage; payments on his truck and Michelle's Merc; school fees for Emily and Jason; violin lessons; the holiday in Cancún; Michelle's hundred-quid-a-time haircuts. It got to him, sometimes, and he wondered what it was all about. He hardly saw Michelle and the kids, and when he did they made him feel ashamed of the way he spoke and ate. And, well, what was it Edward Clare had said? 'Everybody is middle class now.' But Craig knew that he still had a long way to go himself. Meantime, it was him who was in human misery.

Craig looked the Prime Minister in the eye – alarming, since they were overtaking a petrol tanker at the time – and said, 'I took steel plating from Poland to Aberdeen then picked a load of firelighters up from Perth and I'll drop that at Leeds.'

The Prime Minister said, 'It sounds absurd to be constantly moving stuff around.'

Jack answered, 'It's called globalisation.'

A poem from childhood came into the Prime Minister's head, 'Cargoes' by John Masefield:

> Dirty British coaster with a salt-caked smoke stack,
> Butting through the Channel in the mad March days,
> With a cargo of Tyne coal,
> Road-rail, pig-lead,
> Firewood, iron-ware, and cheap tin trays.

'Trading is what made this country great, in the past,' said the Prime Minister.

'Well I'd put it another way, sir,' said Jack, forgetting for a moment to whom he was supposed to be talking. He looked at Craig but Craig was speaking into his mobile phone and talking to someone called Michelle.

'I'd say,' Jack continued, 'that it was exploitation that made us rich, but not great.'

'So what form of economic system would you prefer us to have?' asked the Prime Minister irritably.

'A simpler one,' said Jack.

'You'd have us all weaving our own clothes and growing our own food, would you? And morris dancing round a maypole, would you? And I suppose when we're sick we forage in the hedgerows for natural remedies, do we?'

Jack said, 'You don't morris dance round a maypole, and anyway you're the fan of the middle way.' It was their second quarrel.

On the other end of Craig's mobile Michelle said, 'You said your radio was broken.'

'It is,' said Craig.

'But I can hear the Prime Minister talking in the background,' she said.

Craig laughed. If he did have the chance to get that stupid bastard Edward Clare in his cab, he'd put him right about a few things – the outrageous price of diesel, for a start.

It was dark when they got to the outskirts of Leeds, and a fine rain was falling. Craig pulled into a lay-by at the side of a dual carriageway and said, 'I think it's time Blondie paid me for the lift.'

The Prime Minister tucked his skirt tightly around his thighs and moved closer to Jack.

'I'm up for a threesome, if that's your worry,' Craig said when Jack didn't get out of the cab.

Jack was insulted: did he look like the type of man who would allow his woman to give her sexual favours for the price of a few litres of fuel? He helped the Prime Minister down from the cab, saying, 'Thanks, Craig, we're very, very grateful – oh, and by the way, somebody's obviously been tampering with your tachograph, perhaps while your back was turned.'

Craig threw their bags after them and slammed the cab door. Then he sat for a few minutes and talked to Michelle, saying he'd be home in Sheffield by three a.m. at the latest and that he hoped that she would be nice to him when he joined her in bed. Michelle said she'd been in the gym all afternoon and was totally wiped out and that it would be nicer for her if he let her sleep.

Craig rested his head on the steering wheel. Nobody loved him and for once not even the thought of the money he'd get for delivering his cargo could cheer him up.

In the darkness of the moonless night, fourteen Afghans crept from a hole cut in the soft wall of the trailer and sat around several picnic tables provided for resting motorists by Yorkshire County Council. Their leader, a former ear, nose and throat surgeon, indicated that the group should remain silent until the footsteps of the man and the blonde woman had gone further down the road.

★

Jack couldn't remember a time when he'd felt so tired. He suggested that they should lie down on the grass verge for a while and rest, but the Prime Minister confessed that he was mildly phobic about insects, so they trudged on along the A64 towards Leeds.

In the far distance a fire was burning; as they drew nearer they could see that it was a car fire. The colours of the flames were magnificent rich reds, blazing oranges, heavenly blues and the yellows of the rising sun. There were three police cars at the scene. The policemen were talking excitably about the car chase that had preceded the crash and the fire.

In the back of one of the police cars sat a pale-faced boy. As Jack and the Prime Minister approached they could see the policeman in the front seat give the boy a lit cigarette.

As Jack and the Prime Minister drew closer a young constable said, 'Move along please.'

Jack wondered why policemen always said this. They weren't in the way and as taxpayers they were entitled to see the law in action, weren't they? He stood his ground, but the Prime Minister retreated and stood so far away that he could no longer feel the heat from the burning car.

The young constable said with cold politeness, 'Move on, sir, or I'll book you for obstruction.'

'But I'm not in the way,' said Jack.

'The fire engine might want to park where you're standing.'

'Then I'll move away, won't I. I'm not a bloody fool.'

The Prime Minister said, 'Leave it, Jack, let's go.'

Jack would not move. He didn't like being treated by this young whelp of a policeman as though the public were the natural enemies of the police.

The young policeman still had adrenalin surging through his body. It was his first car chase and he was anxious to get back to his colleagues, who were enjoying an informal debrief. The last thing they wanted was some stroppy civilian muscling in and demanding his rights.

'What's your name and what are you doing out at this time of night?' he asked.

'Jack, leave it, it's not worth it,' pleaded the Prime Minister, sounding like a girlfriend in the build up to a fight.

'I resent your implication that I'm breaking any kind of law. I'm walking along a public highway with my companion . . .'

The young constable's patience snapped. 'You're a civilian rubber-necking and obstructing the scene of a crime, and if you don't move on right now . . .'

A fat sergeant who looked like a Donald McGill seaside-postcard policeman waddled over and asked, 'What's up, Darren?'

'He's refusing to answer any questions, sir.'

A siren was heard signalling that a fire engine was on its way.

'Your name, sir?' asked the fat sergeant.

'My name is Jack Sprat,' said Jack.

The sergeant's face lost its smile. 'Don't try and play silly buggers with me. What's your name?'

'My name is Jack Sprat,' repeated Jack, who carried documentation to prove it. Jack could almost sympathise; in the past, when he was on street patrol, he had often asked suspicious-looking people for their names and had been told they were Engelbert Humperdinck or Bing Crosby. Jack took his wallet out and showed the sergeant his library card.

The sergeant turned it over in his podgy hands then gave it back to Jack and said, 'Right, move along now and I'll let you go.'

But Jack couldn't rid himself of the grievance he felt against these two policemen. He'd done nothing but slow down and look at a burning car. If he had passed by without a glance, what would that have said about his humanity?

The Prime Minister was furious with Jack's obdurance; he couldn't look at his mulish face a moment longer. He switched his attention to the tail end of a conversation a few of the other policemen were having. A middle-aged policeman with a regulation beard said, 'I'm going to have a bad back in two years' time, and because I'll have hurt my back on the job I'll get compo and the full pension, so me and the missis are opening up a bar on the Costa del Crime.'

The Prime Minister was intrigued. How on earth did the constable know he was going to injure his back at work in two years' time?

Another policeman was talking. '. . . if they take me out of cars, I'll do my back in next year. There's no way I'm plodding the fuckin' pavements.'

Everyone moved aside as the fire engine drew up and manoeuvred into position. The Prime Minister was thrilled by the sight of the gleaming engine and the firemen in their masculine uniforms. Did the fire service recruit on good looks lately? Did the requirement for a head for heights state that the head be handsome and heroic? The Prime Minister hastily applied his lipstick and ran his fingers through his blonde curls, but he stepped a little further back into the shadow, aware that his damn beard was coming through again.

Jack was now embroiled in an argument with the fat sergeant about the Human Rights Act, which Jack had sneered about in the recent past but which seemed to him now to be of the utmost importance. But when the firemen had extinguished the flames with a foam spray the argument went out of him, and he moved away to where the Prime Minister was waiting. They began the long walk into Leeds.

After some time they found themselves in the middle of what appeared to be a ghost-town council estate. Whole streets were boarded up. A row of houses had been burned out. Then a taxi drew up outside a boarded house and a couple of teenage girls in crop tops and hipster pants climbed out and let themselves into the metal-plated front door.

Jack ran across to the taxi and flagged it down. The taxi

driver, Ali, sat at the wheel encased on three sides in a steel-mesh cage. He was joyous when Jack asked him to take him and his lady friend to a good hotel in Leeds city centre.

'I'll take you to the best hotel in Leeds, innit,' said Ali enthusiastically. 'They got antiques in the rooms and music and phones in the bathroom and they've even got cats for you to stroke to make you feel at home. They got eighty channels on the TV and the lime and orange juice comes free.'

They drove past more dereliction. At a roundabout the Prime Minister remarked that it was unusual to see council workmen working in the early hours of the morning. Burly men were lifting paving slabs and stacking them in the back of a white van.

Ali shouted, 'They're thieving bastards. Nicking the pavement, innit.'

'York stone,' said Jack. 'They'll fetch fifty quid a slab in London.'

The Prime Minister told Jack that David Samuelson had recently paid £7,000 for a York-stone patio, which was laid by 'contractors' from Leeds.

Ali said, 'This is the Gumpton estate. Only a few taxis will come here after dark – wild people live here. Savages.'

There was a clattering noise overhead, then a bright beam of light illuminated the interior of the taxi. 'The police helicopter is in the sky,' shouted Ali with delight. He made it sound as though he had just heard the first cuckoo of spring.

The helicopter hovered over them for a few minutes but flew away to the east as they neared the city centre. A weary voice crackled over the radio.

'Come in, Ali, come in, Ali, come in. Where are you, Ali?'

'I'm going home to sleep, boss, I'm outside my house now.'

The Prime Minister pursed his lips in disapproval – they were in fact pulling up outside The Falls, a converted grain warehouse that sprawled alongside a canal. Jack booked Ali and asked him to pick them up at o-ten-hundred hours. The weir that gave the hotel its name could be heard as Jack and the Prime Minister walked along the wet cobbles to the front door. A night porter called Norman let them in and switched on the futuristic-style gas fire in the minimalist fireplace in the reception area.

While Jack registered the Prime Minister took one of two dozen red apples that had been arranged in a pyramid shape in a glass bowl. Norman frowned at this; it was understood by the clientele of The Falls that the tower of apples was an *objet d'art* and that only a fool would take one and eat it.

While Jack filled in the registration form – Mr Jack Sprat and Miss E. St Clare – Norman went behind the reception desk and microwaved two glasses of mulled wine. It was far too hot to drink so Jack and the Prime Minister were forced to hang around and talk to Norman while the wine cooled. Norman boasted about the famous and important people who had stayed in The Falls. He mentioned a *Coronation Street* actress, unfamiliar to Jack, who had requested a Mother's Pride and cheese sandwich at four o'clock in the morning. Norman tapped the side of his nose and said, 'Don't ask me how I did it, but at four-twenty-five she was eating that sandwich.'

Jack cut Norman off halfway through an anecdote about Sir Cliff Richard and a pot of Clarins face cream.

The Prime Minister was so tired that he climbed into bed without removing his make-up. He said, 'I know it's sluttish of me, Jack, but I promise to cleanse, tone and moisturise extra carefully in the morning.'

They lay awake in the double bed talking about police reform. Jack suggested that policemen on the beat should be paid on a higher scale than their patrol-car colleagues. The Prime Minister whispered sleepily that he would have a word with the Home Secretary, John Hay, when he got back to Number Ten.

Chapter Nine

Norma was burning bacon in a frying pan. It was how she and James liked it. James had told her how pale and watery the bacon at the children's home had been, how the fat had not been properly cooked and how the rind had been chewy and impossible to swallow. So the small kitchen was full of the smell of burning fat and crispy bacon.

James was flapping smoke away from Peter's cage with a copy of the *Sun*. A headline said, 'Adele: Toe Man Tells All'. James was telling Norma how he'd been sexually abused by somebody who now sat in the House of Lords. 'He bought me a leather jacket one Christmas and a Yamaha keyboard the next. But nobody would pay for lessons so I swapped it for a racing bike and that got stole a week later from outside social services.'

All James's stories were depressing if you listened carefully and ignored the laughter that bubbled through them.

Norma lifted the crisped-up bacon out of the pan with a charred wooden spatula, then laid the crumbling bacon bits on slices of white spongy bread. Then, with a delicate hand, she shook evenly dispensed droplets of HP Sauce over the contents. When the sandwiches had their bread lids in place,

Norma cut across them diagonally. James thought this showed class and he told Norma she was a classy bird – and she was today. She'd been in her wardrobe and brought to the front the clothes she used to save for best. She was wearing the turquoise two-piece she wore to Stuart's ill-fated and short-lived wedding to that beanpole Karen. Even in her flat white silk shoes Karen had towered above everybody else in the registry office, including the bouncers. Stuart had stuffed a layer of newspaper inside his new shoes in a vain attempt to minimise the height difference between them, but there was still sniggering among some of the guests.

Jack had driven from London for the ceremony and brought with him a pretty young woman of average height called Celia. When it became obvious that the fight at the reception was going to go on for a while, Jack whisked Celia away without pausing to say goodbye to Norma, who was in the thick of it. Jack had been up for a promotion with a special services unit and hadn't wanted to be around when the Leicester plods arrived to break up the fun.

In the car on the way down the M1 to London, Celia, who was a clinical psychologist, opined that Stuart, who was obviously an aggressive type, had married Karen because the ridicule she received gave him the perfect excuse to have a fight whenever he felt the need.

It had quickly become a habit for James to read aloud from the *Sun*. Norma couldn't be bothered with reading herself but she had always loved stories.

As told to David Grubb, staff reporter: 'I first met Mrs Floret-Clare in May 1997. My client list was full but she sent word through one of my celebrity clients that she would like me to do her feet. I think Lulu had mentioned my name to her at a Persons of Restricted Growth charity dinner.

Quite honestly, her feet were in a shocking state. She'd been abusing them terribly during the six-week pre-election period. She had multiple problems: corns, hard skin, bunions and the early-warning signs of hammer-toe syndrome were present.

During the first hour-long appointment she worked on her laptop. But on subsequent visits we chatted about this and that. One day my life partner, Gregory, said, "Your little chats with the Prime Minister's wife are of historical importance and should be recorded." So purely for the sake of future historians I began to tape my conversations with Mrs Floret-Clare. She was unaware of the recording device. She might have become stressed had she known about it and stress is bad for the feet, and as a fully trained and certified chiropodist my first priority must be the health of my clients' feet.'

Norma said, 'I'm on the waiting list to get my feet done. But by the time my turn comes I'll have so much hard skin I shan't be able to get into my shoes.'

Peter swung happily on his little trapeze and watched Norma and James tearing at their bacon sandwiches. Norma said, 'You like your little cage, don't you, Peter? It's cosy, ain't it?'

The afternoon before, an angry woman from Victims Fight Back – Marjorie Makinson – had called on Norma and had offered to counsel her about her mugging trauma. Norma had led the woman into the kitchen and explained that she was recovering from the shock now and that James, her new lodger, had found out who the mugger was and had given him a good pasting, but he hadn't managed to get any of her property or money back.

Marjorie was horrified. 'I wholly disapprove of taking the law into your own hands, Mrs Sprat,' she said.

Norma answered: 'We've always taken the law in our own hands round 'ere. You'd get your legs broke if you thieved from a neighbour's house or touched an old 'un or a kiddy.'

For a few moments Norma enjoyed the view from the moral high-ground and remembered the words of advice Trev had given his young stepsons: 'Never shit on your own patch, lads, and never steal from the poor. Go out to the suburbs and hang about until you see one of them happy families going somewhere together – picnic, sports centre, you know the sort of thing. It ain't a crime to take stuff off the middle classes; they're insured and anyway it keeps the economy going.'

Marjorie was eyeing Peter's cage. She was not only a

counsellor of the victims of crime but also an animal-rights activist, and she was sure that Peter's animal rights were being infringed. Not only was his cage smaller than the written guidelines in the proposed Animal Rights bill, but also Peter was entitled by law to have a mate.

Marjorie explained the Animal Welfare legislation, which she had memorised. 'According to RSPCA guidelines, Mrs Sprat, your budgie has the right to a large aviary where he can enjoy the company of other budgerigars in a stimulating environment that includes toys and branches.'

Norma said, 'Peter's happy in his cage and he likes being an only bird.'

'Nevertheless,' said Marjorie, 'the law is the law.'

Adele picked a flake of croissant from her Joseph sweater, then took Wendy's hand and spoke to her in an urgent and evangelical manner. 'Wendy, Barry's leg is – or was, rather – a large part of him, you can't just discard it as if it were a leg of lamb or something.'

Wendy said angrily, 'I wouldn't discard a leg of lamb, would I? I'd cook it and eat it.'

Adele said, 'You're such a bloody pedant, Wendy. It's one of your least attractive qualities. Now, I've had a word with a certain cardinal pal of mine and he's agreed to officiate at the interment of Barry's leg. It would be a quiet affair, just family – and me, of course. An opening's come up at Kensal Rise . . . Say yes now and I can start things moving. All I need is Barry's inside-leg measurement for the coffin.'

Wendy said, 'Doesn't Barry have a say in all this?'

'Of course he does,' replied Adele. 'And he's in full agreement. I spoke to him this morning.'

'But he's off his head on morphine. He's deeply trauma-tised,' said Wendy.

'Yes, and this is a way of reaching closure. He can come to the funeral of one of his significant body-parts. He can talk about what the leg meant to him, his memories of it. You shouldn't deny him this opportunity, Wendy.'

Wendy wondered, not for the first time, if it was Adele who was mad or herself. Was it unreasonable to oppose the burial of her son's right leg or not? Adele was extremely clever and, more importantly, she was an original thinker and a leading amateur theologian.

'I'd like to wait until your husband comes back and talk it over with him,' said Wendy.

Adele's face crumpled; last night the voices had told her that Ed was never coming back.

Alexander McPherson barged into the room and slammed a huge pile of newspapers down on the coffee table in front of Adele. Apart from the *Catholic Herald*, each front page was dominated by Adele's wart story.

'Have you seen them?' He was struggling to control his rage. Adele had broken a sacred rule. She had gone on the *Today* programme and been interviewed by John Humphrys without the knowledge of the press office. It was as if a Christian had volunteered to face a colosseum full of lions and had expected to escape unhurt.

Adele was thrilled to see herself on the front pages of the national press. And she was proud of the context. She was standing up for the sanctity of life and celebrating the holiness of ordinary men and women.

Wendy said, 'Adele's arranged for Barry's leg to be buried by a cardinal in Kensal Rise.' Wendy needed to tell somebody who had his feet on the ground – somebody who, though a bully and a manipulator, was so obviously sane.

Adele picked up the *Independent* and read the front-page leader. Alexander and Wendy exchanged a look, and Alexander put his index finger to the side of his head and twiddled it in an internationally recognised gesture. 'Adele,' he said, 'who is your doctor?'

Chapter Ten

Jack was sitting in the eighteenth-century wet-nurse chair looking out of the window at the unmoving grey water of the canal. A black wooden cat lay at his feet. He had stumbled over it several times in the night. He was trying very hard to be patient, but the Prime Minister had been getting ready to go out for over an hour now. Jack wondered what else the Prime Minister could do to himself. Surely there was a limit as to how much make-up he could apply, and to how long he could primp and rearrange his hair in front of the mirror.

A complimentary copy of the *Daily Telegraph* had been pushed under their door before they were awake. Jack was alarmed to read the headline 'Premier's Wife in Fundamentalist Controversy', but when he showed it to the Prime Minister Edward merely said, 'It's tremendous that Adele has opened up a debate on such an important theological matter,' and went into the bathroom to curl his eyelashes.

The Gumpton council estate lay in a gentle valley bordered on all sides by six-lane highways. A series of long pedestrian bridges and tunnels connected the estate with the outside world. As a resident wrote in the *Yorkshire Post*, 'I know what it feels like to be a hamster now!'

There was a widespread belief among the population of this largely forgotten area that the weather was always worse over the Gumpton – that the clouds were lower and the wind was colder here than in other parts of Leeds. There was no meteorological evidence for this belief, but it persisted and added to the sense of persecution that the residents had been sent or ended up here as some kind of social punishment. Some of the younger inhabitants who'd tried prison said they pre-ferred it to life on the Gumpton; there was more to do in prison.

Looking at the estate, you could be forgiven for thinking that it had been separated somehow from the rest of Great Britain and had never enjoyed any form of governance. It was like a lost civilisation. Travellers occasionally came in from the outside world – social workers, teachers and council officials – but they did their work anxiously and left before night fell. Before descending the hill into the Gumpton, Ali muttered a prayer asking Allah for his protec-tion. On the way he had already told his passengers, the unsmiling man and the pretty blonde lady, that he would not, under any circumstances, leave his taxi unattended. The male adolescents of the Gumpton tribe were culturally programmed to steal any vehicle of any kind. A police Land

Rover had recently been stolen and driven around the estate by two twelve-year-old boys to the cheers and congratulations of most of the population.

First Ali cruised the Gumpton estate pointing out the major landmarks. All the clichés of extreme poverty were there. The Prime Minister squirmed in his seat as they passed the boarded-up houses and the dirt paths where the pavement used to be. He had once visited the shantytown of Rio de Janeiro, where the people existed on a subsistence wage but where, at least, there was an atmosphere of lives being lived and even enjoyed. Here, though, was no evidence that the lives of the Gumpton residents were of any value whatsoever.

Ali parked beside an open space covered in mud and grass that may once have been a park. Heavy rain now obscured the windscreen and Ali switched on the wipers. They watched as a pick-up truck drew up outside a house opposite and two un-athletic, flabby men, both wearing tracksuits and trainers, got out of the cab and struggled to remove a rope that tied an old double mattress to the back of the pick-up. The rain had become a downpour and soon the hair of the two men was plastered to their heads. Their mouths formed violent and obscene words as they hurried to untie the mattress and get it inside the house before the rain soaked it. Jack, Ali and the Prime Minister watched the race as though it was a sporting event.

A tall stocky woman with weightlifters' arms opened the

front door of the house; a toddler wearing only a Spider-Man T-shirt and with a bottle hanging from his mouth clutched at her tracksuit trousers. She appeared to be shouting encouragement to the men, but when Ali wound his window down the trio in the car heard her yell, 'Getta move on, ya fat bastards!'

One of the men roared, 'Do you want this mattress or not, Toyota?'

The men hoisted the mattress on to their heads and staggered blindly up the path towards the front door. The half-naked toddler ran joyfully to greet them.

Toyota chased the toddler, caught him and yanked him into the air by the back of his bunched up T-shirt. The toddler screamed and arched his back and then Toyota slapped at his legs and bare buttocks. The child took a deep breath and held it inside himself. The automatic responses of his small body failed him for a moment.

Inside the car the three men waited for the toddler to draw breath again. The Prime Minister's lips trembled. 'It's utterly barbaric, Jack, you must do something!'

Toyota's strong arms had lifted the bunched T-shirt higher and had brought the child's face level with her own, and she was now slapping at the child in a roughly syncopated rhythm. The words she was screaming into the toddler's face acted as a type of punctuated counterpoint. 'How. many. times. do. I. have. to. tell. you. to. stay. in. the. fuck. ing. house., Tush. in. ga?'

138

'Tush.In.Ga?' queried the Prime Minister, who was pale now under his Max Factor Pan Stik.

'Tushinga,' said Ali. 'It's an African name.'

Jack reflected that it was only the very rich and the very poor who gave their children such extraordinary names.

The two men shifted impatiently under their mattress umbrella, waiting for the toddler's punishment to end. The little one now had sufficient air inside his lungs to scream. The terrible sound propelled the Prime Minister out of the car and up the path. He circumnavigated the mattress and confronted the woman. Tushinga was still hanging in the air with the slap marks showing like red petals against his pale, perfect skin.

'Please! Stop now,' pleaded the Prime Minister.

'Oo the fuck are you?' said Toyota, who was breathing heavily with her exertions. Beating a toddler was harder work than it looked.

'I'm a social worker,' lied the Prime Minister.

'You ain't my social worker,' said Toyota.

One of the flabby men shouted politely, 'Can we get this fuckin' mattress in the fuckin' 'ouse, please?'

The Prime Minister, Toyota and the baby moved aside and the men struggled through the front door and disappeared inside.

The Prime Minister picked up the feeding bottle, which he now saw was half full of what appeared to be Coca-Cola, and gave it to the sobbing child, saying, 'Here, Tushinga, don't cry. Mommy won't smack you again.'

'I'll teck his bleddy head off if he don't do as he's told,' said Toyota. 'He's gotta learn.'

'He won't learn by being beaten, will he?' said the Prime Minister.

'It's 'ow I learned,' said Toyota in a reasonable tone.

'Hello there, Tushinga.' The Prime Minister chucked the child under the chin, but he turned and snuggled his head into his mother's neck. His sobs were subsiding now and his mother began to stroke his hair away from his wet face and made a pattern of little kisses around one of his dimpled hands.

''Ave you took over from Andy, then?' Toyota asked.

The Prime Minister went on with the lie. 'Yes, Andy's had a nervous breakdown and I'm his replacement.' He knew there was a shortage of social workers due to stress and low recruitment levels.

Toyota replied: 'I can't say I'm surprised, he were right jumpy the last time I seen him.' She indicated that the Prime Minister was to go inside the house, saying, 'You'd betta come in for a cup of tea.'

She looked suspiciously at the taxi parked at the kerb and said, 'It's no wonder there ain't any places in the social-services nursery; they're spending all their bleedin' budget on taxis for cowin' social workers.'

The Prime Minister looked back pleadingly at Jack before

Toyota led him inside the house. Jack waved then settled down in the back seat of the taxi to read the *Daily Telegraph*.

Ali pulled a lever under the sagging driver's seat and the back inclined. He was almost instantly asleep. This was turning into the perfect job; the meter already showed £39.40 and it was still only mid-morning.

Tushinga was playing with an empty video case and a few clothes pegs on a threadbare carpet, watched by Toyota and the Prime Minister. The living room was dominated by a large flat-screen television on a smoked-glass stand. It was showing a wildlife programme, and a pack of jackals were tearing a zebra to pieces. There was a black three-piece suite that was almost but not quite leather and hung on the wall above the gas fire was a lurid blown-up photograph of baby Tushinga.

Tens of thousands of cigarettes had been smoked in the room and the ceiling and walls were a fashionable light-nicotine shade.

The Prime Minister was reminded of his own living-room décor. Adele had agonised for days over paint charts with an expensive interior designer who had charged her £500 an hour for a consultation and more for applying a few coats of paint called 'Moody Camel'.

He took a small notebook from his handbag and wrote a few notes. Toyota was being indiscreet about benefit fraud and as he wrote the Prime Minister imagined producing the notes on the floor of the House and silencing the critics in his party of the proposed government benefit-fraud crackdown.

Toyota lit a Berkeley cigarette and politely offered one to the Prime Minister. 'No thank you, I've never smoked,' he said, raising his hand in the stop signal.

'Never?' said Toyota. 'So how do you know you don't like it if you've never tried?'

She made him feel uneasy, as though being a non-smoker was a major flaw in his character.

The fat men stood in the doorway, smoking and watching the television. They remained un-introduced.

'Go on, try one,' urged Toyota. 'Our mam give me my first fag when I were eleven.'

One of the fat men said, 'Right, we're goin' now, Toy; 'ave you got that tenner, then?'

Toyota said, 'I've got nowt in me purse. You can 'ave a look if you like.'

It transpired that Toyota had bought the five-pound mattress plus five pounds delivery from an old relation of one of the men. Her own mattress, now in the back garden, had been irretrievably damaged when Tushinga had got hold of her lighter. Toyota looked at the Prime Minister and said, 'That's why I have to be 'ard on 'im. I don't want him growing up to be a hooligan.'

'You'll have to get us the fiver for the diesel,' said the other man. 'That fuckin' tank's empty now.'

Toyota flew into an instant rage. 'You didn't say nothin'

142

about payin' you on the day. You'll 'ave to wait until I get me social.'

'Me fuckin' tank's empty and neither of us 'as got nothin', an' we've gorra nother job in half an hour.'

'Why ain't you gorrany money?' demanded Toyota.

''Cause we 'ad to pay up front for the scaffold we put up this morning, first thing,' he replied.

'Phone our Derek and see if he'll lend me a fiver,' said Toyota.

One of the men took a pay-as-you-go mobile from out of his pocket, pressed a few buttons and said, 'Toyota needs a tenner to pay for that mattress and the diesel.' He waited for a moment, then grunted and said to Toyota, 'He says fuck off, you still owe him for that baby buggy.'

Toyota screamed, 'The fuckin' wheels fell off outside Lidel's and Tushinga fell on the fuckin' pavement. I were six fuckin' hours in fuckin' casualty!'

The Prime Minister's notes were getting confused. He had written: 'mattress, lighter, fatmen VAT registered?'

One man said to the other, 'You'll 'ave to ask Polio John if he'll let me siphon some diesel from out his invalid car, else we're gonna lose that fuckin' job!'

Polio John was contacted and said that he was at the post office picking up his disability allowance, but he would drive by when he was done.

The lights went out and the television turned itself off with a click.

'I need a lecky card now,' sighed Toyota.

When the Prime Minister looked baffled she explained that the electricity company considered her to be a credit risk, so they had installed a meter. However, since a meter full of silver coinage was a delicious temptation to youth lusting for Nike trainers and crack cocaine, a plastic card had to be bought and inserted instead. The cards were available at certain shops, garages, the police station and even the fire station.

One of the fat men appeared to get an idea and said, 'Ring Lucky Paul and ask him to nip to the garage and pick up a lecky card and a gallon of diesel. He's got credit there.'

Lucky Paul was contacted but said that he no longer had credit at the garage because the old manager had been sacked for selling dirty videos out the back and the new one was 'a stuck up bastard from Manchester'.

A moody silence fell as the three penurious people in the room brooded on their immediate financial problems.

'I wish I could help,' said the Prime Minister.

'S'all right,' said Toyota. 'I know you ain't allowed to give money out.'

Without artificial light the room was very dark. Toyota said, 'I'm gonna run out of fags soon.' She looked genuinely afraid.

One of the men said, 'If we don't get to this job we won't get paid, an' that means we can't pay for the rest of the fuckin' scaffold hire, and then we lose that job an' all.'

The Prime Minister half remembered a poem his father used to recite to him, something about the lack of a nail and a battle being lost.

Toyota had a moment of inspiration. 'Didn't Coughing Tony got his asbestos money through last week?'

'Yeah, but 'e coughed his lungs up on Sunday an' died in the ambulance.'

Toyota lost her temper again. 'Why didn't nobody tell me? I used to do 'is shoppin' and fetch 'is chips when 'e were bad.'

Tears sprang immediately from her eyes and she sobbed noisily for a few moments, watched nervously by the three men. Nobody moved to comfort her. The Prime Minister felt his chest constrict; there was a ringing in his ears and was that a pain in his left arm? He leaned back in the black chair and tried to control his breathing; the problem of the £10 seemed insurmountable. He had been less worried about the billions Britain owed to the World Bank.

Jack was reading with great interest a transcript of the conversation between Adele and her chiropodist, Peter Bowron:

PB   There's a patch of rough skin on the heel . . . Yeah, Graham Norton's got the dinkiest little feet and he really takes care of them.

AF-C   I've been trying to get Eddy to come and see you. His feet are . . . well, unpleasant.

PB   Malodorous?

AF-C   And sweaty.

PB   Yeah, I saw him on the box. Digital shows everything. He was perspiring, well, freely.

AF-C   It's anxiety. He looks like Mr Cool but inside, Pete, he's a mess.

The next minute and five seconds of the conversation is muffled by the sound of a foot-sanding machine.

PB   There, that's lovely and smooth now.

AF-C   Lovely.

PB   I'll tell you who's got great feet and that's Roy Hattersley. He only came the once, he had an ingrowing toenail, but I've never forgotten his feet. They were straight and true. Beautiful instep, fabulously agile toes. He could have been a foot model.

AF-C   But he's a traitor, Pete.

PB   Perhaps, but he's got fantastic feet. Do you want a peppermint massage?

AF-C   Yes please, Pete . . . Is it true you do Posh 'n' Becks? I've heard the rumour.

PB   I can't talk about Posh 'n' Becks, Adele. I've signed a confidentiality clause in the contract.

AF-C   You can tell me. I'm very discreet. Ed tells me

everything. He's not supposed to but he has to talk to somebody. Take Bush's Star Wars defence plan. Ed thinks Bush is crazy to even think about it but . . .

PB   Do you want the half- or the full-leg massage?

AF-C   Full. I've got two hours before I'm at the Palace.

PB   What's the Queen like?

AF-C   The Queen? My God, she could bore for England. It's dogs, horses and postage stamps. Talking to her is like wading through porridge, she'd never even heard of Wittgenstein. Odd, since she's a Nazi! [Laughter]

Jack folded the paper and glanced towards the house, where Toyota could be seen looking out of the window. He got out of the car and went up the path to the front door. A moment later he was inside the house handing a £10 note over to one of the mattress-carriers.

Ali drove the Prime Minister, Jack, Toyota and Tushinga round to the one-stop centre. It was a low, purpose-built redbrick building with a frilly roll of razor wire fixed to the point where the walls met the roof.

A uniformed security guard directed them to a parking space. Next door, connected to the car park by a covered walkway, was the Gumpton Leisure Centre. A family of four were going through the entrance to the swimming pool carrying towels that looked like giant Swiss rolls under their arms. Their accents suggested that they were not residents of the Gumpton estate.

Toyota had talked continually during the ten-minute journey to the one-stop centre, where Jack was going to buy her enough electricity for three days, if she was careful and didn't switch on the fan heater in her bedroom. Though how the fuck she was going to get that mattress dry, she didn't know. She'd been on a scheme to train as a care assistant. She really liked old people; they had more to talk about than young people. Her mam had looked after Tushinga, but he was too much of a handful now he was running about, and her mam couldn't move so quickly with her bad knee. And the social-services nursery was full so, even though there were people crying out for care assistants, Toyota couldn't work. A private nursery cost over a hundred quid a week, so she would have to stay on benefits and live from hand to fucking mouth and buy her and Tushinga's clothes from the Cancer shop.

Tushinga had been asked to a party yesterday but he couldn't go because she had no money for a birthday card and a present. And he needed shoes. Proper shoes, seeing as how he was walking; she wanted his first shoes to be new, not fucked-up second-hand ones.

She'd been good at geography at school. She'd done a project on Africa. She'd given every country a different felt-tipped colour. One day she would like to travel there and see the animals running round free.

She'd done everything to make her money last the week. She'd put it in different jugs and boxes, and kept pound coins in an egg-cup, but did they know the price of disposable nappies? She had to get Tushinga toilet-trained quick. Andy, her old social worker, had told her that Tushinga was too young to control his bladder and bowels, but he understood what it meant when the fucking ice-cream van played 'Greensleeves' outside all right. He were just too lazy to fetch his potty.

Andy had said she should stop smoking, but it were only five a day now – and anyway, he smoked himself so he could talk.

She never went out, and she was only nineteen. Tushinga's dad had only seen him the one time, at the hospital the second day after he'd been born. He'd turned up with his mates and brought a giant teddy that his mam had won in a raffle, so it didn't count as a present. Sometimes he sent some money with Polio John, but he hadn't remembered his baby's first birthday. She knew she was a big girl and she weren't that pretty, but some men didn't mind that. She had a good personality and there weren't nothing about the wildlife in Africa she didn't know. She used to get books on animals out of the old library they had on the estate. It was lovely in there, quiet and smelling of polish, and with them high, curved windows. But that were a carpet warehouse now and the new library were just a room at the one-stop centre, and it were never open when you come to use it.

She didn't know what 'Tushinga' meant in African, but she would find out one day.

While Toyota bought her electricity card, Jack and the Prime Minister read the notices in the entrance lobby. A poster informed them that the Gumpton Youth Club met on Thursdays from seven to nine in the community room, apparently shared by the pensioners' bingo association and the pre-school playgroup (no places available).

Jack said, 'During the war there was a day nursery on every corner so that the women could go to work.'

The Prime Minister replied irritably, 'There are innumerable measures in place to facilitate single parents going back to work, Jack.'

Upstairs, behind coded door-locks, the council workers, urban-renewal workers, social workers, probation officers and the community policeman were meeting with the Gumpton Residents Committee. It was agreed between them that a grant should be applied for and that, should the application be successful, a new ping-pong table, four bats and a quantity of balls would be purchased in an attempt to combat vandalism and joy-riding on the estate.

Jack and the Prime Minister gave Toyota a lift back to her house. Jack carried Tushinga up the path for her. He liked the feel of the kid's arms around his neck. He gave Toyota a £20 note and said, 'I don't care how you spend it, love.'

When he got back inside the car he said savagely to the Prime Minister, 'It was twelve-fifteen on a Wednesday afternoon, so why wasn't the library open?'

The Prime Minister said nothing, but felt vaguely ashamed. His chest tightened again and he could feel pins and needles in the fingers of his left hand, but he remained silent. It couldn't be a heart attack – he was a fit man, and he played tennis and made love twice a week. His heart ought to be in good condition. He picked up Jack's newspaper and scanned the lead story. So what if Adele had called the Queen a Nazi? She was a person in her own right and was entitled to her opinion. He had great faith in Alex McPherson; he would be working like an absolute dog to minimise the damage to the government. He settled back in his seat and pulled the seatbelt over his body. He pushed these unpleasant thoughts to the very back of his mind. He still had three days left of his holiday.

Ali said, 'Where next, boss?'

Jack asked the Prime Minister what he would like to see next. 'Is there a church here?' asked the Prime Minister.

Chapter Eleven

St Luke's was an enormous edifice, now sandwiched between Costcutters and a parade of boarded-up shops. The stained-glass windows were protected by mesh shutters and the roof shone with anti-vandal grease. Confetti had been trodden into the muddy patch of ground near the porch. Music was coming from a building round the back, 'Red Sails in the Sunset'.

Jack and the Prime Minister picked a path through the mud and the rubbish from an upturned wheelie bin and found the church hall. The little building had the appearance of a stockade: it was barred and spiked and razor-wired. The door was locked, so they peered between the bars on the windows and saw old women and a few old men waltzing together. They were wearing sparkling dancing shoes. The women in pretty dresses, and the men in suits, shirts and ties. Their normal, everyday shoes were lined up in a row against the back wall.

Jack was surprised to find that his eyes were wet, though he had never particularly liked 'Red Sails in the Sunset'.

A young black man wearing a dog collar and a dark suit came out of the front door of the hall; he smiled when he saw Jack and the Prime Minister, and asked in a heavy African accent, 'Have you come for the dancing?'

The Prime Minister answered, 'Yes.' Suddenly he longed to twirl and dip in time to the music and get away from the mud and the metal and the cold wind.

The vicar introduced himself. He was Jacob Mutumbo and he had come from Pretoria as a missionary to help the poor people of the Gumpton estate. He had been at St Luke's for only six months, but he had made much progress: he had started the pensioners' dance club because dancing was good for the soul and, he was sorry to say, and please don't take offence, but the souls of the people on the Gumpton estate were damaged and needed to be repaired.

Jack took the Prime Minister in his arms to the Latin rhythms of Edmundo Ross. It was years since either of them had danced a rumba, but they moved well together and Jack was almost sorry when a wheezing old man called Ernie Napier cut in and whisked the Prime Minister away to a far corner of the hall.

Jack sat down to catch his breath and noticed that several old ladies were casting venomous looks at the Prime Minister as he rolled his hips suggestively to the hot Latin beat of 'Guantanamera'.

After Jacob Mutumbo announced a ladies' excuse me, an elderly woman with red spangled court shoes and loose dentures asked Jack to quick-step. As they sprinted around the hall together she told Jack that when she was a little girl she had given a penny of her pocket money towards sending a missionary to Africa. 'Now it's us who needs 'em,' she said.

Ernie Napier was showing off to the Prime Minister, executing steps and turns that he had dropped bit by bit from his dancing repertoire as old age and arthritis had crept up on him. But now, inspired by the Prime Minister's comparative youth and flashy glamour, he pulled out all the stops and the Prime Minister, having taken the unfamiliar woman's part and being hindered by high heels, struggled to keep up with him.

During the interval Jacob spoke to the small group about God. He made Him sound like a benevolent paterfamilias trying to keep his six-billion-strong family on the straight and narrow.

During Jacob's homily, Ernie Napier placed his hand on the Prime Minister's thigh and said, 'I might be seventy-nine but I can still do it.'

The Prime Minister pushed his hand away and said, 'You dance very well.'

Ernie put his wet mouth to the Prime Minister's ear and wheezed. 'Who's talking about dancing? I can still do *IT*.'

The thought of having sexual intercourse with wheezing, slobbery Ernie Napier tightened the Prime Minister's chest and made his palms sweat. He signalled to Jack that he'd like to leave now, but when he stood up his head swam and he sank slowly to the floor.

Pensioners crowded around him, suffocating him with the smell of old clothing and mothballs. He couldn't get enough air into his lungs and felt a rising panic together with a dull pain in his chest. A vision of the Queen with a Hitler moustache came to him. 'I'm dying,' he thought, and closed his eyes.

The ambulance took well over its recommended guideline time to arrive and the paramedics were on the defensive – blaming the anti-joy-ride barricades and their computerised call-out system for the delay.

Jack had moved the Prime Minister into the recovery position; with one hip thrust out and an arm above his head, he looked as though he was posing for a fully clothed version of *Readers' Wives*.

Ernie Napier broke down in tears after the ambulance had gone and confessed to the vicar that he was to blame for his dancing partner's collapse. 'I brought sex into the conversation,' he wept.

Jacob comforted Ernie by saying that God enjoyed sex himself and that he mustn't take the blame. When Ernie was changing out of his dancing shoes he wondered who God had sex with. It was a question that was to keep him awake for most of the night.

Jack had agreed not to contact Alexander McPherson except in the case of a life-or-death matter and now, as he sat in Ali's taxi following the ambulance carrying the stricken Prime Minister to hospital, he thought that this constituted an emergency. He phoned Alexander McPherson and reached him immediately on the designated number.

'McPherson here.'

'It's Jack. Edwina's in an ambulance on his/her way to hospital.'

'Bollocking Jesus! What's up with him/her?'

'The paramedics are treating him/her for a heart attack.'

'Is he/she fighting for breath, sweating, pain in chest and left arm, pins and needles, feels faint, high blood pressure?'

'Yes,' answered Jack.

'Jack, he's hyperventilating. He's always at it. The last time was just before he spoke to Congress last month. Bush's cardiologist checked him out; he was A-1 all round. What was he doing just before he . . . ?'

'Dancing the rumba with a pensioner called Ernie.' Jack couldn't resist adding, 'He/she's in a Marilyn Monroe get-up now.' He was rewarded by a rare sound – Alexander McPherson laughing.

'We're almost at accident and emergency. Shall I ring later?'

'Yeah, keep me posted.' He then did a not-too-bad imitation of Marilyn Monroe and sang breathily, 'Ooo shooby doo.'

It was Jack's turn to laugh, which caused Ali to look at him in puzzlement. If it was his missis who was being taken to hospital in an ambulance wearing an oxygen thingy he wouldn't be laughing, he'd be shitting himself and calling

156

all his relations to come to the hospital and praying, innit. He sometimes wondered if the English felt things like other people. His own kids had been born in England and he had noticed that when their rabbit had died from the cold they hadn't cried for long, nor, as far as he knew, had they mentioned Flopsy's name ever again.

Jack paid Ali what was shown on the meter plus a twenty per cent tip. He also advised Ali to mend his left brake-light.

Ali wrote his phone number on the back of the receipt and told Jack that he would be welcome to come to his house and meet his missis and kids.

Before Jack got out of the taxi Ali said, 'Allah is looking out for your missis, innit, even though she ain't a Muslim.'

Jack thanked him and got out of the car.

The Prime Minister lay on the hard narrow bed in the back of the ambulance and listened to an argument about trolleys between the paramedics and another unseen person. Every now and again somebody smelling of cigarettes and aftershave would bend over him and murmur, 'Keep taking long deep breaths, Edwina.'

The Prime Minister liked the smell of the oxygen and the feel of the mask. It was absolutely marvellous to be ordered about and told not to move. A glorious languor overcame him and he slept aware that, given his status as a bona fide patient, he was absolved for at least twenty-four hours from having an opinion, making a decision, issuing a statement about anything at all.

Jack was surprised to find that the Prime Minister was still in the ambulance; he had expected him to be somewhere inside the accident and emergency department being attended to by doctors. It was explained to him that no trolleys were available, and until one became free the patient would be better off where 'she' was.

Jack noticed the inference that the gender of Edwina was questionable and wasn't surprised. The Prime Minister's beard was visible under the transparent plastic mask, his lipstick had worn off and his feet without the high heels looked decidedly masculine, especially the hairy big toes.

Jack asked, 'Can't you get a doctor to come out here?'

And was told that there was a motorcyclist in resuss and that a man with the end of a vacuum-cleaner suction pipe stuck to his penis had gone berserk in the minor-injury department when the doctor informed him that his wife as next of kin would have to be told he was there.

Jack said, 'So the whole department's ground to a halt, has it?'

He left the back of the ambulance and went to look for a trolley. He pushed through a set of double doors and entered another world – the waiting area of the accident and emergency department.

It was a large, windowless room lit by banks of fluorescent lights into which came the accident-prone, the clumsy, the unfortunate and the innocent. They brought their fractures, scalds, lacerations, sprains, cuts, dull aches, constipations, vomiting, high temperatures, nose bleeds, fits, drug overdoses and listless babies to this room. They had fallen off ladders or roofs, drank bleach or whiskey or nothing. They had tipped boiling water on to their feet and trodden on broken bottles or had stumbled on pieces of Lego and fallen downstairs. Their backs had gone and they had forgotten to take the contraceptive pill and their babies had choked on various small objects. They had been sent by their GPs and telephone help-lines, and none save the occasional sufferer from Münchausen syndrome wanted to be there.

The door hinges gave an agonising piercing squeak that set Jack's teeth on edge.

A large glass cubicle with a sign saying 'Reception' held three women in grey uniforms. A short queue stood in front of each window. A room at one end of the waiting area displayed a sign saying 'Assessment Nurse' above its door. Rows of silent people sat waiting and listening to the confidential information being bellowed through the intercom which connected the reception desk to the waiting room.

While Jack waited to request a trolley he read a scrawled notice written on a white board with what looked like a black crayon.

Welcome to the Casualty Department: waiting times
Children 2 hours
Minor injuries 2 hours
Major injuries 2 hours

He felt insulted – not by the message, though that was worrying, but by the medium. He didn't expect the hospital to employ a calligrapher – though there were enough notices to keep one busy – but surely a little more time and care with the lettering on the notice would give patients and their companions confidence that similar standards prevailed throughout the hospital?

A plump woman, two in front of Jack, was giving her name and date of birth. Emily Farnham, four, five, fifty-three. The intercom whined and the people in the waiting room covered their ears against the banshee-like noise.

'I fell off a horse. I should have let go of the reins but ... . I think I've broken my ankle.'

'Take a seat, the assessment nurse will see you as soon as she can.'

Emily looked round for a seat and hopped to it unassisted.

The man in front of Jack held up his hand. Blood seeped through a white pillowslip wrapped around it. He was in shock and struggled to remember his name and date of birth.

'Is anybody with you?' shouted the receptionist. Feedback distorted her words and they were three times repeated before the man understood.

'My wife, she's parking the car.'

Jack looked around; surely somebody would come and help the man? A woman in late-middle age pushed to the front of the counter. 'I've got my dad in the car outside, he's fell and hit his head. He keeps being sick. He's eighty and he's a diabetic. I can't move him, can somebody come?'

The receptionist said, 'I'm dealing with this gentleman.'

'But he's eighty. He's a diabetic. He's hit his head. He keeps being sick.'

'You'll have to get him out of the car,' said the receptionist.

'He's a big man. I can't move him,' she replied.

'You should have called an ambulance,' the receptionist said.

The woman released hours of tension and screamed, 'I've been waiting for an ambulance for five and a half hours!' She turned away from the counter and said to the man with the bleeding hand, 'I've left the engine running and I'm parked in the ambulance bay.'

He answered, 'I've cut the top of a finger off. I brought it with me. It's in a little plastic bag in my pocket.'

Jack was a strong man but he struggled under the weight of the ex-sergeant major Philip Doughty as he carried the old man from the little Fiat car into the waiting area. Once inside the door he laid Mr Doughty across five plastic seats because there was nowhere else to lay him. The old man's daughter took off her coat and folded it to make a pillow for her father's head.

Jack pushed angrily through a door marked 'No Entry' and found himself in a corridor lined on both sides with sick people on trolleys; some were on intravenous drips, others on heart monitors.

A young man in motorcycle leathers lay pale and still with his head between two immobilising blocks. His red helmet had been placed between his feet. An old woman with white hair called out to Jack as he passed by: 'Help me, son, they're trying to kill me!'

Jack prowled the corridors looking for an emergency trolley or an empty cubicle. Eventually he came to a door marked 'Overnight Assessment'; not knowing what else to do, he asked the sweet-faced girl who appeared to be in charge of the department for help. There were two phones ringing, each with a different tone. The girl told Jack that this was a quiet day, and that she was sure a couple of trolleys would become free soon.

Jack left the department and continued to search the corridors. He saw an empty office and went inside and grabbed a pile of papers. He knew that almost anybody could go anywhere providing they looked as though they knew where they were going and had a pile of documents in their hands. He took off his jacket and rolled up his shirt-sleeves and was able to roam where he pleased.

In the empty X-ray room he found two trolleys and a porter and commandeered all three. Jack was now Dr Jack Sprat and within minutes the Prime Minister and ex-sergeant major Doughty were lying in a corridor waiting to be seen by a qualified doctor.

The Prime Minister slept fitfully; he was disturbed by strange dreams. The Queen was making a speech at Nuremberg, phalanxes of golden-haired youths looking remarkably like Prince Philip when young were chanting 'Mein Führer'. He woke gasping for air and it was some time before Jack could calm him down and reassure him that he wasn't dying and that a doctor would see him soon.

Early evening came and went and by the time night fell camaraderie had sprung up between the friends and relations of the trolley patients. Adversity had revealed to them basic nursing skills that they had not known they possessed.

At midnight friends of the motorcyclist went out and returned with boxes of Domino's pizza, which they distributed to those able to eat. The Prime Minister was given a slice of Napoli thin 'n' crusty. A small piece of pepperoni fell from his mouth and lodged on one of the suction pads that were helping to monitor his heart.

Jack removed the crumb and wiped round the Prime Minister's chin with a tissue given by the woman who had fallen from a horse. He then took a lipstick from the Prime Minister's handbag and asked him to repair his lips.

Dr Singh was not as interested as his colleagues were in the appearance of the man in the blonde wig and women's underclothes. He came from Rajistan and had been taken to Pushkar where a troupe of transvestites – beautiful, exquisitely dressed creatures – had danced for the delight of the male crowd. He was almost sure that this poor chap – who badly needed a shave and whose blonde wig kept slipping to the right – had a sound enough heart, but even so he was sorry that he had to detach the heart monitor from him and give it to another patient, an older man with angina whose need was probably greater.

The man who called himself Edwina had tried to stop the nurse from detaching the rubber pads, and had become hysterical and shouted that he had paid into the National Insurance scheme all his life and that he was entitled to have a heart monitor of his own for longer than a paltry ten minutes. He was the Prime Minister and if he died the hospital would be sorry because Malcolm Black, the Chancellor, was convinced that the NHS had more than enough resources but had no idea how to manage itself. Dr Singh had to smile at the poor fellow; he was obviously suffering from an acute-anxiety neurosis. He would keep him in overnight and let the psychiatrist see him in the morning.

Chapter Twelve

At three a.m. the Prime Minister was admitted to Bevan observation ward. Jack helped an exhausted junior doctor to fill in an admission form then settled back in an armchair to watch over the Prime Minister as he drifted in and out of sleep. It was not quite bedlam on the ward – tickets could not have been sold to gawp at the patients – but there was constant noise and disturbance. Ex-sergeant major Doughty was in the bed opposite and he cried out constantly, thinking himself back in a pontoon about to land on a Normandy beach.

A woman in the next bay said, 'Nurse, nurse, nurse!' But none of the angels came.

The suction-pipe man in the next bed put his head under the blankets and cried because of the pain and humiliation and the awful certainty that his wife would surely leave him now. He told Jack it was the second time this year that he had 'fallen' on to a suction pipe with his trousers round his ankles after the dog had accidentally turned the vacuum cleaner on in the bedroom. It stretched incredulity; even he had to admit that.

Jack was glad when the ward lights were turned on at six

o'clock sharp. The Prime Minister woke and said that he felt much better, but he looked a fright. Jack passed him a lipstick and went in search of a razor.

The Prime Minister lay back against his pillows and watched a dowdy woman in an ill-fitting nylon overall pushing a rancid mop along the middle of the ward floor.

Ex-sergeant major Doughty shouted, 'You should clean under the bed, that's where the germs are!'

Jack bought a bag of Bic razors from the poorly stocked hospital shop, and then went outside to phone Ali on his mobile. Their bags were still at the hotel, and he asked Ali to pick them up and deliver them to the hospital, Bevan ward. Ali said he would do it as soon as he could, but he had to go to the mosque first.

When Jack returned to the ward, he found the Prime Minister talking to the wretched-looking woman with the mop.

'Jack, this is Pat, she's been telling me about her impossible workload. She has to clean two wards all by herself in only three hours. Before they privatised the cleaning service, there were two of them on each ward and they had pride in their work and could even help the nurses. I'll have to talk to the Department of Health when we get back.'

After he had shaved the Prime Minister, Jack arranged some flowers in a vase for a skeletal old woman who had only a few wisps of white hair on her pink head. 'Have you been in here long?' Jack asked politely.

'Five weeks,' she said in a voice that resembled a child's.

'I'm a bed-blocker – that's what the doctor said when he last came to see me. He stood at the end of the bed and said to his students, "Mrs Alcott is a bed-blocker." What does that mean?'

Jack stuffed the last carnation into a vase and said he didn't know, but then the Prime Minister called out, 'It means you can't be discharged because there's nobody at home to take care of you.'

'Yeah, because the bleeding government's closed all the nursing homes to save a few bob,' said a coarse-looking woman in a tartan pyjama suit.

The ward gave the appearance of being busy and efficient, but below the surface confusion reigned. Notes were lost, drugs were given to the wrong people, discharge letters went unwritten and a bouquet of flowers was delivered to the bed of a person who had died two days before. Two people called Smith were prepared for one operation; a diabetic was served a bowl of Kellogg's Sugar Puffs and given sugar in his tea. A patient with 'Nil by mouth' above her bed was asked what she would like for lunch. Meanwhile nurses bustled about busily, though with a slightly martyred air.

Doctors came and went on their rounds, but the only one who stopped to see the Prime Minister was a quietly spoken psychiatrist who had trained in Zagreb.

His report would read that he had attended at the bedside of a male person who called himself Edwina St Clare. He was struck by 'Edwina's' ever-present smile. 'He smiled fixedly throughout our conversation, which lasted an hour. This "Handicapped Smile", as named by Valerie Sinason, the noted psychotherapist, in a recent paper, is where an anxious studied grin is used as a defence mechanism.

'When I asked Ms St Clare if she had any particular worries she said, "Yes, I have worries."'

The report continued:

I asked her to list a few of her worries and she spoke for a full twenty minutes. I have transcribed from the tape only some of those on her list, as time restrictions prevent me from reproducing them in full: the Gaza Strip, electoral reform, fox-hunting, Rail-Track, the Social Exclusion Unit, the Parliamentary Privileges Committee, the last cover of *Private Eye*, the Race Relations Act, the Royal Ulster Constabulary, the former Yugoslavia, the Prevention of Terrorism Act, child poverty, the housing crisis for essential public-service workers, illegal immigration, September the eleventh, constitutional reform, ethnic foreign policy, genetically modified crops, devolution, the tobacco-advertising ban, global warming, the exchange-rate mechanisation, the next G8 Summit, Prime Minister's Questions, Osama Bin Laden, the Euro, Kashmir, the Royal finances, cod quotas and the European Fishing Policy, Air Traffic Control, the national football stadium, Al-Qu'eda, unemployment in the northeast, Robert Mugabe, Saudi Arabia, the reintroduction of foot and mouth, Rupert Murdoch, rogue asteroids, the scarcity of National Health dentists, dead dolphins on British beaches, his compulsion to wrap Bronco toilet paper around his penis, the Crown Prosecution Service, Cornish nationalists, the Financial Services Authority, street crime, identity cards (should they be called Entitlement Cards?), Bush, Iran, Iraq and Star Wars.

I attempted to comfort 'Edwina' by reassuring her that these were not her concerns but rather the government's, and that no one person could be expected to have the knowledge or expertise on so many disparate issues. I joked that even God would have His work cut out to keep up with such an extensive list. 'Edwina' became agitated at this point and said, 'God is a very able deity and I want to make it absolutely clear that He has my full support.'

He shows a fear of differentiation and a marked preference for the ill defined – the androgynous. When I asked him to name his favourite flower he replied, 'Spring and summer flowers.' When asked if he had a favourite rock band, his answer was, 'The bands that everybody likes.' Asked to name a favourite book, he replied, 'The classics.' He is pathologically unable to commit to an opinion for fear of displeasing the questioner, in this case me. I asked him about his childhood. He said, 'I want to make it absolutely clear that I had a hugely enjoyable childhood.' At this point he began to cry.

Mr Jack Sprat, 'Edwina's' companion/partner, confirmed that 'Edwina' had been under an enormous strain for many years. I suggested to Mr Sprat that 'Edwina' would undoubtedly benefit from a holiday. Mr Sprat asked if 'Edwina' would need any treatment. I said that I would let him know.

It was difficult for the patients to distinguish one rank of nurse from another. The Prime Minister committed a major *faux pas* when he asked a nurse with an MA distinction to straighten his pillows.

Jack got sick of waiting for somebody in authority to write a discharge letter and was concerned that the psychiatrist might return and keep the Prime Minister in. At four o'clock in the afternoon he disobeyed hospital rules and used his mobile phone on the ward to contact Ali and ask him to meet them at the main entrance and take them to a country-house hotel. He thought the Prime Minister would benefit from somewhere quiet where he could convalesce.

Ali said he knew the very place – he had once taken a star from *Emmerdale* there after a 'domestic' with her husband. It was miles from anywhere, and it used to be a loony bin.

Jack said, 'It sounds perfect.'

*

Morgan Clare removed the plain cover and introduced the tape to the slot in the video machine. It slid in easily and after a few moments began to play. Morgan glanced at the door to his bedroom. Should he lock it or would a locked door imply that he was ashamed of what he was about to watch? He knew his parents would disapprove but he was entitled to make his own mind up about such things, wasn't he?

During the build up to the main attraction Morgan was aware of a raw excitement building up inside him. His breath was coming fast and his legs felt as though they wouldn't support him if he stood up. The phrase 'weak with desire' came into his mind; he now knew what it meant.

Malcolm Black, the Chancellor of the Exchequer, had slipped the tape to him yesterday: 'Keep it out of the way of your mother, lad.'

Morgan knew a bit about it, of course. There had been a few lessons at school – even his grandfather Percy had been involved at one time, though the family didn't talk about that scandalous episode. So it was time to discover for himself. But why did he feel so guilty?

He crept closer to the television set. The film was in black and white and some of the images were indistinct.

The introduction to the serious hard-core stuff tormented Morgan, but he knew he'd probably have to sit through a lot of tame crap before the really astounding bits appeared.

Morgan got up and slid the bolt across the door. He knew

he was breaking one of the rules of the house: Mum and Dad were not keen on privacy; sometimes Morgan thought they were afraid to be alone.

He took up his place in front of the screen again and was soon rewarded with the object of his adoration, even love. Aneurin Bevan was addressing a Labour Party Conference at Blackpool and entertaining and educating a vast hall full of delegates. Morgan drank in the cadences of his beloved's voice and the wit and wisdom of his words. He was mesmerised by Mr Bevan's passionate championing of the working class and his scathing contempt for the Tories.

Somebody rattled the outside doorknob then his mother shouted, 'Morgan, it's me. Mum. Why is your door locked?'

Morgan picked up the remote and stopped the video, then moved quickly to the door to let Adele in. She hardly ever came to his room – she disliked the musky smell that teenage boys exuded, and she hated the way they kept their windows and curtains closed. Morgan's room reminded her of visiting the souk, but without the pleasure of buying pretty oriental things.

'What were you doing in here?'

When he didn't answer she said, 'It's the wrong time of day to be masturbating, Morgan. You haven't done your homework yet, have you?'

'I've been working on my project,' he mumbled. He hated it when she went on about masturbation. In his opinion she had an unhealthy obsession with it, encouraged it, even, as though it were a healthy pastime like cricket or tennis.

Morgan worried about his mother. She was always *doing* things. She never sat still. He had caught her yesterday breast-feeding Poppy at the same time as she was crouched at a table correcting the proofs of her new book.

She looked around the room suspiciously; she would have made a good CID officer, he thought. Suddenly she picked up the remote and pressed play. Aneurin's beautiful head appeared on the screen and his voice filled the room. 'The language of priorities is the religion of socialism.'

Adele ejected the video and said in a hurt, quiet voice, 'Where did you get it?'

Morgan remained silent.

Adele said, 'You're betraying everything your father stands for. Do you want us to go back to the bad old days of Old Labour with the unions holding us all to ransom, and the rubbish and the dead piling up in the streets?'

Morgan didn't know what his mother was going on about. What was a bit of litter in the streets compared to the glorious ideals that Mr Bevan and his mate Mr Beveridge had spoken of in the olden days?

After Adele had left the room, taking the video with her, Morgan lay on his bed and gave himself up to glories of self-pity. He had become a sort of martyr of the left, he thought, and was being punished for his political beliefs. He didn't care if he never got the Nike trainers; he would go to school barefoot if it came to it, just as children had in Victorian times until the labour movement gave them shoes.

Estelle heard the shouting coming from Morgan's room, something about 'the people' and 'the means of production'. Morgan was turning into a total dork, she thought; he had no idea who was in the Big Brother House or who was in the MTV charts. He was Morgan no-mates. She heard her mother crying and wanted to go next door and tell her to have a rest, to stop being a career woman for a few days.

Estelle didn't want to have a career. She might do a job for a few years – until she had her first baby – but it would be one of those jobs that you could walk away from at the end of your shift and not have to worry about. She might be a plumber, or a painter and decorator – there was supposed to be a skills shortage, wasn't there? Estelle thought careers only made women unhappy. She had seen it with her own eyes. Career women never had enough time to do anything properly. Her mother called it multi-tasking but all that meant was running around doing five things at once before panicking and shouting that you were going to be late for a meeting.

It meant saying to your children, 'Not now.' And some-times crying when you couldn't find your stupid purse and keys. Estelle wasn't fooled by the part-baked bread that Mum sometimes put in the oven. It smelled nice while it was cooking but it wasn't real home-made bread.

Dad's career was worse, of course. It had made Estelle a prisoner. She was like a princess in a tower except that she didn't have long hair because Mum said short hair was quicker to do in the morning. Dad pretended to be interested in what she was doing but Estelle could tell that he was only half listening. She wanted to be the most important thing in his life. But when she complained to him, he said, 'We all have to make sacrifices, Estelle.'

Chapter Thirteen

That morning Alexander McPherson had called a meeting to discuss the management of the crisis that the press had already dubbed 'Barry's Leg'. Present were McPherson; Ron Phillpot, the Deputy Prime Minister; the Chancellor, Malcolm Black; David Samuelson; the head of MI5, Sir Niall Conlon; and Adele's doctor, Lucinda Friedman.

Dr Friedman had landed at the London City airport only an hour earlier before the meeting was scheduled to begin. Alexander had sent a private jet to bring her back from Skýros, a Greek island that was also conveniently a NATO base. It was McPherson's personal opinion that Adele had been going mad in public for the past three days. Even her clothes were mad. That morning she had been wearing what he thought looked like a bollocking clown suit, for Christ's sake. All she needed was an exploding car and she could get a job in the Moscow State Circus.

On her arrival at Number Ten Dr Friedman had gone upstairs to Adele's bedroom and had found her in bed in the foetal position with her hands over her ears. She quickly established that Adele had stopped taking her medication and that the voices were forecasting Eddy's downfall.

'Malcolm Black was behind it all,' Adele told Dr Friedman. He was apparently beaming messages through the party wall that linked Number Ten to Number Eleven. He had demonic powers and was responsible for the floods, the rail crashes and the foot-and-mouth outbreak that had plagued the land in recent years. Did Lucinda realise that Eddy was the new Messiah? He was much better qualified for the job than Jesus had been, Adele had said, combatively. 'And Eddy would not have allowed himself to be crucified before his work on earth was finished, either. He would have come to some sort of agreement with Pilate just as he had done with the Liberal Democrats.'

When Dr Friedman remarked that, so far, she thought the Chancellor had done remarkably well to keep inflation so low, Adele had whispered, 'But don't you see, Lucinda, he's lulling us into a false sense of security. But next time you see him, look into his eyes and see the flames of Hell burning within them.'

Dr Friedman said wearily, 'Are you telling me he's the Devil, Adele? Should I also be looking out for horns and cloven hooves?'

Adele had laughed. 'We live in a post-modern age, Lucinda. The Devil is in the detail and Malcolm Black is obsessed with detail.'

Such religious babble was all too familiar to Dr Friedman. She thought that her profession ought to be grateful to the

177

established religions for providing them with a constant supply of anguished clients.

She stood over Adele and made her swallow a large dose of a new psychotropic drug. Before she left the room she asked Adele, 'Does Eddy think he's the new Messiah?'

Adele said angrily, 'Would I have married a lesser man?'

Lucinda went downstairs and joined the meeting. She informed the distinguished company sitting round the cabinet table that Adele had suffered a psychotic episode, but that she had started her on a new drug regime and was confident that within a week or two Adele would be more or less back to her normal self.

'More or less?' said David Samuelson.

'She could gain a massive amount of weight,' said Lucinda. 'It's one of the side effects.'

'How massive?' asked Samuelson.

Lucinda said, 'Patients have been known to balloon up to twenty-three stone in a very short time.'

Alexander McPherson said, 'It could be good for Ed, to have a fat wife. The average woman in Britain takes a size 16.'

Ron Phillpot screwed up his pugnacious face and shouted, 'She'll be a bleedin' liability until the drugs take 'old. She can't be allowed out attending the funeral of a leg, can she?'

Phillpot flattered himself that he was a pragmatist.

'Don't worry,' murmured Sir Niall Conlon. 'I'll take care of Barry's leg.'

Malcolm Black, aware of the power of silence, said nothing.

Lucinda said, 'She'll sleep for a few hours, but somebody should be with her when she wakes. Does she have any friends?'

'Nobody we can trust,' muttered Alexander McPherson. 'And Wendy's at the hospital with bloody Barry.'

Lucinda sighed and said, 'Oh dear, and I was so enjoying my holiday. I'll grab a few hours' sleep and I'll be here when she wakes up.'

Lucinda excused herself and left.

After she'd gone the men relaxed.

Phillpot said, 'The worst thing a politician can do is to marry a clever wife. My wife's as thick as shit but she looks good on my arm at constituency functions and she keeps me in clean shirts. And as far as I know she hasn't got any opinions about anything, let alone the sanctity or otherwise of extramural body parts.'

Malcolm Black murmured, 'I think you must mean *extraneous* body parts.'

Samuelson said, 'Might this be a good time to change the Party name, I wonder?'

'To what?' scowled Phillpot.

Samuelson formed a pitched roof with his fingers. 'It's been in front of us all the time,' he said. 'It represents gaiety, fun, the loosening of one's inhibitions, celebration, and it also means a group of people united in a cause.'

It was Sir Niall Conlon who supplied the words. 'Is this the Party Party?' he said. 'It was all over MI5 this morning; you really should be more careful with your emails, Mr Samuelson. We live in a time post-privacy.'

Ron Phillpot laughed, showing two rows of mean little teeth. 'So you want to call it the Party Party, do you?'

Alexander said, 'The Party Party.' He imagined the words as slogans on billboards and posters draped in streamers and balloons. It could give respectability to the vilified phrase 'champagne socialist'. On the other hand, it was bollocking naff.

Malcolm Black gave a dismissive bark of a laugh. 'The Party Party, so good they named it twice, eh.'

'It would certainly appeal to the young, don't you think?' said Samuelson, who had demolished his roof and was now massaging each finger in turn.

Malcolm Black said, 'I wouldn't care to lead a party that felt it had to repeat two words in a two-word title. Bearing in mind the demographics of the future, in that we're all going to live longer, maybe we should appeal to the elderly – my own preference is that we call ourselves Old Labour.'

He looked around and waited for a response, but nobody met his eye. Each man was thinking about his own political future.

Chapter Fourteen

The Grimshaw was a former lunatic asylum that had been converted in 1987 into a character hotel. A group photograph of the last lunatics to live there before they were turned out to live in the community hung on a panelled wall in the majestic reception hall. A framed straitjacket provided another amusing touch.

The owner, Clive Bostock, stepped forward to greet Jack and the Prime Minister. He was wearing tweeds the colour of Oxford thick-cut marmalade. His greeting was so effusive, with handshakes so warm and so long, that both Jack and the Prime Minister wondered if this little man with a bushy grey moustache could be a close friend they had failed to recognise.

Mrs Daphne Bostock was equally delighted to see them; she appeared to be enthralled by the details of their journey and was apparently agog at Jack's observation that they were lucky the rain had kept off.

Clive Bostock poured the guests a glass of sherry from a decanter kept on the reception desk. Jack was longing to get into their room and take his shoes off, but when he asked if he could register and proffered a credit card Bostock waved it away as though it was a stick of dynamite and said, 'Good God, man, you don't need to pay now, you're our guest. Now, let me show you around the house and introduce you to the dear people who help us run the place.'

'We don't like to differentiate between us and the staff,' said Daphne. 'We're just one big happy family.'

They were taken down a long corridor to the vast kitchen where half a dozen surly Eastern Europeans stopped their work to shake hands. Out of the corner of his eye Jack saw one of the workers make an obscene gesture behind Mrs Bostock's back.

Mr Bostock talked without needing to draw breath. 'When Daph and I first saw this place it was a mess, wasn't it, Daph? Roof fallen in, brambles in the isolation cells, but we saw the possibilities. It had been a dream of ours to run a truly hospitable hotel, one where the guests could come and go as they pleased, could wander into the kitchen and help themselves to a bit of cheese and a chunk of fresh-baked bread, where meals were taken with the family, where guests could read the papers in our drawing room and watch the box with Daph. You won't find a mini-bar in your room, no, none of that nonsense; if you fancy a tipple you come down and jolly well help yourself. We run an honesty bar, though we do ask you not to finish a bottle if you can help it, in consideration of the other guests.'

Jack's heart sank; he glanced at the Prime Minister and noticed that, like Daphne Bostock, he had lipstick on his teeth.

'You won't find a breakfast-menu card to hang outside your door like those anonymous chain hotels, either. Breakfast is taken in the kitchen. Most people opt for the continental, though, if you insist, a full English can be arranged – but we need to know the night before so that the cook can come in especially on the early bus. Some of our guests feel so at home here that they wash up after meals and take the dogs out. Most people make their own beds and whiz a lavatory brush round the bowl.'

Jack looked out of the window and saw in the distance a man mowing a lawn. He wondered if he was a paid employee or a paying guest.

They were shown to the Ophelia suite. On the way along the first-floor corridor they had passed the King George III suite and rooms named after famous lunatics of the past.

The suite comprised three small, interconnecting rooms. One of the rooms, a large walk-in closet, still had bars at the window. Rolls of pink and green rose- and chintz-patterned drapes had been swagged around the window and bed. Hideous articles of furniture stood defeatedly against the walls.

A depression settled on the Prime Minister and he felt his smile begin to slip. He fought to keep it in place and went into the bathroom to see how he was doing. He knew that if his smile went he would be lost, swamped by childhood unhappiness and adult anxieties. The smile kept him together and formed a protective ring around him, like the toothpaste advertisement had promised.

Jack said, 'Why don't you have a soak in the bath with some of that bubble stuff you nicked from The Falls?'

The Prime Minister had emptied the basket of aromatherapy oils and herbal extracts and other toiletries into the bottom of his travel bag. Jack had watched him at the time and thought that he'd never before seen anybody quite so excited by these small gifts.

Jack turned the bath taps on but nothing came out. He waited impatiently for a few moments, then a thin stream of lukewarm water trickled out of the hot tap.

The Prime Minister waited nearby with a little bottle of Lavender for Stress bath oil. He yearned for a long soak in a scented bath now that Jack had mentioned it, and when it became obvious that he was not going to get it he blamed Jack. It was not fair to do so, that was clear, but Jack had made a sort of promise and had then sort of broken it.

In the violent row that followed, Jack shouted, 'You can bloody well talk about broken promises – what about your bloody promises not to raise taxes?'

Other cruel things were said that both men almost immediately regretted. Jack was the first to apologise and said he would ring down to reception and complain to a Bostock. He dialled from the large institutional-looking phone by the bed. There were various extensions to choose from. He pressed the Reception button and waited; the phone rang but nobody answered. He tried other extensions, including one marked 'Electro-convulsive Therapy'. An American voice answered: 'Sissy Klugberg.'

'There's no hot water in the Ophelia suite,' said Jack.

'We don't gotten hot water either,' she answered.

Jack asked, 'You're a guest, are you?'

'Well, I guess so, but my husband's been out there trimming the lawns almost since we gotten here, so . . .'

Jack interrupted: 'Mrs Klugberg, do you have washing facilities in your room?'

'No, we don't have a bath tub or a shower. We're in the Napoleon room and Mrs Bostock explained that Napoleon didn't allow Josephine to wash. I guess it's some kinda reason . . .' Her voice trailed off as she once again tried to fathom Mrs Bostock's explanation for the lack of any washing facilities. 'Oh. Mrs Bostock reminded me that we had chosen to stay at a character hotel and that cold-water baths were responsible for forming the British character.'

Jack said he looked forward to meeting Sissy and her husband . . .

'Glade,' supplied Sissy.

Apparently a gong was going to be struck to inform guests that they should be dressing for dinner; another would be sounded when dinner was about to be served.

Once again Jack thought longingly of the Holiday Inn. He wanted to lie on the bed in his underpants eating the vegetarian choice from room service and watching CNN.

*

Poppy Clare lay on her back in her cot and practised kicking with her fat right leg. Her gaze was fixed on a clockwork mobile which turned slowly above her and played the 'Yellow Rose of Texas'; it had been a gift from the President and First Lady of the United States.

As each component of the mobile came into sight she stretched out her short arms in a spirited attempt to grab the cowboy boot, the Stetson, the oil rig, the heifer, the cactus, the star, the yellow rose and the big fat dollar sign.

The clockwork mechanism would keep it turning for eleven minutes, then it would stop and Poppy would start to cry. She was learning that if she made a loud enough sound somebody would come into the room. The best person was her mother – she had the milk and the soft breasts and the warmth – but Estelle was good too. Estelle would pick her up and throw her in the air and would dance with her in the mirror and pretend to be her mother.

Su Lo was kind to her and she was the one who took her into the outside world and showed her the trees and allowed her to feel the wind and the sun on her face.

Daddy smelled nice but he held her too tight, as though he was afraid he might drop her and do her harm.

The mobile started to slow down, the notes of the music becoming more widely spaced, and Poppy knew it would stop soon. She began to whimper then grizzle, then she heard Su Lo say through the little speaker of the baby alarm next to the cot, 'Hello, Poppy, I can hear you, Poppy. Mummy can't feed you any more, Poppy; she is sick and her breast milk is full of medicine. So I am here in the kitchen, Poppy, making you a nice bottle of Cow & Gate. You will soon get used to it, Poppy.'

Poppy didn't know what a bottle was – milk had come from only one source before: her mother. All she knew was that everybody in her world was kind.

The mobile stopped and Poppy became still and watched as the big fat dollar sign swung slowly to and fro above her head.

The Prime Minister sat at the table which served as both dressing table and desk, and began to compose a poem called 'Pamela'.

Who is Pamela, who is she?

He crossed it out when he realised that there was a famous poem with more or less the same construction.

He didn't know why Pamela had come into his head at all. She lived near Bourton-on-the Water with her husband, Andrew, an unpleasant man who did something with dogs, but Edward hadn't seen her in three years. When Edward had become Prime Minister his sister had sent a card of congratulations. On one side was a picture of a ferocious-looking Dobermann, and on the other she had written: 'Dear Ed, So you're top dog now. Congratulations. Let's make a bargain – you don't talk about me and I won't talk about you. Love Pamela.'

Jack said, 'I'm sorry about this; we should have gone to a Holiday Inn.'

The Prime Minister smiled into the mirror and said, 'The Bostocks are tremendous people and this is a tremendous place, everything is tremendous. I'm enjoying myself tremendously.'

Dinner was served in the converted laundry, now a dining room. Mr Bostock carved a gristly lump of meat and distributed pieces of it on cold plates to the guests.

The Prime Minister had dressed for dinner in his sequinned sheath dress and looked almost womanly in the dull light given out by the low-energy bulbs in the wall lamps.

The surly kitchen assistants came and went with various dishes of tepid root vegetables. A heavy stone-ground loaf weighed down a wooden board.

Glade Klugberg, an American man in a tartan cashmere jumper, said, 'This is just great.'

His wife, Sissy, said, 'We have nothing like this in the States.'

Jack asked, 'Will there be hot water in the morning?'

Clive Bostock said, 'That depends on the vagaries of our somewhat eccentric boiler, I'm afraid, Mr Sprat.'

Jack swallowed a morsel of the filthy food and said, 'At 260 quid a night I don't expect there to be vagaries, I expect there to be hot water.'

Silence fell at the table until Daphne Bostock said, 'This isn't the Holiday Inn, Mr Sprat.'

Jack answered, 'I know, every Holiday Inn I've stayed in had hot water twenty-four hours, round the clock.'

Clive Bostock gave a little laugh and said, 'Really, Mr Sprat, one might almost think you had a fetish about hot water.'

The Prime Minister looked down at the table found by the Bostocks in the old occupational-therapy department. It had been used for basket-making and other soothing handicrafts. He hated this sort of conflict. He could cope with the unpleasantness in Kosovo and Sierra Leone, abstractions that didn't touch him personally, but right now in the Bostocks' dining room he felt that he should mediate in some way. Bostock reminded him uncomfortably of his father. 'Personally I think that hot water is a bit, y'know, overrated.'

'Quite,' said Clive Bostock. 'At my school only the nancy boys whined for hot water!'

It suddenly became imperative to Jack that he beat Bostock over this hot-water issue. He felt as if he and Bostock were at Wimbledon on the centre court, so he hit the ball back to Bostock, saying, 'The toughest man I ever knew was Mitch Bates, a captain in the commandos; he used to take a hot bath twice a day.'

Bostock hovered on the base line for a split second then rushed to the net and sliced the ball back. 'I believe it's been scientifically proven that too much exposure to hot water weakens the sperm. Excuse me, ladies.'

Jack caught the ball and smashed it back. 'Mitch Bates has got twelve children, eight boys and four girls, all of them over six foot tall.'

Bostock failed to get to the ball in time and Jack muttered to himself, 'Game, set and match.'

Daphne Bostock left the table and went out into the kitchen, where she could be heard shouting at the foreigners that they must make coffee and take it into the drawing room.

The Prime Minister was refusing to speak to Jack or to look him in the eye. He had been ridiculously pedantic about the hot water. What was the matter with him? The Bostocks were the salt of the earth.

The Bostocks led everyone into the drawing room. Jack noticed a pair of Clive's socks lying on the carpet next to the empty fireplace. Daphne's embroidery lay on the sofa, and photographs of gormless-looking Bostock children and grandchildren stood around in silver frames. A huge television was showing *Who Wants to be a Millionaire?*

'Sit down and make yourselves comfy – you're friends of the family, remember?'

Jack noticed that the Bostocks took the most comfortable chairs and that, when the coffee was brought in by a mournful-looking woman called Eva, Clive Bostock poured a cup for himself and his wife first.

Jack infuriated Clive Bostock by answering all of Chris Tarrant's questions correctly and winning a million pounds. The Americans were impressed. Glade said, 'Hey, what are you, some kinda genius, fella?'

Jack was equally surprised. Until tonight he hadn't realised that he knew that panama hats were originally made in Ecuador.

'Jack is a product of Britain's comprehensive-school system,' said the Prime Minister.

Daphne Bostock wrinkled her nose as if the word 'comprehensive' was a bad smell and was in the room.

Jack said, 'Edwina, if you think they're so great why don't you send your own children to a comprehensive?'

'We scrimped and saved to send our children, Mark and Gillian, to a good private school,' said Mrs Bostock.

Jack took a sip of coffee and said, 'It's years since I've tasted acorn coffee.'

Bostock took this as a compliment. Jack motioned to the Prime Minister that it was time they went to bed. As they were climbing the stairs they heard Clive Bostock's voice booming out telling Glade and Sissy that Robin Hood had invented acorn coffee in Sherwood Forest in the eleventh century.

When they got to their room Jack rang Norma. She said she couldn't talk for long because she'd got company, and in the background Jack could hear young voices and the occasional burst of laughter. She told Jack that James was like a son to her and Jack felt a surge of jealousy. Norma said her dinner was getting cold, so Jack let her go and put the phone down after reminding Norma that she could ring his mobile at any time. She said, 'Thanks, but I don't suppose I'll bother.'

Jack had wanted his mother to ask him how he was; he sometimes missed such small attentions. He took the zip-up shoe-cleaning kit from his bag and cleaned his brogues and the Prime Minister's high heels. He asked the Prime Minister what he'd like to do tomorrow.

'I want to see Pam,' the Prime Minister said. MI5 had warned him when he became leader of the Opposition that his sister was a 'cause for concern'. He wanted to know why. Suddenly he wanted to talk to her about their mother.

Chapter Fifteen

Norma had a houseful again. 'It's like the United Nations in here,' she said to James, looking around at the boys and girls sitting in the front room eating chips off white polystyrene trays. Norma had asked James to fetch her a bit of cod, but James had come back with a piece of battered trout and told her that cod was now a luxury fish that only the rich ate.

'The world's gone bleedin' mad!' she said.

She had buttered a sliced loaf and cut the bread nicely and placed the halves on a dinner plate decorated with a silver doily. She had offered the plate around and the boys and girls had made chip sandwiches. They had all said 'please' and 'thank you' and most of them had made use of the kitchen towel she had provided in place of serviettes.

James teased her and said that his young friends were nesbits who'd been dragged up and didn't appreciate such refinements, but Norma could tell that he liked these things himself.

There were a few things that Norma didn't like about these evenings, and one of them was all the swearing. It was fuck this, fuck that, them fuckers and fucking everything else. One girl had said 'motherfucker' in Norma's presence and she had rounded on her angrily and shouted, 'You foul-mouthed little bleeder. Mother is a special word; it's mothers what bring life into this world!'

James had made the girl apologise. Norma was proud of him; all the boys and girls seemed to be a little bit afraid of him and did more or less what he told them to do. He was a natural leader. He had explained to Norma that since the youth club had closed on the estate the local boys and girls had nowhere to go in the evenings. It was much better for everyone concerned if they came to Norma's and smoked a bit of dope, instead of walking the streets and getting into trouble.

Another thing she didn't like was the music. For one thing she couldn't see what was musical about that thump, thump, thump. To her it seemed like a lot of angry men shouting about smacking up their bitches. But it was easier to listen to after she'd smoked a few joints – in fact, everything was easier then. She stopped thinking about Stuart, worrying about Yvonne and about Jack being lonely. Even her arthritis had stopped bothering her and when she went to sleep she had beautiful dreams.

When the boys and girls had gone and James and Norma were cleaning up in the kitchen, James said, 'How'd you like to do a bit of social work, Norma, at the weekends? There'd be a hundred quid in it for you.'

Norma said, 'I'm too bleedin' old to go out to work!'

James said, 'Now that's the beauty of it, you don't have to go nowhere. I'd bring the poor unfortunates here from Friday night to Sunday evening.'

'What's up with 'em?' she asked. She thought about the minibus that used to pick up the mongol boy from the bottom of the street.

'They're committed to taking an illegal substance,' he said. 'And they need a mother to take care of them while they're under the influence. They need to be somewhere safe, Norma, where they won't hurt themselves or other people.'

'What would I have to do?' she asked.

'Nothing much,' he said. 'Just feed them and do a bit of washing. Sometimes they lose control of themselves, down below, if you get my meaning.'

She said, 'Are we talking about crack, James?' She had read in the *Mirror*'s pull-out 'Parents' guide to drugs' about crack. One of the signs was uncontrollable diarrhoea; crack-users mixed the stuff with bicarbonate of soda and that made them shit themselves.

James said, 'You'd be brilliant at it, Norma. I mean, you're not judgemental, are you? I mean, you've got compassion for druggies, haven't you? I mean, you did your best for Stuart, didn't you? You would have liked Stuart to be looked after by somebody like you, wouldn't you, Norma?'

'Are you one of these poor unfortunates, James?'

'To be honest, Mother, I am,' he said.

'Since how long?' she asked.

'It's only been a couple of weeks, Norma,' he answered. 'But since I first took it, my first hit, it's all I've been able to think about.'

Norma tried to recall what she had read in the *Mirror*. Didn't crack send them mental? And violent? Or was that ecstasy? She couldn't remember.

She couldn't bear the terrible look in his eyes, and said, 'If I'm going to be washing shit-up pants, James, I'll need more than a hundred quid.'

James said, 'Sorted.' He kissed her goodnight and went to bed.

When Norma heard the door to the donkey room bang shut, she kicked off her shoes and unfastened a few of the hooks and eyes on the corset she been wearing under her cocktail dress. One of the girls had complimented her on her slim figure earlier and told her that she didn't look seventy-one.

Norma said to Peter, who was swinging on his trapeze, 'Don't tell our Jack, Pete, it could get him into big trouble.'

Peter jumped off the little swing with a flurry of his wings and hopped to his water dish, hoping that Norma had remembered to fill it. But it was still empty.

The Bostocks were quarrelling in the kitchen when the Prime Minister and Jack went down to breakfast the next day. Glade and Sissy Klugberg were at the sink washing up what looked like last night's pots.

Bostock was saying to his wife, 'You'll have to get on the phone and order more foreigners, Daphne. You're responsible for driving the last lot away.'

Daphne turned to Jack and the Prime Minister to elicit their sympathy. 'All I said to the foreigners was that it wouldn't hurt to see a smile now and then, considering how good we've been to them. I know they'd been through difficult times, torture, having to flee their villages and so on. But Clive and I have been very good to them. I mean, we gave them a perfectly good dormitory to sleep in, and food. OK so it wasn't the same food we ate, but it was food. And they got pocket money, and if they'd smiled more that would have earned them tips from our guests. They should have been grateful.'

Clive pushed the remains of last night's loaf towards Jack and the Prime Minister, followed by a sticky jar of marmalade. He said, 'It's a bit of a scratch affair this morning, due to the foreigners escaping in the night, and we've a conference today – I don't suppose you could help us to put the chairs out?'

Before the Prime Minister could speak Jack said, 'We've both got bad backs, sorry, and we're leaving for Gloucestershire as soon as our car arrives.'

Sissy said, 'Glade and me would be happy to help.'

The conference was being held in the old gymnasium

where the lunatics once danced with the staff at the annual Christmas parties. Photographs on the walls showed happy people wearing paper hats. It was impossible to tell the warders from the inmates.

Jack and the Prime Minister stood in the doorway and watched Glade and Sissy unstacking chairs and lining them up in rows in front of a small stage.

A banner backdrop said, 'The Entitlement Card – a corporate opportunity'.

Jack said, 'Not so much Big Brother, but big sister and the whole bloody family.'

The Prime Minister snapped, 'That's just paranoid hysteria.'

Jack said to the Prime Minister, 'Ed, surely you can see the point in being anonymous occasionally, of being able to just sod off without anybody knowing who you are or what you're doing?'

The Prime Minister said, mantra-like, 'If you've got nothing to hide what's there to be afraid of?'

Jack said, 'But I have got things to hide. My credit rating, my taste in library books, the political party I support, my stepfather's criminal record, how my brother died, how much booze I buy in a week, my genetic code. Why should some insurance company know all that?'

The Prime Minister grew thoughtful. Would the Entitlement Card scheme find out about the Bronco lavatory paper? He was absolutely sure that Adele was the only

198

person who knew of the use he put it to. But he would die, die if his idiosyncrasy became known to the *Daily Mail*.

While the Prime Minister packed Jack went outside to ring Ali and find out how long he would be. He longed to get away from this place. While there he saw a fleet of minibuses transporting dark-suited men and women down the drive. He watched as the delegates got out and gathered together at the front of the house. Clive Bostock came out to meet and greet them before leading them inside.

Adele drifted in and out of a blissful sleep. The bed was deliciously soft and warm and she felt weightless, as though she was enveloped in the substances of fairy tales – goose down, swans' feathers and the fine thread spun by glowworms.

Three swans were holding the silken ropes in their beaks and were pulling her *bateau lit* through a sky streaked pink and blue as the sun set over a medieval landscape.

She was being transported to Fairyland, a utopia with a landscape designed by Vita Sackville-West, where her fellow fairies would drink the morning dew from flowers and eat berries and where all sustenance was provided by the natural world.

Adele sat up in her bed and said to the swan leading the formation, 'I think you've taken a wrong direction – shouldn't you have turned left at the Milky Way?'

The swan said, 'Excuse me, but I've been on the Fairyland

route for a thousand years, don't try and teach me my job.'

Adele spoke to the swan again: 'When do I get my gossamer wings?'

'They'll be allocated on arrival,' said the swan irritably. 'Try to relax.'

But Adele couldn't rest. 'What will I do in Fairyland?' she said.

The swan replied, 'The same as the other fairies: you'll sleep in a cobweb hammock slung between two blades of grass; you'll wake in the morning and rinse your face in a washbasin made from an acorn cup; you'll breakfast on nectar and berries and then you'll choose what to do with the rest of your day.'

Adele said tentatively, 'Would it be acceptable if I simply sat and did nothing?'

'That would be perfectly acceptable,' said the swan. 'Idleness is a condition much admired in Fairyland.'

'Ignorance is venerated,' said another swan.

As the swan's wings flapped her towards the horizon, Adele planned her future life. She would wear an upturned bluebell on her head and commission a fairy dressmaker to fashion a dress made of rose petals. She couldn't possibly make her own fairy clothes; she was hopeless with a needle and thread.

Lucinda sat in a chair at the end of Adele's bed and read an article in that week's *Spectator* which praised Adele's courageous position on one of the most important issues of the day, Barry's Leg. Lucinda was interested to be informed that the Pope had been heard to remark in several languages, 'Barry's Leg was given by God, removed by God and must be disposed of by God.'

Adele looked over the side of her bed. Fairyland twinkled below and she couldn't help worrying: as far as she knew, Fairyland's socio-economic system might be similar to the world she was leaving. Was there a class system? Did some fairies live in large toadstools, in exclusive enclaves on prime sites, while others slummed it in small mushrooms on the edge of bog land?

Adele asked the lead swan, 'Will there be books?'

'No, there are no books in Fairyland,' said the lead swan.

'I'll have to write my own books, then,' Adele replied.

'You'll be thrown out if you do,' said the swan. 'Books cause nothing but trouble.'

'But I must have something to read,' Adele said.

'What have all your books and magazines and inventions and schools of philosophy and political systems led to?' asked the lead swan.

They began to descend. Adele heard tinkling laughter and saw thousands of fairies looking up at her and smiling. Each of them had a nose exactly like her own.

★

Lucinda noticed that Adele's first gesture on waking was to cover that enormous nose of hers. 'I dreamed I lived in Fairyland,' Adele said sleepily.

'What was it like?' said Lucinda with professional interest.

'It was heavenly; there was absolutely nothing to do,' said Adele.

Lucinda pressed: 'And the other fairies?'

'Delightful,' said Adele.

Lucinda sensed, however, that Adele was holding something back, and asked, 'Was Ed there?'

'No, but it was all right,' replied Adele.

'So what was wrong?' Lucinda pressed further.

'Nothing.'

'Come on, Adele, I've been your shrink for too long – I know when you're holding back from me,' said Lucinda.

Adele put her hand up to her nose.

Lucinda took a chance and said, 'Adele, there's only one thing we've never discussed, though it's as plain as the nose on your face – in fact, it *is* the nose on your face.'

Adele pulled up the sheet so that only her eyes could be seen.

'Adele, that thing on your face has to go! I know a plastic surgeon who . . .'

Adele was outraged. 'That's body fascism,' she shouted. 'Why should I have to fit into the media's idea of beauty?'

Lucinda said, 'Admit it, your nose is a huge problem. It's psychologically crippling you.'

An hour later, Lucinda and Adele were turning the pages

of a plastic surgeon's catalogue and choosing a new nose for Adele. There were noses of every imaginable size and shape.

Chapter Sixteen

When Norma and James returned from the cash and carry with the supplies for their weekend guests, the exterior of her house had been transformed. The front door had been reinforced with steel plate and security bars had been placed over the downstairs windows.

'It looks like a prison,' she said. 'Where's my letterbox gone?'

'You don't need a letterbox,' said James. 'You never get no letters.'

They carried the boxes of supplies from the car into the kitchen and found three of James's friends about to bolt a sheet of steel on to the back door.

Norma offered them a cup of tea and one of the youths said, 'We helped ourselves to a cup of coffee, Norma, I hope you don't mind; an' we gave Peter a drink of water an' all.'

Norma said, 'Do you lads work for the council, then?'

James laughed and said, 'No, they work for me. I want my mother to feel safe in her house. Gotta keep the Yardies out, eh?'

Jack rang while the bars were being fitted to the kitchen

window. He told Norma that he might call in on her sometime over the weekend.

Norma said, 'Which day? Friday, Saturday or Sunday?'

Jack said he wasn't sure about his arrangements and asked if it mattered.

James had been listening; he shook his head at Norma and mouthed, 'Not this weekend.'

Norma said, 'Don't come this weekend. I'm going to be busy.' Then, because she didn't know what else to do, she said, 'Bye,' and put the phone down.

Norma and James unpacked the boxes and stacked the cans of lager, frozen pizzas, beefburgers and bags of oven chips on the table.

James had bought enough food and drink for eight people, including himself and Norma. He said, 'When we've been up and running a few weeks we'll buy a proper freezer and a new washing machine.'

Norma nodded, but she wasn't entirely happy telling Jack that he couldn't come to see her at the weekend. Sometimes she felt that James was taking over her life, but she didn't want to say anything to him. She wouldn't want to go back to the times when she spent every day alone with nobody to talk to except Pete. She was disappointed that James had stopped doing the cleaning, but, as he had explained to her, 'Norma, at your age you need the exercise; it'll stop you having a heart attack and stuff.'

★

After leaving the Grimshaw Hotel, the Prime Minister had suggested that they should take the scenic route and drive through the Peak District on their way to Bourton-on-the-Water. A map had been purchased from a petrol station and the Prime Minister had volunteered to map-read. But after only a few minutes he had directed them down a farm track and Ali had been obliged to make a five-point turn in the forecourt of a farmhouse, watched by the startled farmer and his wife. After a few more false starts the Prime Minister handed the map to Jack and said girlishly, 'You'll have to do it, Jack, it's a well-known fact that we women are hopeless with maps.'

Ali said, 'My missis is brilliant at map-reading. She got us from Islamabad to Karachi – that's 900 miles – without one wrong turn, innit.'

The Prime Minister looked out of the window at the spectacular moorland and felt humbled by Ali's wife's expertise.

Jack took the map reluctantly. He'd been enjoying sitting back and looking out of the window. He liked the look of this countryside; there was something elemental and wild about it, and he thanked God there wasn't a thatched cottage in sight.

But Ali's patience was being tested, by the highest road in England: the Leek to Buxton road. One minute they were in bright sunshine and the next they were driving through dense cloud. Convoys of caravans crept ahead, buffeted by the unchecked wind, and immediately in front of them was a pensioner in a Reliant Robin who appeared suddenly to lose his nerve and slowed down to fifteen miles an hour. Unable to overtake because of the constant stream of motorcyclists roaring past in the opposite direction, Ali became dispirited and for the first time since their acquaintance he lost his temper and swore and raised his fist to the old man in the little three-wheeled vehicle ahead of him.

When Jack saw a sign advertising traditional cream teas just outside Bakewell he asked Ali to pull into the small car park. The Prime Minister and Jack got out but Ali remained seated behind the wheel.

Jack leaned into the taxi window and said, 'Ali, come inside with us, nobody will nick the car out here.'

Ali said, 'No, I couldn't go in there.' He looked anxiously at the grey-stone cottage clad in wisteria, as though it were the KGB headquarters.

Jack asked, 'Why not?'

Ali answered, 'It ain't my kind of place, innit. It's for the English.'

'But you're British, Ali,' said the Prime Minister. 'You're as free to have a cream tea as any other British citizen.'

Ali laughed a laugh devoid of humour or amusement. 'I went in a country pub once with two of my brothers-in-law. It was noisy with talking, but when we walked in it went quiet. Before we could order, the landlord said, "I thought you chaps couldn't drink." I says, "We can drink orange juice." We was only in there for five minutes, innit, and a woman comes in an' said to the landlord, "Crikey, Eric, they've started coming out of the towns."'

The Prime Minister said, 'Did you report her to the Race Relations Board?'

Ali and Jack laughed. Jack said, 'Your faith in the institutions is very touching, Ed.'

Ali said, 'If I went to the Race Relations Board every time I was called a fuckin' Paki, I'd have to pitch a tent on their doorstep. No, I just keep to my own streets when I ain't working. It's a shame, 'cause my missis, she likes the countryside, cows an' that . . .'

The Prime Minister said, 'I insist that you accompany us, Ali. The cream tea is a British custom and should be freely available to everyone with a valid British passport.'

'Or an Entitlement Card,' muttered Jack.

Ali got out of his cab reluctantly and allowed himself to be led inside the cottage tea room. Those taking tea inside turned to stare, but it was not Ali they were staring at, it was the Prime Minister. Transvestites were rarer than Pakistanis in the Peak District. They sat down at a vacant table. Ali looked miserably down at the pink gingham tablecloth. It was bad enough being the only brown face in here, but look who he was in here with! He'd known after a few hours that the woman with the blonde hair was really a man, and everybody else knew an' all, innit. He'd told his missis that if Jack called again he'd say he was booked. If word got out into the community that he was hanging out with perverts it could give him a bad name at the mosque. He was already under pressure to make his missis wear a burka. When he had mentioned it to her she had quoted the Koran at him, the bit that said women were as good as men, and then she'd said, 'You know I can't stand anything round my face, even my hair gets on my nerves.'

He wished his wife was here now; she would know what to order from the menu. She read better English than he did. She had taken GCSEs and had worked in a bank until she'd got married to him.

The Prime Minister asked Ali what he would like to order from the menu. Ali said, 'I'm all right, thanks.' It wasn't true but he could hardly tell them he couldn't understand some of the words on the menu, could he? Even though he was starving and hadn't eaten since breakfast.

Jack said, 'We'll get a mixture of things and share.'

A lanky schoolgirl with round shoulders came to their table and said robotically, 'Hello, my name is Emma, I am your waitress for today, how may I help you?'

Jack said, 'Hello, Emma, I am your customer this after-noon, and I would like to order.' Jack looked at the olde English script in the menu and read, 'A platter of fresh-picked salad nestling inside slices of oven-baked bread, traditional farmhouse scones with a serving of finest dairy cream and a selection of fruit from the hedgerow, preserves, and a large pot of Earl Grey.'

After the order had been repeated a few times and the

girl finally understood, the Prime Minister said, 'I'd like to talk to you, Ali, about your experience of living in this country, racism, integration, and ethnicity.'

Ali said, 'I'd sooner talk about cricket, if you don't mind, Edwina.'

The Prime Minister had been warned by Alexander McPherson, who had said to him, 'Steer clear of bollockin' cricket and force yourself to follow football. New Labour, New Football.'

The three men sat in an uncomfortable silence for a while. Jack pretended to read the menu. Ali traced a pattern on the cloth with his forefinger and the Prime Minister tried desperately to remember the last time he had been briefed about cricket. Eventually he said, 'The English Cricket Board has approached us for guidance on whether the forthcoming test between India and Pakistan should be played on neutral grounds, in England.'

Ali laughed. 'Neutral,' he said. 'There'll be blood on the outfield at Headingley, I'm telling you, innit. Don't get me wrong, I ain't prejudiced – some of my best friends are Indians.'

When the food came it failed to live up to the cream-tea ideal that Jack had envisioned. The inside of every sandwich was slimy with mayonnaise, the scones had been incompetently microwaved and were sizzling on the plate, the cream had been squirted from a can and the jam came in little plastic containers that required piercing with the prongs of a fork.

Jack called Emma over and said, 'These sandwiches are covered in mayonnaise.'

Emma mumbled, 'They came with mayonnaise.'

Jack asked, 'Came from where?'

The girl said, 'The sandwich factory, in Buxton.'

Jack said, 'That must be ten miles away.'

Ali, the professional, said, 'Nearer fifteen.'

Jack said, 'Who bakes the scones?'

The girl didn't seem to understand. 'Bakes? They're from Iceland.'

'Iceland?' said the Prime Minister, who had recently been in Reykjavik. 'Now that is, clearly, absurd.'

Ali explained that Iceland was a nationwide retail chain that specialised in frozen food.

Emma said, 'Shall I clear the table, then?'

Jack said, 'Leave the Earl Grey.'

When Emma brought the bill over to them Jack paid it in full; he didn't want to have an argument with a nervous girl who didn't know the true meaning of the words 'fresh', 'traditional' or 'hedgerow'.

As they left the tea room Emma said gloomily, 'Missing you already.'

Jack said, 'I beg your pardon?'

Emma repeated, 'Missing you already.'

Jack said, 'Emma, you're not an American and this is not America. Whoever told you to use that expression is a monumental fool.'

Emma said, 'Whatever.'

The microwave pinged and Emma turned away.

They stopped a mile down the road at a garage and bought sweets, crisps, bottles of pop and a copy of the *Daily Mail*. Ali never missed reading his horoscope; these childish treats cheered them up. When he inserted his *All-Time Soul Greats* compilation tape into the car stereo the three men sang along with Eddie Floyd and 'Knock on Wood' as they drove towards Stafford and the horrors of the M6.

Four junctions later, after joining in with 'Under the Boardwalk', 'Rainy Night in Georgia', 'Soul Sister', 'Brown Sugar' and 'When a Man Loves a Woman', traffic from the M54 joined them and they came to a standstill sandwiched between a tanker displaying a skull and crossbones on its rear and a lorry stacked with three tiers of bleating sheep.

'Why have we stopped?' asked the Prime Minister.

'Volume of traffic, innit,' said Ali. 'It's always like this at Walsall. Last time I done this journey I got stuck for three and a half hours. I read the paper, went to sleep, and when I woke up people had got out of their cars and were walking about on the motorway talking to each other. It was quite nice really,' he said dreamily. 'A bloke in a red Astra gave me a can of Lilt when I said I was thirsty. But I tell you what, if that prat Edward Clare had turned up he woudda been tore to pieces.'

The Prime Minister looked around at the stalled traffic

and said nervously, 'Traffic is not the Prime Minister's responsibility; Ron Phillpot is the Minister for Transport.'

Ali said, 'Ron Phillpot's a tosspot, innit.'

'Yes, it's quite clear to me that he is in fact a tosspot. He was only made Deputy Prime Minister as a sop to the left,' said the Prime Minister.

Jack asked, 'Aren't the government building the Northern Relief Road somewhere around here?'

The Prime Minister said, 'It's a public/private partnership; it's going to be a toll road.'

Ali said, 'Why should I pay ten quid to drive along a bit of road? I pay road tax, income tax, council tax and fuel tax already, innit.'

Jack said, 'It's highway robbery. Dick Turpin was doing the same thing 200 years ago.'

They drove at walking pace for the next two hours, listening to Five Live Drive on which a debate was raging about the role of the Prime Minister's wife. Should Adele be seen and not heard or should she be able to express an opinion on matters of national interest?

When Peter, a caller from Truro, rang in and said that Adele Floret-Clare had more balls than her husband, the Prime Minister surreptitiously adjusted his testicles inside his wife's knickers and nodded in agreement.

Hassin from Kettering asserted that Adele was right about the question of Barry's Leg, though he thought that the burial of warts was a step too far.

Sandra from Cardiff rang in to suggest that a compromise be found whereby wart burial could be centralised; she wasn't sure how many warts could be fitted into an average-size coffin but she was sure that it would run into hundreds, if not thousands.

When a Doctor Singh, a Lecturer in Mathematics from Brunel University, rang in to say that approximately 51,842 warts would fit into the average coffin, Ali switched off the radio and reinserted the *All-Time Soul Greats* tape.

By the time the traffic was moving again the three men had memorised the words of 'Knock on Wood' and had even perfected an in-car dance routine which included synchronised knocking on each other's heads.

The Prime Minister had a moment of epiphany. He had never been so happy in the whole of his life. Each time 'Knock on Wood' finished he begged for it to be played again.

Eventually Ali said, 'No, my head's hurting, innit. Jack, read me out my horoscope – I'm Capricorn.'

Jack read aloud. '"Storm clouds are gathering in your life. A person of the opposite sex is feeling resentful – have you told them lately that you love them? Failure to act could lead to a serious life change, one you may regret."'

Ali picked up his mobile and phoned home. He spoke urgently to his wife in Urdu. When Ali was driving with two hands on the wheel again the Prime Minister said, 'What do the stars say for Pisces?'

Jack said, 'I thought you were born in May.'

'I was,' said the Prime Minister. 'But Malcolm Black's Pisces.'

Jack read: ' "Seize the opportunity for self-fulfilment this week. You have the courage, you have the talent; now go ahead and take what is rightfully yours. If planning to move house this week you may find a short delay – don't be dispirited." '

The Prime Minister whispered, 'The bastard, as soon as my back is turned . . .'

He nodded his head when Jack asked if he should read out the forecast for Taurus, the Prime Minister's own sign.

Jack read: ' "Your old feelings of insecurity continue to haunt you. Don't give up on your quest. Perhaps now is the time to rest on your laurels. Let others do the dirty work. Family matters need your attention." '

The Prime Minister sat in silence.

Ali asked, 'Jack, what are you?'

Jack said, 'I'm Cancer and it's all a load of rubbish.' But to please Ali he read: ' "Romance is just around the corner. However, if you scuttle back into your shell when it appears, you could miss the opportunity to be truly happy. Is your pet insurance up to date?" '

They pulled in at Frankley Services on the M5 for a toilet stop. Jack and Ali went into the men's together and the Prime Minister joined the women in the ladies'.

The Prime Minister remained seated on the lavatory long

after he had finished urinating. He couldn't bear the fact that they were driving south and that in two days he would once again be immersed in the troubles of the world. He felt that he could remain seated in this cubicle for ever, listening to the sounds of flushing water, the roar of the hand-dryers and the bright chatter of women as they primped in front of the mirrors. He put his head in his hands and sat there until he heard Jack's voice calling to him.

'Edwina, are you in there?'

Chapter Seventeen

Malcolm Black was sitting on the sofa with his arm around his wife, Hannah. His huge head lay heavily on her delicate shoulder. He had told his office manager and his private secretary that he wanted one uninterrupted hour alone with his wife.

She said to him, 'It's time you had your hair cut, Malc. It looked awful on the telly last night, like an NHS wig.'

'That bad?' he said.

Their hour together was coming to an end and still no decision had been made. Did she want him to be the next Prime Minister or not? If she said no, he would concentrate on stabilising the economy and eradicating child poverty. If she said yes, he would change the face of Britain for ever.

He began to bite his nails, until she slapped his hand away from his mouth. 'It's nice sitting here,' he said.

'It could be an adventure,' said Hannah.

He laughed. 'Yes, one of those glorious British adventures that end in failure and defeat. I could be the Ernest Shackleton of British politics.'

Hannah sat up straight and looked him in the eye. 'How much do you want to be Prime Minister, out of ten?'

'Ten,' he answered.

'Then you better had be,' she said. 'You've not done bad for a smart-arsed Govan boy, have you?' She laughed. Precocious as a child, Malcolm could recite all of the Thomas the Tank Engine books from memory by the age of three. He asked endless questions, so that those questioned fled at the earliest opportunity. He seemed to inhabit a different world to that of his classmates; he shrank from being touched. At sixteen he'd entered Edinburgh University, where he'd fallen in love with a Balkan princess – had he married her he could have ended up as king of her country. He was hopelessly disorganised and kept a filing system in various pockets. When he watched a football match on the television, he threw himself into the game with such ferocity that Hannah feared he would burst a blood vessel. He had grown up in the Govan shipyards, and the poverty he had seen there had made him a socialist. He had a deep and tender affection for babies and small children.

He didn't believe in God, and found it astonishing that the Prime Minister, the Home Secretary and the Foreign Secretary were all members of the Socialist Christian Movement. All three of them seemed to be such rational men. Malcolm had once come across them in a room, each man with his hands pressed together and his eyes closed, and he'd fervently hoped that they were thinking, not praying.

Hannah Black left to attend an evening function. Malcolm

pulled Morgan Clare's homework folder on to his knee. *'Public–Private Partnerships are less efficient and more costly than publicly funded projects. Discuss.'* Malcolm Black wrote: 'There is nothing to discuss. PPPs are a proven disaster. Extreme prudence must be used when considering future projects. National and regional devolution and PPPs increasingly absolve central government from responsibility when things go wrong, but allow them to claim the credit when things go right.'

Ali's taxi came to a board at the side of the road that said in Gothic lettering, 'The Haven: superior boarding for dogs. First right'. Next to it was a For Sale sign featuring the name of an estate agent and a telephone number.

Ali waited for a slow-moving tractor to pass by, then he turned the car and crunched down a long gravel drive. They heard the distant sound of many dogs barking.

Ali said fearfully, 'That sounds like a lot of dogs, innit? I ain't happy with dogs; my uncle was bit by one in Lahore an' he got the rabies.'

The Prime Minister said, 'I doubt if any of the dogs at Pamela's kennels are rabid. It costs £100 a day to board here.'

Ali said, 'You're jokin' me!'

They drew up outside the pretty Georgian house; a tall woman with blonde hair tied up on top of her head came through a side gate carrying a plastic bucket. Even from a distance she looked disconcertingly like the Prime Minister.

She wore a grey fleece jacket, tight faded denims and green Wellingtons.

She put down the bucket when the Prime Minister got out of the taxi, and said, 'Christ, Ed! You look better in a frock than I do!'

Her laugh was attractively low and husky and sounded as if she was recovering from a throat infection. She took a packet of St Moritz cigarettes from the top pocket of her jacket and lit one with a pink disposable lighter. She immediately started to cough and said, 'These bloody things will kill me.'

Her accent was posh but not intimidating. Jack loved her immediately.

He didn't notice at first that her fingernails were dirty, nor that her hair was tied up with a man's sock. The Prime Minister introduced them, they shook hands and looked each other in the eye and smiled. She said, 'I knew you would come one day.'

Jack thought at first that she was talking to him, but if she was it was the Prime Minister who answered. 'Pam, I'm not here.'

'I know,' she said. 'You're in a bunker playing at being the great war leader.'

The Prime Minister led her away from the car and whispered, 'Ali, the driver, doesn't know who I am, Pam – don't spoil things for me.'

Ali sat behind the wheel waiting for the English to go

through their strange greeting ceremony. He wondered if his children would learn to pretend not to be pleased to see their relations or to meet new friends. The beautiful sister of the strange man in the blonde wig knocked on the window and invited him to come inside the house to have a cup of tea.

He asked about the dogs and told her about his uncle in Lahore. She was most interested and assured him that all the dogs here were in secure accommodation.

Since shaking Jack's hand she had avoided looking at him directly, but spoke mostly to Ali, asking him for details of his uncle's lingering death.

They came to a low whitewashed building. 'That's where the boarders live,' she said. 'I was just about to give them their supper. Eddy, go inside and make Ali a cup of tea. Jack can help me to feed the dogs.'

The Prime Minister was relieved to get away from the barking and growling dogs; his father had not allowed him to keep pets, on grounds of hygiene.

Jack had expected the smell of disinfectant, stone floors and cages. He was astonished to find cubicles, carpets and soft lighting. Each dog had an outside run and a colour television; a few of them were watching *Crossroads*.

As Pamela went from room to room distributing Pedigree Chum into the dogs' bowls, Jack found himself talking to her about the dog he'd had as a boy. How the dog hadn't minded being used as a footstool.

'What was he called?' asked Pamela.

'Bob,' said Jack. He didn't tell Pamela that he had never called out the dog's name in the street; if he had the dog would have been subjected to abuse and ridicule by the neighbours – the local euphemism for excrement was bob.

She was almost as tall as he was and he liked that; smaller women intimidated him with their frailty. He couldn't stop looking at her lovely face. She said everything with half a laugh. He tried to work out how old she was, but in the end he asked her.

She told him immediately. 'I'm forty-one,' she said. 'They lied about the forties being the best years of your life.'

'It's only been one year,' said Jack.

'Yes, and it's been fucking awful. My husband left me in January, my financial advisor is now living in Tangier, and Eddy's bloody government has allowed corporate Britain to steal my pension scheme.'

Jack was pleased to hear all this; it meant that she was available and vulnerable. He thought he might stand a chance of making her happy and building up her pension plan again.

Jack asked if she had any children and was relieved when she said no.

'I like children too much to have one for myself,' she said. 'I would have made a terrible mother. I'm fundamentally lazy, I'm horribly selfish and anyway, I hate pain. I've seen too many cowboy films and watched cowboys' wives

screaming the ranch house down giving birth to the cowboys' sons.'

Jack said, 'It was always a son, wasn't it?'

Pamela said, 'Yes. I was a double disappointment to my
father. Not only was I a horribly ugly little girl, I also killed
my mother.'

'Indirectly,' said Jack.

He had to stop himself from touching her, putting his
arms around her and holding her tight. He almost settled
for simply putting his hand on her shoulder but he didn't
want to alarm her.

They went into the house by the kitchen door; an old
black Labrador padded up to Jack and dropped a rubber
Santa Claus at his feet.

'That's Bill,' Pamela said.

Jack stroked one of the dog's velvety ears and said, 'Hello,
Bill.'

There was a recycling box on the floor of the small utility
room; half a dozen Stolichnaya bottles were visible. Jack
asked her if she lived alone.

She kicked at the box and said, 'Yes, and I drink a bit
because I'm lonely.'

Jack was almost relieved that she had a fault and wasn't
perfect; it gave him some hope that she might need his
help. He wanted to take care of her. And anyway, he
thought, he didn't drink enough himself. He saw them
together in Spain, perhaps, maybe even at a bullfight; she

was Ava Gardner, he was Ernest Hemingway, they were drunk and brawling in public. He asked if he could have a glass of vodka. He felt quite capable of downing a tumblerful in one go.

She said, disappointingly, 'There's not a drop in the house. I keep forgetting to buy it when I'm in the village.'

'So she's not an alcoholic,' thought Jack, and was relieved. She could be anything she wanted to be. He didn't care.

'I've got wine,' she said. 'But that doesn't count as drink, does it? It's more of a medicine since the bloody doctors said we could drink two glasses a day.'

Everyone sat at the big table in the middle of the kitchen; it was covered in books, newspapers and a pile of final demands. Ali fell asleep almost immediately.

Pamela said, 'He's fucking shagged out. I'm not allowing him to drive back to Leeds tonight.'

Jack wondered if her bad language would eventually get on his nerves after they were married. She didn't look the type of woman who would take criticism lying down.

The Prime Minister said, 'Why did Andrew leave you, Pam? Was there another woman?'

She said, 'He probably got bored. I'm a very boring person, Ed. It's the reason I don't go to parties: I bore everybody to tears. I've got absolutely no conversation.'

Jack vowed never to go to another party, ever again. He wanted to stay at home and be bored by Pamela.

She said to the three men, 'I never, ever cook. But there

is food.' She waved vaguely towards a larder and a fridge. 'I'm sure you'll find something.'

She lit another St Moritz and said to Jack, 'You're a policeman, aren't you? I had a burglary last week.'

Jack said, 'What did they take?'

'The usual things,' she said. 'Telly, video, bit of silver, all my jewellery.'

'Did you report it?' asked the Prime Minister.

'There was no point,' she said. 'The burglar alarm wasn't working, so the bloody insurance company won't pay out.'

Jack wanted to tell her that he would be willing to withdraw all of his savings and replace the jewellery she had lost.

As if reading his mind she said, 'I don't miss any of it. I've got too many things as it is. Look at this house. I've got five bedrooms, two bathrooms, three reception rooms and a kitchen all stacked with *things*. I'm sick of it all. I shall never buy another thing as long as I live. What I long for is a white room, a little white bed, an ashtray and a few books.'

The Prime Minister said, 'You've just described a prison cell. And if you carry on associating with your trouble-making friends, that's where you'll end up.'

He opened the door of the fridge and looked inside. There was a bowl of red apples, two leeks, a bag of sprouting potatoes, a pot of cream, a packet of only slightly mouldy cheese and various little wrapped-up parcels in the dairy compartment.

She said, 'You make me sound like an anarchist; it's just that we're against everything you stand for, Ed.'

The Prime Minister slammed the fridge door shut and went into the pantry. They could hear him walking around on the stone floor in his high heels. When he came out he said, 'There is absolutely nothing to eat, and I'm hungry.'

Pamela said, 'Don't whine, Eddy. It reminds me of our God-awful childhood.'

The Prime Minister said, 'I had an idyllic childhood.'

'You're not talking to David Frost now,' she said. 'It's me, Pamela; I was there some of the time, remember.'

Jack said, 'We could send out for pizza.'

Pamela said, 'Domino's don't deliver so far out and there's nothing in the village; it's almost dead now since Ed closed the post office.'

The Prime Minister said, 'I didn't personally close it, Pam, those little rural post offices are no longer viable concerns.'

'It was viable to me,' she shouted. 'I now have to drive into Stow-on-the-Wold to buy a fucking stamp.'

The Prime Minister said, 'Pamela, please don't swear.'

While Pamela and the Prime Minister snapped and growled over the bones of their political differences, Jack got up and began to gather together the ingredients for an evening meal. He cleared a surface, assembled some utensils

226

and began to cook. Through close study of her books, he had been taught by Delia Smith to prepare a repertoire of seven fail-safe dishes. He wanted to dazzle and seduce Pamela with his skills. He wanted to demonstrate how good he was at baking a tart, putting up a tent, ironing a white linen shirt, driving through London traffic, doing the cross-word in the *Independent*, and hitting the bull's eye with a variety of guns – he could kill an assassin at a range of 500 metres with a high-velocity rifle.

He was astonished to find out that falling in love was like the songs and the books said it would be. Colours were brighter; life seemed full of amazing possibilities. He rarely sang and before today in the car had never done so in company, but now the words to 'Try a Little Tenderness' came into his head, then he found himself singing 'Wearing the same shabby dress . . .' Nobody heard him. Ali was still snoring and the Prime Minister and his sister were still raging at each other about the successes and failures of global capitalism and who had received the most attention from their father.

When the leek and onion tart was ready Jack put it on the table in front of Pamela as if it were the Holy Grail. He was rewarded by her saying, 'Fucking hell, that looks good.'

He set out the side dishes, sautéed potatoes and a bowl of minted petits pois.

Pamela opened a bottle of wine with well-practised ease. She said, 'Does Ali drink?'

Jack woke him up and Ali said, 'When in Rome, innit,' and had half a glass.

Jack was gratified when every last morsel had been eaten.

At Pamela's suggestion Ali phoned his wife to tell her that he wouldn't be home that night. Salma didn't believe him when he told her that he was staying in a house next to some boarding kennels in the country, so he took the phone outside into the cool April evening and let her listen to the sound of eleven dogs barking. She was not placated.

'Ali,' she said. 'Don't do this to me; you're with another woman. I know who she is – it's that fat whore who works in the greengrocers.'

Ali came back into the kitchen and said to Jack, 'Talk to my missis, Jack. Tell her I'm on a job.'

Jack took the phone and spoke to Salma. He told her that providing she gave her permission he would like to engage Ali for a further two days.

She said to Jack, 'We have never been apart for more than one day; it will be hard for me. You must take care of my husband, make sure that he eats – sometimes he forgets.'

Jack said he would do that. Then he thanked her and handed the phone back to Ali.

Ali would have preferred to have slept in his car – the driver's seat folded flat and he had a blanket in the boot – but Pamela wouldn't hear of it. She took him upstairs and gave him a choice of four bedrooms. He chose the nursery. There was a bed in there that looked about the right size for him. He was only a small man.

The Prime Minister was drunk. He was so drunk that he kept repeating to Jack and Pamela that he wasn't drunk. He also told them repeatedly that he loved them both very, very much. Then he cried and said he wanted his mum. 'I don't remember her, Pam,' he said. 'I used to have a picture in my mind of her face and her hair but then I realised that it wasn't Mum at all, it was Jean Simmons the actress. I'd got the two of them mixed up somehow. Mum was fat, wasn't she? I remember her going off in the car to the hospital, she was more like Hattie Jacques.'

Pamela said, 'Mum wasn't fat, Ed. She was pregnant with me.'

Jack said, 'Isn't there a photograph?'

Pamela said, 'There were a few. Mum didn't like being photographed; in every one I've seen she'd turned her head away and her face was just a blur. Andrew took the photo albums.'

'Why?' shouted the Prime Minister. 'Mum was my mother, not his.'

'Mum shared the album with his favourite Labrador bitch, Patsy,' said Pamela.

'What was she like?' pressed the Prime Minister.

Pamela said, 'I don't know. Ask somebody who knew her. Uncle Ernest lives in a care home near Cheltenham.'

The Prime Minister said, 'I want to see him now.'

'Tomorrow,' said Jack.

The Prime Minister pulled off his blonde wig. His own hair lay flat and distorted on his scalp. Pamela and Jack supported him up the stairs and led him into a handsomely furnished bedroom. The Prime Minister insisted on undressing himself. Pamela said, 'Do you want to borrow pyjamas or a nightie?'

Jack said, 'There's a nightie in his bag, I'll see to him.'

When Jack rejoined Pamela at the kitchen table he saw that she had opened a third bottle. She wanted to talk about her brother.

'I hate it when people have a go at Ed,' she said. 'I know I disagree with practically everything he stands for, and I hate the way he kowtows to the Yanks, but he's my big brother and I suppose I love him.'

At ten o'clock she put her jacket on and said, 'It's time to put the dogs to bed.'

Jack went out with her. It was years since he'd been in such complete darkness; he looked up, expecting to see stars, and there they were – the sky was full of them. As he and Pamela walked towards the kennels he said to her, 'We don't see the stars in the city.'

She threw her head back to look up. 'They're a small compensation for living in the God-awful countryside,' she said.

'You're not happy here,' he said.

'No, I'm a city girl. Andrew kidnapped me and brought me here. I'm not even a real dog person, either,' she said.

She went from room to room switching off the dogs' televisions and wishing them goodnight. Eleven pairs of eyes watched as she turned and said, 'See you all in the morning,' before closing the door.

Under cover of darkness Jack took her arm and walked her along the path towards the house, though it was he who didn't know the way.

Jack asked if he could make some coffee.

'Andrew may have left some beans,' she said. Then she added, as if finally realising that three months had passed since he'd gone, 'They're probably a little stale.'

Jack knew that after they'd finished their coffee he should have gone to bed. Pamela had been yawning throughout their conversation and had mentioned several times that she had to be up early in the morning to see to the dogs. But Jack couldn't tear himself away. It was Pamela who got up from the table first, saying, 'I'm dead on my feet.'

He apologised for keeping her up. She said, 'Jack, do you know that Chinese proverb, "After three days, fish and visitors stink"?'

He said, 'I do.'

'Well,' she said, 'it's been my bitter personal experience that after only one day fish and visitors stink.'

Jack said, 'Don't worry, we'll leave before lunch tomorrow.'

'You'll be bored with me by then anyway,' she said.

This would have been a good opportunity for him to make some kind of declaration of his interest in her, but he said nothing and she went upstairs to her bed. He remained seated at the kitchen table for a long time, trying to get used to the idea that he was now living in a new universe.

Chapter Eighteen

Ali was woken by his mobile phone. He opened his eyes and saw that he was lying under a Lion King duvet. The caller was Sedek, his eight-year-old son, who asked him for the name of the longest river in the British Isles. Ali said it might be the Thames, but he wasn't sure.

He heard voices outside and got up and looked out of the window. Jack and Pamela were clipping leads on to the dogs' collars. Ali opened the window and asked about the river. Jack and Pamela answered simultaneously: 'The Severn.'

Ali gave his son the answer to his homework question, then asked to speak to each of his children in turn. He told them that he had slept the night in a wonderful bedroom that had been prepared for a child. 'It was fit for the child of a king,' he said. 'Everything that a kid could want was there, apart from a television and video.'

Pamela divided the dogs between her and Jack, taking six herself. They walked away from the house down the gravel drive; she was smoking her first cigarette of the day. The noise of barking was terrible; the dogs were ill disciplined and refused to walk in a straight line. When they reached the end of the drive the sun came out and Pamela pushed her dark glasses down from the top of her head to cover her eyes. She was wearing a different-coloured sock in her hair this morning, Jack noted.

'Are we walking far?' Jack shouted over the row.

'To the village and back,' she said. 'I need some fags.'

There was very little traffic and they walked in the middle of the narrow lane. Every now and again they had to stop to disentangle the leads. Jack admired the wild flowers in the hedgerows. The sun was shining.

Pamela said, 'This is my land. I had to plant those wild flowers. I had to send away to a specialist nursery; the bastard farmers round here had killed everything off with their bloody chemicals.'

'So you don't hate the countryside?' said Jack.

'I hate what they've done to it,' she said passionately.

A brand-new olive-green Land Cruiser, driven by a man wearing mutton-chop whiskers and a tweed cap, passed at speed, forcing them almost into the ditch. It was some time before the dogs were calm enough to proceed with their journey.

'That's the farmer who owns the land next to mine,' Pamela said. 'He was on television last year crying about his bloody sheep. About how they were like members of his family, about how much it hurt him to see his livestock destroyed. Well, the half-a-million-quid compensation he swindled out of Ed soon put the smile back on his face. The same flock of sheep were moved from farm to different farm so often they must have thought they were on a fucking Cook's tour.'

They approached the village of Swale-on-the-Wold; it was evident from the glances that the villagers directed at Pamela that she was not popular. She came to a stop outside the old post office. Two men were fitting a double-glazed PVC unit into the gap left by the old sash window.

They walked on and Jack wondered if he could live with somebody who existed at such a high level of indignation and anger. He held on to the eleven dogs while she went into the small Spar shop. When she came out she was carrying a box of Vesta Chow Mein. Jack said, 'You'll have to come to London, Pamela, and I'll take you to Gerrard Street and buy you a proper Chinese meal.'

To his surprise she said, 'When?'

He said, 'As soon as Ed is back at Number Ten.'

She said, 'Jack, it's fairly obvious to me that Ed is a burned-out case.'

As they passed the old post office on their way back they saw that a workman was fixing a wrought-iron sign over the front door: 'Ye Olde Poste Office'.

Ali had worked out how to boil a kettle on the stove and had made tea. He was telling the Prime Minister why he would never vote Labour again. 'First they wasted all that money on the Armouries Exhibition – I mean, who wants to spend thirty quid on taking his kids to see a few old guns and swords, innit? And then there's the stupid one way system an' all them bus lanes, and why did they have to close the swimming baths down before my eldest lad got his bronze medallion?'

The Prime Minister sat with his head in his hands and raged inwardly. Why was the British electorate unable to differentiate between the responsibilities of national and local government?

Pamela came in and said, 'Congratulations, Ed, you were a good, classic drunk last night, ten out of ten.'

The Prime Minister blinked rapidly and mumbled an apology.

Jack went upstairs to collect their bags; he passed the open door of the nursery. On his way back he went inside and looked around. The furniture and the toys were new but obviously unused. Jack opened the top drawer of a chest and found it to be full of pale, small articles of clothing. He closed the drawer gently and shut the door behind him as he went out.

Pamela was busy when they left; a woman with a Caribbean tan was being reunited with her small dog. Jack kissed Pamela on both cheeks and smelled her perfume and said he would be in touch about that meal.

She had given him such a beautiful smile that he felt warmed by it, and even the prospect of visiting eighty-one-year-old Uncle Ernest in a nursing home did nothing to diminish the heat.

Jack asked Ali to slow the car down and pointed out Pamela's wild flowers growing at the side of the road. The Prime Minister said, 'Y'know, Jack, there's nothing as beautiful as the English countryside – except Tuscany, of course.'

Ahead a tractor was skirting the perimeter of a field adjacent to the road. A pipe on top of the enclosed cab was spraying a fine mist, and before they could wind up the windows of the car the mist had wafted inside and was stinging their eyes and making them choke and cough. Ali braked and turned the engine off, unable to see the road ahead. Not only were his eyes full of moisture, but also the windscreen was covered in an opaque film that the windscreen wipers couldn't remove.

A quarter of an hour later a 999 call was received at police headquarters in Cheltenham from a farmer at Swale-on-the-Wold who claimed to have been dragged from his tractor and assaulted by three ramblers: a tall white male, a blonde transvestite and a Pakistani man. The officer who took the call warned the farmer about the penalties for making hoax calls: a large fine or imprisonment.

When the officer had disengaged the call, she said to her colleague seated next to her, 'Another crazy call from a farmer. It's all the chemicals they use.'

Chapter Nineteen

In the reception area of the Rainbow Residential Home for the Elderly, where the smell of uric acid intermingled with the scent of industrial disinfectant, Jack and the Prime Minister were greeted by the proprietor, Harry Rainbow, a man who could have been a retired heavyweight boxer. An obese black cat slinked around his pinstriped trousers as he shook their hands vigorously. 'This is Blackie,' he told them. 'The residents love him.'

'I've never seen such a fat cat,' said Jack.

'He's a monster,' agreed Harry Rainbow. 'I've asked the residents not to feed him but they're killing him with kindness. We get through a cat a year on average; they're all called Blackie, 'cause it saves getting new identity discs made. So, have you come about the closure?'

'No,' said the Prime Minister. 'We've come to see Ernest Middleton.'

Rainbow was surprised that Ernest had visitors. 'His niece, Pamela, comes every Sunday,' he said. 'But nobody else. Sad, really – he's the uncle of the Prime Minister, you know. But the poor bugger doesn't get so much as a

Christmas card from him. Ernest has taken the closure very badly. He could do with cheering up.'

The Prime Minister said, 'Why are you closing, Mr Rainbow? Isn't there a demand for places in residential homes?'

'Yes, but me and Mrs Rainbow are in business first and foremost and the profit margins on old people are not worth the candle, to be honest. I need another fifty quid a week per unit to make it worth me and Mrs Rainbow's time. And then there's all this new legislation coming in. I've got to widen all the doors by an inch.'

'But where will they all go?' asked the Prime Minister.

A stoop of old ladies crept on Zimmer frames across the reception area. Harry Rainbow shouted, 'It's the Zimmer-frame gang, run for your lives!'

The old ladies laughed politely at Harry's familiar joke. Harry said, lowering his voice, 'I don't know where they'll go, but in three months' time this place will be a private clinic: breast augmentation, Botox, liposuction, that's where all the money is now.'

He introduced them to Lauren, a care assistant. Lauren looked directly at the Prime Minister from behind her green-rimmed spectacles and said, 'Where do I know you from? Is it Weightwatchers?'

Jack diverted Lauren by asking her if it was possible to see Ernest now.

'You can see him,' she said, 'but he might not talk to you. He's sulking, bless him. It's come as a terrible shock to them all, this closure.' She continued to walk as she led them down a corridor and into a large room where wisps of old people sat in plastic armchairs corralled by bib-like tables. 'Mind you, I'll be sorry to see the old people go, but Mr Rainbow's told me that private patients'll tip well providing we bow and scrape a bit.'

A large television was showing a children's programme. Four actors wearing primary colours and genial monster heads were miming to a song about the delights of cake.

Lauren went up to a scrawny old man with a clever face who was wearing a suit, shirt, tie and waistcoat and said, 'Ernest, you've got visitors.'

'*The Visiters* by Daisy Ashford,' said Ernest. 'A delightful book. It could have been tiresomely *faux* naive but she pulled it off, I think.'

Lauren said, 'He talks gibberish sometimes.'

Jack said to Ernest, 'It's a very funny book.'

The Prime Minister said, 'Uncle Ernest, do you remember my mother, your sister-in-law, Heather Clare?'

'She can't be your mother, my dear,' said Ernest. 'Heather only had two children. One of them is the Prime Minister and you're obviously not him, and the other is the beautiful Pamela and you're certainly not her. So who are you?'

The Prime Minister sank momentarily into a pit of self-doubt. Who was he?

Jack came to his rescue: 'This is Edwina, Heather Clare's love child.'

Ernest said cheerily, 'I'm not surprised. Your mother enjoyed a bit of rumpy-pumpy; she mixed with a fast set in the thirties, when she was young – musicians, you know.'

This account of his mother did not in any way accord with the Prime Minister's memories. 'Do you have any photographs of her?' he asked.

'In my room,' said the old man.

They helped him as he struggled to get up from his chair, and escorted him to the lift in the corridor. As they slowly ascended two floors Jack asked, 'How long have you lived here, Ernest?'

Ernest replied, 'I've forgotten. All I know is that I had to sell my house to pay for my care, and now all that money is gone and I'm completely dependent on the state.'

His room was small but pleasantly furnished with a well-stocked bookcase and a Dansette record player.

Jack looked out of the window and saw Ali washing his car clean of pesticides with a bucket of hot soapy water he'd begged from a kitchen assistant.

Ernest rummaged through a drawer and eventually he brought out a handful of photographs. 'That's rather a lovely one of Heather,' he said, placing it on the Prime Minister's lap. 'It was the winter of 1936.'

The Prime Minister looked at the pretty, vibrant-faced

girl walking alongside a column of flat-capped, poorly dressed, pale-faced men.

Jack, looking over the Prime Minister's shoulder, said, 'The Jarrow Marchers. They stopped off in Leicester at the Co-operative Shoe-works; my granddad was one of the blokes who volunteered to stay late and mend their boots.'

The Prime Minister took in every detail of his mother's image. The cigarette she held between the forefingers of her right hand, her dark-lipsticked mouth, the ridiculous ankle-strapped shoes she wore on the cobbles, her tiny waist and the excitement shining in her eyes.

Ernest passed the Prime Minister another photograph, this one of his mother standing in front of a theatrical poster laughing and pointing to a name in the middle of the bill. She now held the cigarette in her left hand. He tried to read the name but the letters were too small.

Ernest said, 'She was a rhythm guitarist in an all-girls jazz band. Miss Monica's Hot Seven.'

'Guitar? Jazz?' said the Prime Minister. 'No, not my mother – she was a very quiet, devout woman. She wouldn't let me listen to popular music of any kind.'

Ernest lowered himself on to his bony knees and said, as he pulled a box out from under his bed, 'That was before she married that Stalinist Percy.' He took a seventy-eight rpm record in a yellowing sleeve out of the box, passed it to Jack and asked him to put it on the record player.

Jack carefully removed the shellac record from its sleeve and using only his fingertips lowered it on to the turntable.

Ernest said, 'Your mother has rather a good solo, about two minutes in.'

After a few seconds of hiss and crackle, 'Stomping at the Savoy' filled the room. Miss Monica had arranged the music so that each of her girls had the chance to shine with her instrument, albeit briefly. When the guitar solo began the Prime Minister leaned towards the record player nervously, willing his mother to do well.

When she finished the Prime Minister applauded and accepted Jack's congratulations as though he had played the solo himself.

The next photograph was more conventional. His mother was standing next to his father. They were in their wedding clothes. Her dress was like a draped white column and she held a huge bouquet of flowers in front of her belly. Ernest said, 'She was five months pregnant, though one would never have known.'

The Prime Minister said, 'So Edward, her first child, was illegitimate?'

'A bastard,' said Ernest. 'But it was awfully good of Percy to marry her, considering the morals of the time.'

The Prime Minister said, 'What do you mean?'

'Edward's real father was a refugee called Shadrack Vajansky.'

'Crikey,' said the Prime Minister. 'What was this chap's nationality?'

'Czechoslovakian,' said Ernest. 'He was a handsome fellow with black eyes and a couple of gold teeth who did a bit of knife-grinding in the neighbourhood. There were rumours that he came from an aristocratic Romany family. Though I rather think he started those rumours himself. He certainly had the gift of the gab.'

'Blimey. Is he still alive?' asked the Prime Minister.

'I don't know,' Ernest answered. 'The poor chap was deported and sent back behind the Iron Curtain. Heather was terribly upset; she made inquiries but nothing came of them.'

Sweat had broken out on the Prime Minister's forehead. Jack took out a white handkerchief from his pocket and handed it to him. The Prime Minister mopped his brow then excused himself and went to find a lavatory. He was glad of the support of the disability rails that surrounded the toilet bowl. He sat down and took a piece of Bronco lavatory paper from out of his handbag.

So the foundations of his childhood had been blown up by Ernest's revelations. He was the child of a Romany; he had bona fide Bohemian blood flowing in his veins. His mother sounded like a fabulous woman. He wished he'd known her better. He threw the Bronco into the bin and tore off pieces of soft pink paper from the roll on the wall and he blew his nose and wiped his eyes, then looked into the mirror and repaired his make-up. He didn't bother washing his hands.

Clarke and Palmer knew about the Prime Minister's mother's career with Miss Monica's Hot Seven, but it came to them as a surprise to learn about his natural father. Palmer tapped a few details into the laptop in front of him and within minutes found out that Shadrack Vajansky was still alive and was living in the outskirts of Bratislava in a Romany encampment. According to immigration records, he had made two attempts to settle in Britain, the first in 1951, when he was fleeing from Soviet Communism, and the second in 1998, when he got no further than Heathrow in a vain bid to claim asylum because of persecution by racist skinheads in Slovakia. Apparently he told immigration officers that he was the father of their Prime Minister and asked if he could be allowed to make a phone call to Edward, the son he had never met. Permission was refused.

Clarke said to Palmer, 'You know what, Palmer; I look nothing like my dad.'

After the Prime Minister had left, Jack said, 'Are there any photographs of Pamela, Ernest?'

Ten minutes later even he was growing tired of looking at the constant stream of photographs that Ernest passed to him. There she was, a true beauty, sitting on Santa's knee, paddling in her knickers at Black Rock Sands, in her Girl

Guides uniform, tearing up L-plates on the day she passed her driving test, and getting married to Andrew, a tall man with a thick neck whom Jack disliked on sight.

A bell rang as the Prime Minister re-entered the room. Ernest said, 'That's the lunch bell.'

Jack helped Ernest to put the photographs away and took the opportunity to steal one and palm it into his pocket. He didn't know which one he'd stolen. He would look at it later when he was alone.

The Prime Minister was more direct. He asked Ernest if he could have a photograph of his mother to keep.

Ernest said, 'Take all three, I'll be dead soon.'

The Prime Minister said, 'Uncle Ernest, you could live another twenty years.'

Ernest said, 'With any luck, my dear, I shall be dead in a fortnight.'

There was a queue of old people at the lift, so they half-carried Ernest down the stairs and into the dining room and sat him at a round table for six.

Lauren and other care assistants bustled about delivering plates of pale stew and vegetables to the residents.

'I'll let you eat your lunch, shall I?' said the Prime Minister to Ernest.

'I shan't be eating lunch,' said Ernest. 'I shan't be eating ever again. I'll tell you a secret: I haven't eaten for two days; I'm starving myself to death.'

He picked up the plate of food in front of him and with

246

difficulty bent down and placed it on the floor. It wasn't long before Blackie padded over and began to lick delicately at the watery stew.

Jack said he wanted to stretch his legs and went for a walk in the grounds. He saw why Ernest didn't want to leave this place – the gardens were lovely, with daffodils and crocuses shining through the grass under the mature trees. Jack sat on a wooden bench that displayed a brass plaque inscribed, 'In loving memory of Elsie Stafford who was happy here'. He took the stolen photograph from out of his pocket. He didn't recognise Pamela at first; she was being dragged across the village green in Swale-on-the-Wold by two uniformed policemen, and in the background was a pack of hounds and a huntsman on a horse who looked remarkably like Prince Charles.

Jack phoned Pamela because he wanted to hear the sound of her voice. He could hear the dogs barking in the background, and a man's voice. Jack said, 'You've got company?'

Pamela said, 'It's my neighbour, Douglas. Something dreadful happened to him today. He was minding his own business spraying pesticides on to the hedgerows when for no reason at all a towny dragged him out of his cab and threw him into a drainage ditch where he was verbally abused by a female impersonator and a Pakistani.'

Jack could tell she was trying very hard not to laugh.

He told her that her Uncle Ernest was starving himself to death.

Pamela said, 'He's a fool. I've offered to look after him here, but he said he's had a dog phobia since reading *The Hound of the Baskervilles*.'

Jack wanted to tell her that he loved her but he was conscious of her neighbour's aggrieved presence in the room. It was Pamela who said she had to go; somebody had turned up to collect a female poodle called Harrie.

He looked at the photograph again, searching for reasons why he should forget about this woman. Her view of the world was different from his own. He had previously thought that foxes were vermin, but now he was beginning to see the fox's point of view.

He remembered a fox stole that his mother used to wear around her neck on winter mornings; he had always hated its glassy-eyed stare. He phoned Norma but there was no reply. He would ask the Prime Minister if they could call in at Leicester on their way back to London.

Ali shouted to him that they were ready to go; the Prime Minister was already sitting in the back of the car, holding the record of 'Stomping at the Savoy' as though it was nitroglycerine about to explode. Jack said, 'Ed, you can't sit and hold it for two days.'

The Prime Minister said, 'But these shellac records shatter so easily.'

Ali was hurt. He said to the Prime Minister, 'Look, if

you've got somethink to say about my driving, just say it, innit. When I was eleven years old I used to drive a TaTa truck full of eggs round Islamabad and I never broke one egg, not once.'

Jack thought that Ali was overstating his case about being a careful driver, but he said nothing.

After asking the Prime Minister's permission Jack directed Ali to turn left on to the A46 and head towards Leicester.

Ali said, 'You can trust me with your precious record. Just put it on the seat next to you – Allah will keep it safe.'

The Prime Minister did as he was told. He thought that Ali would make a very effective chief whip.

After a few miles Ali regained his good spirits and the atmosphere inside the car lightened. The Prime Minister said, 'Can we stop somewhere for a drink? I could murder a Campari and soda.'

Jack said, 'Ed, the expression is, I could murder a pint.'

Ali said, 'Stratford's on the way.' Then he added, 'William Shakespeare was born there, you know.'

Jack said irritably, 'You'll be telling us the Prime Minister lives in Downing Street next.'

Ali laughed triumphantly and said, 'He don't any more; he's supposed to be in a nuclear bunker, but I reckon he's dead.'

'Dead?' said the Prime Minister.

'Yeah,' said Ali. 'I reckon he tried to walk on water and drowned himself.'

The Prime Minister forced himself to laugh along with the others.

Ali said, 'My eldest boy, Mohammed, is doing Shakespeare for GCSE.'

The Prime Minister said, 'How did he do in his SATS?'

'Don't talk about SATS to me,' said Ali. 'All my kids have had their hair turned grey from worrying about them tests.'

'What Shakespeare play is he doing?' said the Prime Minister.

'It's not a play,' said Ali, 'it's a sonnet; that's like a poem,' he explained helpfully and told them that he sometimes wrote poetry himself. It were no good, though – he wouldn't never show it to anyone except for his wife. He usually did it late at night after the last kid had gone to bed. His wife had bought him a notebook and a pencil case and they were kept on a shelf in the old meter cupboard in the front room. He had started off making rhymes but then Mohammed read him a poem that had made him and Ali laugh; it was by a bloke who was still alive, Simon Armitage, he lived near Leeds. He was quite famous and Ali was pleased that Jack had heard of him. Edwina, the bloke in the blonde wig, hadn't. So Ali explained to him that this Armitage bloke wrote about ordinary things and Ali had wrote a poem about his taxi, comparing it to a cowboy's horse. It weren't good enough to put in a book, but his wife liked it and she had copied it out for him in her nice handwriting and sent it to his father in Pakistan.

Jack was scowling across the road at Anne Hathaway's cottage where lines of tourists were tramping up and down the path to the front door.

'I don't understand it,' said the Prime Minister.

Jack winced at the Prime Minister's pronunciation of 'it' as 'ut'. He noticed it more frequently now that they had been in each other's pockets for seven days, and almost waited for it. Jack said, 'Understand what?'

'Your antipathy to thatched cottages,' said the Prime Minister.

'They're so bloody smug and self-satisfied,' said Jack. 'Let's go for that drink.'

'I wanted to be an actor when I was a boy,' said the Prime Minister.

He and Jack were sitting in the Dirty Duck in Stratford-upon-Avon. A group of actors were eating lunch at an adjacent table.

'They say that politicians are just ugly actors, don't they,' said Jack with a laugh.

The Prime Minister looked crestfallen. 'Who says that, Jack?'

'They!'

'But who are they?' pressed the Prime Minister.

Jack replied, 'It's just a figure of speech.'

'But politicians are no uglier than most of the population,' said the Prime Minister.

Jack said wearily, 'The point is, Ed, that politicians are primarily actors.'

Ali was looking through the multi-paned window of a gift shop in the pedestrianised shopping centre. It was his eldest son's birthday next week and he had bought him a William Shakespeare T-shirt but he was having doubts now – what fifteen-year-old boy would want to be seen wearing a T-shirt what had a picture of an old bald-headed git on it, innit. And he couldn't just buy a present for Mohammed, could he? The others would expect something an' all.

The Prime Minister was happy to be in the Dirty Duck with a Campari and soda on a little table in front of him; he felt sure that his mother would approve of him, drinking at lunchtime in the company of theatrical folk.

An actor with a familiar pock-marked face leaned over and said, 'Aren't you Victoria Rotherhide? Weren't we on *The Bill* together in 1988? I'm Guy Sutherland.'

The Prime Minister blinked rapidly and said, 'Hi, Guy, I'm Edwina St Clare.'

'Yeah, course you are, I'm crap at names,' said Guy. 'You were a woman whose kids were abducted and I was the nutter.'

The other actors at the table laughed and one said, 'Typecast again, Guy.'

The Prime Minister said coquettishly, 'May I join you?'

He wanted to get away from Jack for a while and be with creatures of his own kind. After all, he had the theatre in his blood. Jack was behaving like a moody adolescent lately, and such cynicism – how could anybody find a thatched cottage less than charming?

He sat next to Amaryllis, a dark-haired actress with intense black eyes and artfully arranged scruffy clothes. She said, 'I assume you are here for the audition, you're terribly like Edward Clare.'

Jack looked over from the bar and saw that the Prime Minister was laughing with his head thrown back showing his Adam's apple. Jack frowned; he had warned the Prime Minister not to do that, it was a dead giveaway. Still, at least he was laughing.

The Prime Minister and Amaryllis were swapping their life stories: according to the Prime Minister, he had studied at RADA with Helen Mirren and shared a flat with Simon Callow. After working in rep in Nottingham and Bristol he had worked mostly in TV and films but theatre was his first love. 'One feels, y'know, legitimised by the audience.'

Jack saw one of the actors at the table turn his head and stick his fingers down his throat.

Opposite the pub in a stage manager's tiny office in the back of the Royal Shakespeare Theatre sat Sir Digby Priest, celebrated theatre director. He was due to start rehearsals in three days on a play called *The Life and Spiritual Death of*

Edward Clare by Wayne Sparrow, a left-wing playwright who had won critical acclaim for his first play, *Fart*.

Sparrow had been commissioned three years before but had missed deadline after deadline and had finally delivered the Clare play two nights ago. He had been drunk or drugged and had mumbled, 'It's fucking rubbish and it's only twenty-seven minutes long. I've been having trouble with my identity.'

After reading the manuscript Sir Digby had considered paying to have Sparrow's legs broken. As a boy Digby had helped his uncle to deliver milk to the Krays, and he still had contacts in the East End.

However, the brochure advertising the production had been printed and the posters were up in the shops around Stratford, so the show would have to go on.

Digby was still searching for the lead actor; he turned the pages of *Spotlight*, in which he had been desperately scanning the photographs of leading men for anyone resembling the Prime Minister. Why did the bastards keep the same photograph in the book for twenty years? He had auditioned leading men who had served at El Alamein, for Christ's sake.

As he left the rehearsal room he took a call from a casting agent who told him that she was lining up a couple of likely Edward Clares, but one would have to have time off for a telly job and the other was a bit on the short side, though he was prepared to wear lifts in his shoes.

Digby said, 'How short is on the short side?'

'He's almost five foot one.'

'It's not a lift he'll need in his shoes, darling, it's a fucking escalator,' shouted Digby.

The phone rang again. It was Amaryllis, whom Sir Digby had once directed in *Streetcar*. She had been a disaster as Blanche; her southern accent had sounded as if it had come straight from the Welsh valleys. Amaryllis said, 'Digby, darling, the definitive Edward Clare is sitting in the Duck. He's a woman, but she is he.'

Sir Digby took a small brush from out of the shoulder bag he carried everywhere and brushed his hair and goatee beard. He was between wives and was ever hopeful of finding female companionship. As he hurried through the building and out into the street he was greeted, or at least recognised, by almost everybody he passed. He had often spoken in interviews about his 'absolute need for privacy'. However, his flamboyant Falstaffian appearance and booming voice meant that, tragically, he was unable to melt into a crowd. Brian Blessed had once been heard to remark, 'I adore darling Digby, but Christ is he loud.'

Jack watched as Sir Digby Priest strode into the bar. He had read Priest's published diaries and felt as if he knew the man. Because of this familiarity Jack raised his hand in greeting, then dropped it again when he realised that Priest was in fact a stranger to him. He wondered why a man who was in his sixty-fifth year would rig himself up in jeans, cowboy boots, a Rolling Stones T-shirt and a black leather jacket.

He watched as Sir Digby cleared a path through the bar towards the Prime Minister.

Digby saw at once that the creature in the gypsy dress and cheap blonde wig was awesomely suitable to play the Premier.

Amaryllis introduced them, Sir Digby boomed out, 'Get lost, cattle,' and the actors got up obediently and moved to the other side of the room.

He took the Prime Minister's hands and held them inside his own great paws. He looked deep into the Prime Minister's eyes and said in what he thought was a confidential whisper, though Jack heard it at the bar, 'I'm quite used to transsexuals, my dear; my first wife was a man. I went to a Catholic school so I knew nothing about women and was a bit of a lemon sexually, but it was the sixties and one didn't like to admit to being less than clued up about women's bodies, so I assumed that my first wife, sweet, sweet girl, Cassandra, had a larger than usual clitoris. However, the poor love was in private despair because she was actually a man who had an absurdly small penis. I paid for her to have the chop and the marriage struggled on for a while but one day there was an ugly row about something silly – she'd used my shaving brush and hadn't rinsed it – and we divorced. But tell me about yourself, my dear.'

The Prime Minister talked for a few moments about the

highlights of his career – a suicide in *Casualty*, the Inspector in *An Inspector Calls*, Gwendolyn in the *Importance of Being Earnest* – 'But I've always longed to work at the RSC.' Henry V was a part he was born to play.

While the Prime Minister had been talking Digby had been watching every movement of the Prime Minister's face and listening to every nuance of his voice, that mixture of hesitation and command. Digby tried to calm himself; he had been in this perfect casting situation before, when Sylvester Stallone had almost signed up to play Bottom in the *Dream*. That had ended in tears when Stallone's agent had requested that it be written in the contract that Stallone would be allowed to kill a mother-fucking swan if it came near him. When Digby had phoned LA to say that the swans at Stratford were owned by the Queen and were protected by law the agent had screamed, 'The deal's off! Doncha know a fucking swan can break a man's arm?'

Sir Digby said to the Prime Minister, 'Shakespeare bores me rigid. I will only work on contemporary plays by living authors. I want you to audition for the lead in a play called *The Life and Spiritual Death of Edward Clare*.'

The Prime Minister said, 'The lead?'

Digby said, 'You bear an uncanny resemblance to our esteemed leader and your voice is remarkably similar. Are you available?'

'Yes,' said the Prime Minister. 'I'm resting at the moment.'

'Then let us go and see what you look like in a suit, shall we, my dear?'

'Blimey,' said the Prime Minister. 'This is rather exciting.'

Jack followed Sir Digby and the Prime Minister over the road to the rehearsal rooms; he allowed himself to be introduced as the Prime Minister's agent and was grudgingly admitted into the rehearsal room where the audition was to take place. The Prime Minister was led away by the wardrobe mistress and reappeared ten minutes later dressed in a blue suit, a white shirt, a red tie and lace-up shoes, and wearing his own hair. The little crowd of theatre workers in the room applauded spontaneously as the Prime Minister made a shy entrance.

Sir Digby paced the room issuing instructions to the Prime Minister: the Prime Minister had to laugh, cry, get angry, talk to God, address the UN, pretend to be a dog, sing, dance and be a ten-year-old boy.

Jack cringed with embarrassment. In his opinion the Prime Minister was completely unable to play himself. And he had no idea of what to do with his hands. But Sir Digby announced after a few minutes of conferring with his assistant director and others in the production team that the Prime Minister would be expected at rehearsals at ten o'clock on Monday morning. He addressed the room with a voice trembling with emotion: 'This is a fucking important play; it is about the spiritual degeneration of a political leader and his capitulation to American imperialism.'

The Prime Minister looked nervously over at Jack and said to Sir Digby, 'I'll need to talk to my agent, of course, but crikey it's very nice of you to give me the part.'

Ali was inside one of Stratford's multifarious gift shops immersed in an English world of childhood iconography. He was surrounded on all sides by Winnie the Pooh, Eeyore, Roo, Peter Rabbit, Rupert the Bear, Thomas the Tank Engine, the Fat Controller, Noddy, Big Ears, Alice in Wonderland, the Mad Hatter, Toad of Toad Hall, Ratty, Badger and Mole. He was sweating with indecision – would Areefa, his three-year-old, prefer Winnie the Pooh to Rupert Bear? Would Sedek be insulted by the floating Noddy soap dish? Would his missis be offended if he bought her a Toad of Toad Hall soft toy? (Ali's private name for her was Froggy ever since she'd had thyroid trouble in the late '90s, though thanks be to Allah that was cleared up now.) Hassina, the eldest daughter, at thirteen, would be impossible to please anyway, but maybe she wouldn't object to Peter Rabbit.

Chapter Twenty

Norma woke up and lay for a moment before she remembered that today was the big day. She threw the heavy bedclothes back; she could take a few off now that the room was lovely, gorgeous, like it was summer. Since James had come she'd agreed to have the heating on all day and all night. It was daring, she knew, but it was true what James had said: 'The electric bill comes four times a year but we could die tomorrow.'

She liked the way he always said 'we', always included her, like they were partners in business and in life. She loved James. She knew it couldn't never be *that* kind of love – she was seventy-one and he wasn't even twenty. Although there had been a couple on *Jerry Springer* who said they were happy; he was bald and dribbling out of the side of his mouth and she was just sixteen and a bit retarded, poor kid.

Anyway, she was glad she didn't have to do *that* ever again. She'd only enjoyed it with Trevor, and he hadn't bothered her that often. Christmas, Easter, Blackpool Illuminations week and other odd times when he'd had just the right amount to drink. Too little and he'd be a bit shy, too much and he'd have a bit of a struggle to get a purchase on it.

The love she and James had for each other was the pure type but more exciting than the love she felt for Stuart, Yvonne and Jack, and James needed her help. He was like a life and business partner, and as soon as he was cured of crack he was going to take her travelling abroad. A cruise first, just to break her in – she'd never been out of England before, though she and Trev had planned a holiday to Disneyland but then Trev had fallen off that roof. If you get the right ship where everybody speaks English it's just like being in England, James had told her.

They cleaned the house together; she liked it clean for visitors. Then James said, 'Let's do some cooking, Mother.' He led her into the kitchen and sat her down. He took a roll of aluminium foil out of the cupboard drawer and used it to line the surface of the table. He then searched for and found a baking tray, a Pyrex bowl, a little milk pan, a roll of clingfilm, a large metal spoon, a sharp knife, a cola tin partially scraped clean of its paint and a hole-punch. In minutes the table was transformed into an alchemist's work bench. She watched him like she used to watch her mother as he sifted and mixed a bit of white powder, a sprinkling of bicarbonate of soda and a few drops of water in the Pyrex bowl. Then he took the little milk pan and heated the mixture until it snapped, crackled and popped.

Sir Digby was reluctant to let his astonishing new discovery leave without giving him a firm commitment. 'Edwina, stay in Stratford with me. I'm renting a delightful thatched cottage; we could work on the script together. I've done a little research myself and I think I've got the measure of our celebrated PM.'

'What are your own politics?' asked the Prime Minister.

Sir Digby was surprised to be asked. His name regularly appeared immediately after Palin and Paxman on petitions and round-robin letters to the press on every conceivable radical issue from prison reform to the war against Iraq.

'I'm afraid I'm rabidly anti-Establishment. I was thrown out of the MCC last year for trying to start a Mexican wave in the members' enclosure at Lords.'

Jack laughed.

Sir Digby said testily, 'I know it's not akin to throwing oneself under a tank, but there are very few opportunities to do so in the streets of this country.' He looked almost regretful, then said, 'Edwina, together we could make a difference, we could bring down the Clare government. Please say you'll play Edward Clare.'

Then Jack said, 'Edwina and I need to discuss it. We'll be in touch – don't call us, Sir Digby, we'll call you.'

Jack then escorted the Prime Minister to where Ali was parked with his hazard lights flashing on a double yellow line. Before they could pull away from the kerb, Sir Digby thrust a copy of the script through the open window saying, 'We've almost signed Sharon Stone to play Adele. She's being a bit precious about the false nose, but I'm sure once she's tried a few on . . .'

Jack said, 'Drive on, Ali,' and the car drew away slowly and joined the tourist traffic leaving Stratford. The Prime Minister read aloud from Wayne Sparrow's skimpy script. One of the liveliest scenes was set in the Oval Office at the White House and involved the Prime Minister of Great Britain and the President of the United States wrestling naked by firelight; the victor would win the dubious honour of issuing the command to rain missiles on to the major cities in all the troublesome 'Axis of Evil' countries.

Jack said, 'Sparrow's obviously a D. H. Lawrence fan. I'll ask Sir Digby to double the money if he's expecting you to show your arse, Ed.'

Ali said, 'It sounds like a film my missis was watching the other night.'

In another scene, Sparrow's Prime Minister was dressed as a poodle and was jumping through a burning hoop held at arm's length by the Statue of Liberty. The dialogue throughout was littered with obscenities and expletives.

When Jack took the script and read out a monologue Ali said, 'Ain't you read the notice on the dash, Jack? No bad language!'

Lately, Palmer and Clarke couldn't wait to get to work and resented having to hand over to the night shift. They had offered to work around the clock, sleeping and eating in the office, but the boss had refused them permission, citing Health and Safety regulations. They had grown fond of their surveillance subjects and had cheered loudly when Jack had pulled that mutton-chopped bastard farmer from out of the tractor cab and duffed him up.

They were tracking Ali's car as it moved along the A46 towards Leicester, where Jack intended to call in and check on his mother. There were intelligence reports that there had been a lot of unusual activity in and around her house lately, but the CCTV pictures had been indistinct. They had picked up the registration of a Mercedes Coupe that had been parked outside for several days guarded by two small boys in hooded tops and baggy trousers. The number plates belonged to the owner of a chain of sportswear shops in Reading; the car had been stolen from the Pink Elephant car park at Stanstead airport and hadn't been reported missing.

Adele and Lucinda were being driven to Harley Street. Their car was followed by another in which sat Adele's bodyguard, Sergeant Sandra Lock, and her colleague Sergeant John Harvey.

Adele had yet to find, either in brochures or on the Internet, the perfect nose. Lucinda was growing bored with the subject of Adele's new nose. She was hoping that Sir Nigel Hambleton would carry the baton from now on. Their appointment was for seven o'clock in the evening so they had allowed over an hour to travel the short distance of only two and a half kilometres from Downing Street to Harley Street. However, the traffic became gridlocked at several places along the route. At Piccadilly Circus Adele had time to watch the crowds as they milled around the tourist hub of the world. She looked across to Eros and saw now how young he was. He was a teenager in love, and below him on the steps sat other teenagers with beautiful faces, the neon lights reflected in their eyes. A boy who looked remarkably like Morgan was sitting with his arm around the shoulders of a black girl in a combat jacket and khaki trousers, but it couldn't be Morgan – he had volunteered to put Poppy to bed before writing an essay about child labour.

Lucinda yawned and tried to calculate how much she ought to charge for her time. If she paid her plumber £65 an hour, would it be unreasonable for her to invoice at £150 an hour? After all, she had studied for ten years.

At Cavendish Square the car again came to a complete standstill. In the gardens of the square marquees had been erected and flaring torches illuminated wooden walkways, people in evening dress were showing invitations to dinner-jacketed security men. Adele saw several faces that she knew and felt a pang that she hadn't been invited to whatever it was that was going on. Lucinda murmured, 'It's a charity do to provide water wells in Swaziland.'

The car inched forward and Adele asked the driver to

telephone Sir Nigel Hambleton's secretary and to tell him that the Prime Minister's wife was stuck in traffic.

Adele said to Lucinda, 'What would you say to me if I told you that I want to resign from my unpaid voluntary position, that of being the Prime Minister's wife?'

Lucinda said, 'Are you telling me that you want to divorce Ed?'

'No,' said Adele. 'But I want a trial separation from the job.'

Lucinda said, 'It'll be at least two months before your new nose is fit to be seen in public; you should go away, Adele, somewhere warm, take Poppy with you. Do no work, get fat. We women knock ourselves out and for what? I mean, what's it all about, Alfie?'

Sir Nigel was waiting for them in the entrance lobby of his consulting rooms. He had often seen the notorious nose in photographs and on film and had once murmured to his wife, 'By Christ, Betty, I'd like to get my hands on that.' And now here it was. He could hardly restrain himself from feeling its contours, testing the cartilage and accessing the nostrils. He led Adele and Lucinda into his office, where he chatted urbanely about reconstructive surgery. He had recently repaired the septum of a minor royal who had snorted more cocaine than was wise.

The moment came when all three of them had to address the reason for Adele's visit. Sir Nigel overcame any potential embarrassment by retreating into science and technology.

He measured and calibrated Adele's nose to the nth degree. He examined it internally with a tiny light on a flexible tube. He asked Adele many nose-related questions. He then pretended to weigh up the advantages and disadvantages of giving Adele nasal reconstructive surgery and, unsurprisingly, he suggested that Adele was a suitable candidate. He asked her if she had a particular nose in mind. When she said, 'I'd like it a lot smaller, something like Barbra Streisand's,' he said, 'I think we can do better than that, Mrs Floret-Clare.'

He sat her in front of a computer and ordered her to keep absolutely still, then he tapped a few keys and Adele's face appeared on the screen. He then superimposed a menu of noses on to Adele's face. She quite liked the Cleopatra; it made her look confident and imperious. The Sophia Loren didn't work; it made her eyes look too small, though it was beautiful in itself. The Greta Garbo was perfect. She ordered it and insisted on paying a deposit, and asked if it could be given to her the following day.

Sir Nigel said he would shift things about a bit. He would admit her at once and he ordered her not to eat or drink anything after midnight.

Morgan had taken down Poppy's American mobile. If he was in charge of putting her to bed and getting her to sleep, he would do it on his own terms. She lay on her back watching him through the wooden bars of her cot. He pulled up the low nursery chair and began to tell Poppy a bedtime story.

'Once upon a time in 1856 a boy was born in Scotland called Keir Hardie. He left school and went to work when he was eight. And at the age of ten was working down the mines. Think of that, Poppy, a little kid of ten working in the dark, deep under the ground. He went to night school and became a journalist, then stood for Parliament like Dad. He started the Independent Labour Party.'

Poppy began to whimper. She kicked the blanket off and began to thrash her arms and legs about inside her peppermint-green Babygro. Morgan was amazed at how quickly she worked herself up into a frenzy of open-mouthed screaming, unable to stand it for long; he re-hung the American mobile and set the clockwork in motion.

They entered the outskirts of Leicester. They were 100 miles from London. The Prime Minister said, 'I don't want to go home, Jack. Is there any chance of extending our holiday?'

'This is not a holiday for me,' said Jack. 'I'm doing a job of work.'

'C'mon, Jack. It has been absolutely terrific, tremendous fun.'

Jack hated the word 'fun'. In his opinion it had nothing to do with having a good time and was overused by people who thought practical jokes such as shoving people into swimming pools were funny. It was a word Richard Branson used a lot.

'Have you learned anything?' said Jack bluntly.

'Only that, y'know, people seem to kind of plough their own furrow, regardless of what we in the government want them to do.'

Jack said, 'They could plough a straighter furrow with a better plough and a healthier cart horse.'

'Cart horse?' said the Prime Minister. 'I'm talking about high-tech computerised farm machinery.'

Jack said, 'I tell you what, Ed, it would be an interesting experiment to see how democracy would work in this country, wouldn't it?'

The Prime Minister said, 'Britain is celebrated as being the very cradle of democracy.'

Jack said, 'Well, the baby's fallen out of the cradle into the bathtub and been thrown out with the bathwater.'

Ali was sick of listening to such tangled metaphorical exchanges. He turned the radio on.

'. . . A hospital spokesman admitted today that the amputated leg at the centre of what has become known as the Barry's Leg Row has been disposed of by mistake due to an administrative blunder. A mortuary technician has been suspended pending further inquiries. Our medical correspondent, Martha Tree, is at the hospital now. Martha, what can you tell us?'

'Well, very little. As you've just said, the leg has been

269

accidentally disposed of and a member of staff has been suspended pending further inquiries.'

'Do we know how the leg was disposed of?'

'No, not at this stage.'

'Do we know how the family feels about the disposal of the leg?'

'No, not at this stage. But I expect they are devastated. People usually are.'

Jack turned to see how the Prime Minister had taken the news. He appeared to be unconcerned and was fiddling with the hooped gypsy earrings he'd bought from Accessorize in Stratford earlier in the day.

They drove past rows of large detached houses. In the garden of one a woman in a sari was pruning a shrub; in another a brown-skinned family were admiring a new-looking car. There were very few white people around.

The Prime Minister remarked on this and Jack said, sounding like a tour guide, 'Leicester's well on the way to being the first city in Britain to have an ethnic majority.'

Ali laughed and said, 'Your women don't want kids, innit.'

Jack, suddenly conscious of his own childlessness, said defensively, 'Our women want to have a life outside of child-bearing.'

The Prime Minister said, 'My wife, Adele, has managed to juggle work, children and a social life brilliantly. I don't know how she does it.'

Ali drove past shops with Indian and Pakistani names. A cinema was showing a Bollywood film. The Bank of India was flanked by Rahki's shoe shop and Aman's translation service. Ali said that after he'd dropped Jack and the Prime Minister off at Norma's house he would visit his second cousin who lived next to the flyover in Belgrave.

'I expect you'll enjoy eating your own food again,' said the Prime Minister, looking at the restaurants and take-aways.

Ali looked puzzled. 'I can get my favourite food any-where,' he said. 'It's seafood pizza.'

The taxi drove into the estate where Jack had been born and where he had brought himself up. As they passed poorly executed community murals Ali said, 'I ain't happy leaving you here. Are you sure you don't want me to drive you straight to London?'

The Prime Minister was keen to delay the hour of his return: the weight of his responsibilities was already pushing down on him. He said, 'No, we must visit Jack's mother and find out why she's not answering her phone. We'll be perfectly safe, we are protected by CCTV.'

The cameras were everywhere, swivelling their inquisi-tive heads slowly in 360-degree turns.

Jack said, 'CCTV is a joke, Ed. You get badly trained security officers watching a bank of blurred, out-of-focus screens which make everybody on the street look like the abominable snowman. You got caught up in the hysteria

271

whipped up by the private security firms who are hungry for contracts.'

The Prime Minister had come to dread Jack's lectures and wished he hadn't encouraged Jack to talk more. Over breakfast at the Grimshaw Jack had grown alarmingly angry on the subject of the paucity of day nurseries.

Jack failed to recognise the fortified exterior of his mother's house and he allowed Ali to drive by it twice before he realised that it was in fact Number Ten. He had phoned on and off throughout the day but still received no reply. As he and the Prime Minister walked down the path he thought he saw a face looking through a gap in the curtains at the barred front-room window. The dark beats of drum and bass reverberated through the brickwork.

He banged on the steel-plated door and noticed that the letterbox had disappeared. He wondered how his mother was able to receive the junk mail she was so fond of. She had often rung him in the past to tell him that, according to Mr Tom Champagne of *Readers Digest*, she had won hundreds of thousands of pounds.

From inside the house came the sound of James shouting. He appeared to think that the drug squad were at the door. The Prime Minister looked around fearfully; he had not expected to find Jack's mother living in such a depressing area. There was nobody on the street and most of the houses looked unoccupied. It was getting dark and he wished that he had asked Ali to wait for them. Since the beginning of their journey, seven days ago, he had never once felt afraid. Jack had been like a pillar beside him, but a pillar made of cold marble. He sometimes wished that Jack had no political opinions, but he had never doubted Jack's ability to cope with any situation. Now he saw that Jack himself was afraid and he didn't like the tremor in Jack's voice as he shouted, 'Mam, Mam, open the door.'

Norma sat behind the closed kitchen door. She could hardly hear herself think, what with James's music being so loud, but she could still hear Jack shouting from outside. She wanted to run and let him in but James was standing spreadeagled against the kitchen door talking to her in a voice she had come to fear. He was smoking one of his special roll-ups – not the ones with dope in but the other ones, the ones he said would kill her, the kind that made him forget his manners and use terrible words then made him whimper and cry and shit himself.

Jack said to the Prime Minister, 'Wait here,' and hoisted himself over the side gate. The Prime Minister wanted to run but the two little hooded figures leaning against the nearby Mercedes did not answer his tentative friendly half-wave.

Jack padded stealthily alongside the house and went into the back garden. The kitchen curtains were closed and the back door had also been reinforced. He pressed close to the window and heard his mother shouting over the music, 'Please, I'll have to let our Jack in.'

273

Inside, James drew the smoke deep into his lungs, where tens of thousands of tiny capillaries took the chemicals swiftly into his blood stream. And when it hit the section of the brain that produces a feeling of pleasure it destroyed a million cells. James's pleasure in music, food, sex and the joys of the natural world would be further diminished for ever.

He quickly went through the options that the crack-induced paranoia made available to him. He had a gun he'd bought second-hand for £40; it was inside a cream-cracker tin on top of the kitchen cupboard and he had never fired it yet but he thought he would know what to do. He could shoot Jack and try to escape in the car; he could take Norma hostage; he could invite Jack in and explain to him that his mother was running a crack den from a council house, which was surely grounds for eviction.

He chose to let Jack in and walked to the front door. He drew on the last shreds of his roll-up then began to unfasten the chains and shoot the bolts. The music thudded through his body, his teeth were rattling inside his mouth. He opened the door but Jack wasn't there; instead he found on the doorstep a blonde woman with hooped earrings, who on closer inspection turned out to be a man in drag. He almost laughed out loud; the Drug Squad filth could never get it right. 'Where's Jack?' he said and pulled the man inside. He shouted into the Prime Minister's face, 'Where's Jack?'

The Prime Minister had often wondered how he would stand up to interrogation or torture. Then Norma and Jack came to the kitchen door, Jack said 'I'm here!' and the Prime Minister was saved from finding out.

Norma was saying inappropriately, 'Shall we all have a nice cup of tea?'

Chapter Twenty-One

Alexander McPherson went downstairs to the press office and gathered his team around him. They were mostly young and some of them were clever, but not all – one had been chosen because of his obvious stupidity. He was a nice twenty-four-year-old called Ben Fossett who had been carefully selected to represent the gullible, respectable British taxpayer. He had once said, when speaking as a delegate at a Labour Party Conference, that professional politicians should be able to rise high in the Party ranks only if they were totally honest in word and deed.

Fossett's innocently idealist words were repeated end-lessly at New Labour get-togethers and were always accompanied by helpless laughter. Nobody was more surprised than he when he was summoned to the press office at Number Ten and given a job as a special advisor. During his time there he had remained free of cynicism. McPherson used him much as a sea captain of old used a barometer before setting out to cross the Bay of Biscay.

McPherson leaned up against a tall filing cabinet and said, 'Right, here's the facts: One, Adele Floret-Clare has had a psychotic episode or, in other words, she's gone barmy, she's been given medication and she's in a private hospital.

'Two, Barry's Leg. An injunction has been taken out against publishing anything at all about Barry's Leg so this is a story that can run no further. I need a statement about Adele to catch the six o'clock news; you've got twenty minutes and we haven't got time for your bollocking laptops to warm up.'

Fossett sat at a desk and chewed at the rubber on the end of his pencil. He thought for a moment then wrote:

Dear Mr or Mrs Editor,

Our mummy has been poorly with a nervous illness, she needs piece and quiet, so please don't write anything in the newspapers or say anything nasty about her on radio or television. Our Dad is not here to help us, he is away trying to make the world a safer place for children everywhere.

Love from the Clare kiddies.

When it was Fossett's turn to read his paragraph out loud he introduced it by stammering, 'I, er . . . just sort of, er . . . put myself, y'know, in the mind of a child . . . er.'

'Not difficult,' muttered McPherson under his breath.

'If you could get the kiddies to sign it, er . . . perhaps there is a photograph . . . And by the way "peace" is deliberately misspelled.'

McPherson tore the paper from Fossett's sweaty hands, scanned it quickly and ordered a secretary to write it out in a childish hand on Number Ten stationery and to be sure to misspell 'peace'. When it was done he ran upstairs and entered the Clares' living quarters, where he found Morgan and Estelle bickering over the TV remote control.

He ordered them to read the letter and to sign it. Morgan refused, stating that it was a crap letter and he would hardly, at his age, be unable to spell the word peace. Estelle, however, had recently been experimenting with her signature and signed with a great flourish. McPherson took the letter and signed for Poppy and said to Morgan, 'I know all about your plans to join the anti-globalisation protest next month, Morgan. You should be more discreet with that pay-as-you-go phone of yours.'

Morgan said, 'It's a free country, isn't it?'

McPherson didn't answer. Estelle and Poppy would look good on the front of the *Sun*; Morgan would only have spoiled the picture with his miserable, spotty face.

Palmer was at a meeting where plans to assassinate Saddam Hussein and thus precipitate a regime change were being discussed. A foreign office official had just said, 'Nobody apart from the Prime Minister and his Christian Socialist pals are keen on attacking and invading Iraq. It would be rather expensive and not a little dangerous given the situation in the Middle East and would engender a tiresome amount of paperwork given that none of the MoD computers are up to facilitating a war.'

There was general laughter, and it was agreed that other options should be explored.

Palmer, himself a confectionery lover, said he had read in the *Spectator* that Saddam Hussein had a passion for Quality Street chocolates. 'Apparently he's especially fond of the Country Fudge.'

A young black woman representing the CIA said, 'Sir, latest intelligence reports he's now swapped his allegiance to the new one, Orange Chocolate Crunch.'

'Typically opportunistic of him,' murmured the Foreign Office official.

The meeting lost its focus for a few moments as the members discussed the relative merits of orange creams, hazelnut and caramel and the coconut éclairs. An Iraqi specialist argued for the toffee penny until the meeting was brought back to order.

Palmer suggested, 'Why not ask Porton Down to adulterate the Orange Chocolate Crunch ones with one of their deadly bacteria and send Saddam one of those festive tins for Christmas?'

There were several objections to this. Somebody said the Quality Street people might not cooperate and could sue the government. Somebody else said that Iraq didn't celebrate Christmas. Another said Saddam might offer the tin to one of his grandchildren and that they could not condone the killing of an innocent child.

Since nobody at the meeting could condone the accidental poisoning of a small child with a chocolate, it was agreed that a surprise missile attack on areas of major population seemed inevitable – unless the Prime Minister had undergone a change of heart during his week's absence.

The only sounds in the kitchen came from the zips and metal buttons of the denim jeans as they scraped and turned across the porthole of the washing machine. The four of them watched the kettle and waited for it to boil. The music from the next room dominated them; the Prime Minister wished that somebody would turn it off.

The reek of marijuana and crack hung in the air. Peter stood on the floor in a corner of his cage cheeping repetitively and monotonously. Jack said, 'The poor little bugger's off his head.'

James stood with his back against the kitchen door and Jack got the uncomfortable feeling that to ask him to move aside might exacerbate the violent atmosphere already present in the room.

The Prime Minister looked around with interest. It appeared to him that he was in a typical working-class kitchen. Cans of lager were stacked on the draining board next to boxes of microwave food. There was even a mangy-looking budgerigar whose cage floor was lined with a copy of the *Sun*; the headline read, 'Saddam likes Quality Street'. An ashtray on the kitchen table held a small pyre of cigarette ends, and next to it, almost touching, was a donkey pulling a cart containing salt and pepper pots. There was nothing in the kitchen of any taste; Adele would find it amusingly kitsch.

Jack's mother, a slattern wearing too much make-up, did not appear to be pleased to see her son. She shouted over the music, 'And I don't know why you're looking so bleedin' mardy, our Jack. I told you not to come, I said I'd be busy.'

The Prime Minister noticed that Norma looked at James when she said this, as if absolving herself from blame.

As his mother poured boiling water into a metal teapot Jack spoke with absolute banality about the weather, trying to neutralise the tension in the room.

The Prime Minister wrinkled his nose. He had just identified the acrid smell; some of the more dissolute students at Cambridge had smoked dope. He never had, knowing instinctively that he wouldn't like it – he had to keep himself under control. He wondered now if his mother and his real father had ever shared what he believed used to be called a jazz cigarette.

Norma said, 'So you'll drink this tea then you'll go, will you?' It was more order than question.

Jack said to James, 'How's college?'

James said contemptuously, 'College is for pygmies. Only little people go to college. I operate on a need-to-know basis; why should I clutter my head up with facts I ain't gonna need?'

The Prime Minister had once heard Michael Heseltine make a very similar statement.

Norma said, 'James will get by without an education; he's the cleverest person I know. He's got a Mercedes and he's only nineteen.'

The Prime Minister said tentatively, 'Well, y'know, Mrs Sprat, I kind of think that education is not only about equipping us with the tools for material gain. A good education should also enhance our lives and enable us to contribute to society, to make a difference.'

James said, 'Where were you educated?'

'At Cambridge,' said the Prime Minister, lowering his eyes modestly.

'Well, it ain't done you much good, has it?' said James. 'Look at the state you're in. You ain't a man, you ain't a woman, you ain't no class, what are you?'

The Prime Minister adjusted his wig and ran a hand over his bristly chin. He had meant to shave before entering the house, but there hadn't been a suitable opportunity.

James said, 'I've seen you before; do you work in the cloakroom at the Powder Poof?'

There was a violent banging on the other side of the kitchen door. James shouted, 'Get back in that room and stay there.' He could have been yelling at a dog.

'Who's that?' said Jack.

'One of our guests,' said Norma. She was clattering cups and teaspoons into saucers. She said to James, 'Shall I take our guests in the front room a cup of tea?'

James shouted, 'No! Stay out of there.'

Jack saw his mother's frightened face and stood up and said, 'I'm not staying out of there! I've got to turn that music off.' He asked politely for James to move away from the kitchen door, and when James refused and called him a fascist Jack behaved fascistically: he took James's right arm and bent it behind his back with such ferocity that it almost broke. James screamed with pain and sank to his knees.

Norma cried out, 'Don't hurt him, Jack!'

Jack pulled James to his feet and pushed him along the hallway and into the front room. It was completely dark but he could smell the presence of other people. The music was like a living thing thumping at Jack's body. His hand went to the light switch on the wall by the door, but somebody had taped over it.

Jack tore off the tape and flicked the switch and the centre ceiling light came on and revealed four men and two women who protected their eyes from the sudden glare. They were an ex-manager of a carpet shop, an ex-hospital nurse, an ex-tyre-fitter, a car salesman, a doorman and a girl who lived in a probation hostel. They had begged, stolen and taken out loans that they could never repay so as to give James £500 each to weekend at his house, all found. A huge speaker stood in each alcove either side of the fireplace. Speakers smaller than these were used in the Palais de Danse where Jack had taken ballroom lessons with 300 other people. All he could think of was to stop the noise; he looked around for the source and saw that the speakers were connected to a CD player standing on his old desk next to his reference books and a donkey vase containing a bunch of dead daffodils. He fumbled with various switches. Eventually there was silence, and Norma's guests looked at this newcomer who had blundered into their dreams.

James stood in the centre of the room and looked at Jack with contempt. He pitied the little people who were afraid to take crack – they were pygmies. They would never know the ecstasy that James had experienced the first time he'd taken it. He affected the stance of a world statesman, both commanding and patronising, and started to preach to everyone in the room.

'The purpose of life is to take crack,' he explained. 'It is the reason we were born, and it is all we exist for. Only a few superior people are allowed to know the wonders of crack, and we are the true elite. These privileged people –' here he gestured towards the tyre-fitter – 'are holy and must be allowed to gather together to worship crack. Everything is allowed in its name. Rape, murder and torture will happen to people who try to prevent the worship of crack. If a crack-user has no money they must be allowed to steal from the pygmies like you and your mother, Jack. To kill a pygmy is no crime, to rape a pygmy is no crime, to bugger a pygmy is no crime, to kidnap and torture a pygmy is no crime. A crack-head knows the truth and the truth is a pleasure so exquisite as to need a new form of words before the degree of the pleasure can be understood.

'Imagine infinity, the immeasurable distances of space stretching into a forever future, and then imagine pleasure so large. Who wouldn't want to feel so gooooooooood, so hiiiiiiiiiiiiiiigh, so loooooooooooovely, so wooooooooonderful . . . ?

> 'God is crack.
> Jesus is crack.
> Allah is crack.
> Buddha is crack.
> Krishna is crack.
> Abraham is crack.
> Moses is crack.
> Martin Luther is crack.
> Mandela is crack.
> Beckham is crack.
> Puff Daddy is crack.
> Crack is crack . . .'

James's voice faltered slightly. 'This is the promise of crack; this is why we take it again and again and again and again and again . . .'

The ex-nurse said, 'But it is a broken promise and we can never, never, never, never get that same pleasure again, no matter how much we take and how much we spend.'

James continued, 'But we have to keep on trying. There is always hope, we must have faith.'

The car salesman said, 'And we got to be prepared to lose our families, lose our wives and husbands and children, lose our jobs, our friends, lose our money, our property, our houses, our self-respect, our pride, ourselves.'

James said, 'Yeah, and we will live in a dark world where everybody is our enemy as shadows wait to kill us, where every sound threatens our lives and the sun only reminds us that we will soon be thirsty yet we have nothing to drink and nobody to moisten our lips.'

James felt the energy leave his body and he lay down on the half-moon rug in front of the fireplace and seemed instantly to fall asleep.

Jack switched the light off and closed the door quietly behind him as if he had just been checking on sleeping children. He went upstairs and pulled Norma's largest suitcase from the top of the wardrobe in her bedroom.

Norma was telling the Prime Minister how much he looked like the Prime Minister: 'You're Edward Clare to a T,' she said. 'The voice, the blinking, the smile, even the crooked teeth, everything,' she said.

The Prime Minister, unnerved by James's rant from the other room, tried to remember how one spoke to a genuine, old-style working-class person. What were the key points? Ferrets? Bingo?

Norma told the Prime Minister that he could be a million times better at being the Prime Minister than Rory Bremner. She said, changing the subject, 'I'm glad our Jack's come to take charge.'

The Prime Minister said automatically, 'Our policemen do a wonderful job.'

He asked Norma how she thought the government was doing. She didn't appear to understand the question. 'I don't know,' she said. 'I'm not interested in politics, except for Ron Phillpot; I liked it when he gave that bloke a good pasting.'

The Prime Minister was strangely comforted by Norma's indifference. What was the point of him lying awake at night fretting about the Kyoto Agreement when the vast majority of people slept for eight hours in blissful ignorance of the dangers of power-station emissions?

The telephone rang on the kitchen wall. Norma looked at it fearfully; James had discouraged her from answering the phone or making her own calls.

Upstairs Jack heard the phone ringing and ran down to answer it. It was his sister, Yvonne.

'Where are you?' he asked, genuinely interested – after all, she could be anywhere in the world.

'I've just landed at Luton and I'm on the motorway,' she shouted. 'Why hasn't Mam been answering the phone? Has owt happened to her?'

Jack didn't know how to begin to explain to Yvonne what had happened to their mother during the past week, so he said, 'I'm so glad to hear your voice, Vonnie.'

She said, 'Is Mam all right, then?'

Jack said, 'She's here in the kitchen smoking a fag.'

Yvonne shouted over a badly connected line: 'Tell her I've brung her some money.'

Jack said, 'Is Derek with you?'

'Who?' Yvonne seemed to have forgotten that she had once been married to a man called Derek for twenty-six years.

'No, I'm on my own,' she said. 'And I'm driving my own car.'

Jack couldn't imagine his sister driving, driving her own car or driving her own car on the motorway having 'landed at Luton'. The last time he'd seen her she'd been cleaning the windows of her semi-detached wearing a wrap-around apron and fluffy slippers while Derek held the back of the chair she was standing on.

Norma panicked slightly when Jack told her that Yvonne would be there in an hour or so. She said, 'Vonnie won't like all these guests here, Jack.'

Jack was amazed at his mother's capacity for self-deception. Calling the people in the front room 'guests' was like describing ants in the jam as 'welcome visitors'. Jack said, 'Where does he keep the stuff, Mam?'

'I can't tell you,' she whispered. 'I've promised him I won't tell. He made me swear on Pete's life; he said he'd put him in the microwave and eat him with a poached egg. He said he'd wear Pete's feathers in his hair. I'm glad you've come, Jack.'

Jack whispered, 'Don't tell me then, Mam, show me.'

Norma pulled open the cutlery drawer of the kitchen table and took out an Old Holborn tobacco tin; wrapped inside a piece of dark-blue velvet were small glittering rocks. 'Crystals?' said the Prime Minister.

'Crack!' said Jack.

The Prime Minister drew back as if expecting one of the tiny rocks to insinuate itself inside his body to send him mad and propel him on to the street to rave and mug and commit unspeakable acts against his fellow human beings. He felt better when Jack covered the little rocks with the velvet, replaced the lid and put the tin into the inside pocket of his jacket.

Norma said, 'You can't keep it, Jack; the guests have paid for it up front.'

Jack said to his mother, 'I've got your suitcase off the top of the wardrobe and put it on the bed. Go upstairs and pack it; you're leaving here tonight.'

'Where are you taking me?' said Norma.

'I don't know,' said Jack.

'I can't leave Pete,' she said.

'We'll take him with us,' Jack said, though in his opinion Peter didn't look strong enough to withstand much of a journey.

With Jack standing guard in the hallway Norma went upstairs and began to pack. The Prime Minister said to Jack,

289

'Jack, I'm a tolerant kinda guy but I sort of draw the line at crack, and I'm feeling pretty uncomfortable right now with this situation. I realise that this is nothing out of the ordinary for you, Jack, but I must confess that I'm sort of, y'know, shocked. Jack, it's your duty to take me away from this place. Call Ali, tell him to come now.'

Jack said savagely, 'I blame you for this. You've known about crack for ten years and you've done fuck all about it. You've run away and shoved your fucking moderate head under the duvet and pretended that crack was a nasty thing that would go away all by itself if we kept still and pretended it wasn't there. Well, it's here,' he shouted, 'in my mother's house.'

Statistics came to the Prime Minister's lips. He reeled off the millions spent on drug education and prevention; he said that X per cent of something had been spent on something and that X per cent had been allocated to something and that X per cent of X per cent was due to be spent over the next spending cycle.

Jack shouted, 'Yeah, and eight and a half per cent of the Disciples betrayed Jesus. Percentages mean nothing, statistics are balls.'

The Prime Minister said, 'The government has spent four and a half million pounds funding research.'

Jack roared. 'Crack-related crime costs this country billions. I'll tell you what, Ed, my mam's front room is full of drug experts – why don't we go in there and pick their brains? It won't cost your government a fucking penny.'

Yvonne was getting used to the controls of the BMW car and she dared to move into the fast lane where she put her foot down until she reached ninety miles an hour. The weather was crap and she wished now that she'd worn the yellow cashmere cardigan she'd bought in Marbella. She turned up the car heating and twiddled with the radio trying to get some decent music: Frank Sinatra, Neil Diamond, Queen – something with a tune she could sing along with. But all she got was depressing news about England. That they'd lost at cricket, floods had engulfed the West Country, the M25 had been closed for seven hours and that Edward Clare would be resuming his Prime Ministerial duties the next day, that the Prime Minister's children had issued a statement pleading for their mother's privacy. Yvonne wondered how she could have lived in England for so long. Compared to Marbella it was total crap. Was it possible in England to breakfast on a warm balcony surrounded by bougainvillaea, sipping fresh orange juice and eating croissants with proper coffee while looking at a blue sea? No, it bloody well wasn't. Could you walk about in a white denim skirt suit with gold sandals and matching shoulder bag in Leicester in the winter without looking like a prat? No. Could you eat dinner on the street at ten o'clock at night without freezing your tits off in England? I don't think so.

Yvonne touched the gold shoulder bag that lay on the passenger seat next to her; inside it was a bulging envelope full of Euros and she was longing to see her mother's face when she gave her it. She wanted to show Mam the apartment on the beach complex, to parade through the white rooms with the marble floors and cream furniture, to demonstrate the fridge with the ice-making machine, to adjust the air conditioning to Mam's taste, to show Mam into the guest room with the en-suite bathroom, to prove to her that Jack was not the only success story in the family. She might be forty-eight but Pedro, her current lover, had told her that she looked at least twenty years younger, and she had to admit that having a tan suited her, as did the Mia Farrow haircut. A man in the check-in queue at Malaga airport had accused her of pushing in and had called her Eurotrash. This was quite a compliment: she had always wanted to be European, ever since she'd heard Edith Piaf sing 'La Vie en Rose' and seen Audrey Hepburn sitting on the back of a Vespa in *Roman Holiday*. She passed the fields of radio masts of the listening station near Daventry, then, looking around at the drivers of the cars she was overtaking, she thought how pasty-faced and ill dressed they and their passengers looked under the sodium lights. The whole of the English population appeared to have let themselves go.

Yvonne remembered the precise moment in 1990 when she let herself go. She'd been upstairs recovering from the flu and had overheard Derek on the phone to one of his mates having a desultory conversation about a second-hand garden shed. She then distinctly heard Derek say, 'Well, I'd better ring off now, *I've gotta go up to the lump in the bed.*'

The lump in the bed. His words de-sexed her and made her ashamed. When she was better, she lumped around the house in elasticated clothing that stretched to accommodate her spreading figure. She stopped colouring her hair and tied it back with an elastic band. Her eyebrows went un-plucked, she wore Derek's socks and the hairs on her legs showed in the gap between her trousers and shoes. She joined the ranks of the other women who had let themselves go – they were everywhere, standing outside the junior-school gate, waiting at bus stops, sitting in outpatient departments.

Mrs Thatcher had saved her from herself. Yvonne had watched her heroine leave Downing Street crying in the back of that limo, a finished woman.

'She'll let herself go, like me,' Yvonne had thought, but within a few months Maggie was back as beautifully groomed and defiant as ever. Yvonne had been inspired by Maggie's crazed self-belief and the fact that she could earn £20,000 an hour for the Thatcher Foundation, a charity that apparently promoted capitalism as a force for good. Yvonne had sent a cheque for £10 to the Thatcher Foundation as a gesture of support. She had told this to Jack at a Christmas do at Mam's house and Jack had laughed, 'She won't be grateful for your pathetic tenner; she's as hard-bitten as a bar of peanut brittle.'

Yvonne couldn't stand that Edward Clare, and if she'd been tortured by having bamboo shoved under her fingernails she still couldn't have told you what he stood for. He talked a lot about the middle way, but middle meant nothing – whoever paid big money for a ringside seat to watch a middleweight boxer?

She had never regretted leaving England; she had vowed to do it if Labour got in. It had taken her a few years and now she had done it, unlike Frank Bruno and Paul Daniels who as far as she knew were still here.

She and Derek had always voted Labour – until Mrs Thatcher had exploded on to the scene in all her majesty. There was nobody to touch her. You could understand everything she said, for one thing. She'd cut the unions down to size, hadn't she? The union at Derek's factory always used to be causing trouble, agitating for more money and better health and safety. If somebody got their fingers caught in a machine, that was their own stupid fault; Derek had survived with all his fingers present and correct. Mrs Thatcher had swept the old trouble-making unions away, Derek hadn't minded at all taking his own toilet paper to work; why should his boss pay to wipe Derek's arse? Maggie had allowed Derek's firm to buy their sheet steel from India instead of the foundry down the road. OK, the quality wasn't as good, but it was five times cheaper, five times! And the union could say nothing because the order books were full, and Derek worked overtime in the evenings and at weekends and they eventually bought the council house they'd lived in since they were married, at eighty per cent off the market value.

The Prime Minister was surprised at how normal-looking the crack-heads were. He had expected overt signs of depravity and evidence of moral turpitude.

The nurse said she was in court next week accused of stealing from the bedside lockers of the patients in her care; her only worry was finding enough crack in prison to satisfy her habit.

Jack said, 'From what I've heard you'll have no problem; it's easier to get crack inside than it is to get an aspirin from the prison doctor.'

The doorman said he didn't know for how much longer he could hang on to his job; he owed money all over the town and gangsters kept coming to where he worked, threatening to shoot his kneecaps off. It was Friday night and he should be on the door of the Starlight room and he'd left his wife at home with no money and three kids to feed. He'd ordered her never to open the door to anybody at any time; the Yardies had started to punish druggy debtors by throwing acid around and he couldn't stand it if his wife's pretty face was ruined, he couldn't live with a scarred-up woman.

The Prime Minister said, 'Why don't you go to the police?'

This cheered everybody up and made them laugh.

The Prime Minister looked around and waited for somebody to explain the joke.

The car salesman was mostly incoherent and the Prime Minister had to strain to understand that his habit was costing him more than he earned; he had spent the £11,000 earmarked for his wedding and honeymoon on crack. His fiancée was unaware that he had a habit and she wouldn't know until the morning of the wedding when the hire car failed to turn up to take her to the church that hadn't been booked.

The Prime Minister said, 'Have you tried drugs counselling?'

The nurse said, 'There's only one place in the country and there's a six-month waiting list.' She then said to Jack, 'Kick that bastard awake, I need another hit.'

They all turned to look at James, who lay on the floor dreaming.

The Prime Minister said, 'He looks dead.'

Jack felt his pulse and said, 'No, he's alive. Pity.'

The Prime Minister asked them all, 'Why have you done this to yourselves?'

The girl living in the probation hostel said, 'I dunno, when I was a little kid, just learned to walk, I drunk bleach from the bottle, I dunno why I did that either. I was at a house an' James was there an' we was, like, seeing who could drink the most tequila without passing out, an' I won, an' James showed us these pretty little rocks, that was the first time. In the morning I wake up and, like, I'm happy, and then, like, I remember. I gotta go out first thing and I've gotta suck a bloke's dick or frighten a stranger to get me some money, an' it's hard work, I can't never relax, I always gotta be thinking an' planning an' I'm dodging people all the time. My mum is after me 'cause I had her rent for crack and I'm, like, hassled the whole time, there's some streets I can't walk down and places I can't go. The police know me; they drive by in their cars and shout out of the window that I'm too ugly to turn a trick. They call me Crack Alice. I run away to Nottingham but I got beat up bad, an' I come back on the train without a ticket and, like, the guy what collects the tickets showed me no respect, so I pushed him, only pushed him, and they said it was assault, but it weren't – like, ask anybody in this town, I wouldn't hurt a fly, not unless it hurt me first. I despise that ticket collector; I've got nothing but despisal for him.'

The ex-tyre-fitter said angrily, 'I didn't come here to talk. I want the lights out, the music on and another rolley and more ice; I've paid for it and I want it. I borrowed the money from a loan company. I've consolidated my debts; I've just got the one debt now and with the compound interest I'll be paying them back until I'm sixty-five.' He started to laugh. 'But they'll never get their fucking money; I'll be long dead by then.'

The Prime Minister said to him, 'Citizens' Advice Bureau runs debt clinics where you'll get sensible, practical advice.'

The nurse said, 'Either I get another rock or I want my money back.'

Norma had filled her suitcase with her prettiest things; there were a lot of sequins and three evening bags but very few warm comfortable clothes. Jack heard her dragging the suitcase down the stairs and ran to help her.

Yvonne turned off at Junction 21 and navigated a series of dual carriageways and several roundabouts the size of small offshore islands. She passed the single-storey, windowless buildings where things were made or warehoused, and the out-of-town shopping centres where identical shops sold identical goods and where a constant wind blew across the flat landscape. She drove by the multiplex cinema and its surrounding franchise restaurants where badly cooked processed food was sold to customers who lacked the confidence to complain, until she reached the mean single carriageway ring road which had cut established communities in half.

It had been good to hear Jack's voice on the phone; he was straight but Yvonne liked that about her brother. Whenever she was faced with a difficult decision or a moral conundrum she would ask herself, 'What would Jack do?'

Soon she was driving past familiar landmarks on the edge

of her old estate. The only good thing about the place where she'd been brought up was that it was only a mile and a half from the M1 and was easy to get away from. She slowed down and looked at the engineering factory where Derek, her estranged husband, had worked since leaving school at fifteen. He'd been as good as chained to a machine in there for eight hours a day, five and a half days a week. He'd earned a certificate for good time-keeping – he'd hung it on the wall in the kitchen of the house they had lived in together – but however hard he'd worked they'd still been poor. Not hungry or cold poor, but always having to be careful poor. There had only ever been the one week in the caravan at St Leonard's-on-Sea, never two. They hadn't been able to work out why they had not been able to save for their old age, or buy a car. In the end she had come to loathe him for being the first worker on the factory floor in the morning and the last to leave it at night.

Yvonne and Ali drew up outside Norma's house at the same time, blinding each other with their headlights. They walked up the path almost together. Yvonne said to Ali, 'Who called a taxi?'

Ali said, 'I'm not just a taxi. I'm private hire, innit.'

Jack opened the door to them. When he saw his sister he was amazed once again at the ability of women to transform themselves. It was as though the Yvonne on the doorstep had stepped out of the pod of the old Yvonne – she was younger-looking, sleeker, and the blurred outlines of the old Yvonne had been rubbed away, leaving a sharper, more angular woman.

He sent Ali through to the kitchen and detained his sister in the hall. Yvonne took the news reasonably calmly from Jack that her mother was now hostessing a crack house and was in love with a nineteen-year-old dealer called James, and that James and six other druggies were presently sitting around in the front room either coming down from the effects of crack or urgently wanting more.

Yvonne had once come home from school to find an escaped prisoner called Kevin O'Dwyer eating spaghetti hoops in front of the television. That evening she had watched the prisoner's delight when he was the top item on the regional news. A police spokesperson had said that the public must not approach him. O'Dwyer had rolled a joint and passed it to Norma, saying, 'You're a true friend to the friendless, Norma; you'll receive your reward in Heaven.'

Yvonne had almost been proud of her mother's Christian charity, but had been relieved when O'Dwyer had been caught on his way to early-morning Mass and returned to prison.

On going through to the kitchen Yvonne was introduced to the Prime Minister. She said, 'You must get sick of people telling you that you look amazingly like that prat Edward Clare.'

Jack said, 'The Prime Minister's not a prat, Vonnie, he's a decent bloke who's worked like a dog and he just made the mistake of trying to run a country without having any politics.'

The Prime Minister looked at Jack almost gratefully.

Norma said to Yvonne, 'Where's my money, you thieving bitch?'

Yvonne took the envelope out of her bag and threw it on to the kitchen table; 38,400 Euros spilled out.

'It's Monopoly money,' said Norma.

'It's the Euro,' said the Prime Minister.

Ali said, 'I had a German bloke tried to pay me in Euros. I drove him round to the police station but they told me they'd do me for wasting police time. So I had to take 'em and change 'em at a bank, innit.'

Jack said, 'How did you make that much money, Vonnie?'

'It's my women-empowering-women scheme,' she said. 'I get two women at a time to put in £3,000, and each of them get two other women to put in the same, and them two get another two, and them two get two more and so it goes on.'

'It's pyramid selling,' said Jack.

'The Department of Trade and Industry are looking into it,' said the Prime Minister. 'They've been flooded with complaints from women who have lost their savings.'

'I operate in Marbella where people have got a bob or two,' said Yvonne.

'Like me,' said Norma. 'I gave her £3,000.'

'And I've brung you back £24,000,' shouted Yvonne.

Jack said, 'Vonnie, you don't get anything for nothing in this world.'

'But you're wrong there,' said Yvonne. 'Some people do get something for nothing. Bankers do, an' it all works so long as everybody believes. It's like when we went to see *Peter Pan*, Jack, we all had to clap our 'ands real loud to prove we believed in fairies, well, that's how business operates, including mine. You just have to hope that not everybody asks for their money back at the same time. And people don't, they're all too busy clapping 'cause they want to believe and they love Tinkerbell.'

Jack said, 'I was never taken to see *Peter Pan*.'

Yvonne said, 'No, you're right, it was Stuart.'

The Prime Minister said, 'Is everybody guaranteed to win then, Yvonne?'

'Sooner or later,' she said. 'Why, are you interested in investing?'

Ali said, 'I wouldn't mind a few more details.'

Yvonne snapped, 'It's women only. As soon as men get involved it turns nasty and there's trouble.'

'Anyway, Mam,' she continued, 'I want you to come and live with me in Spain. I saw the *Leicester Mercury* in Marbella – one of my clients gets it posted out to her – and I nearly dropped dead when I seen your picture on the front page all battered and bruised, so you're coming back with me.'

302

'What about Pete?' said Norma. 'He can't fly, can he?'

Yvonne had never been a bird- or animal-lover and admired the Spanish authority's indifference to them. 'I'll buy you a bigger, more colourful bird, one with more life about it,' she said. 'And we'll keep it in a three-tiered cage on the terrace.'

Norma said, looking at Peter, 'No, I can't leave Pete. He's stuck by me through thick and thin so I'll have to stick by him.'

The Prime Minister said, 'Norma, y'know, I think that's, y'know, rather heartening.'

Jack said reluctantly, 'I'll look after Pete, Mam.'

Ali said, 'My kids would love a bird.'

The Prime Minister said, 'I'd gladly give it a home.'

Norma said angrily, 'But it's me Pete loves.' She talked to Peter directly: 'I'm your mam, aren't I, Pete.'

Jack said, 'Mam, go and get your passport, you're going to Marbella for two weeks tomorrow with our Vonnie while I sort everything out here. Pete will be famous. He'll be the first budgie to live in Downing Street, though not the first bird-brain, of course.'

There was a commotion in the hall and Jack went to investigate. James was pushing the guests out of the front door, throwing their shoes and clothes after them. The carpet salesman was already walking along the pavement barefoot; the nurse was picking up the contents of her handbag. James seemed to be under the impression that they were government agents. He came into the kitchen and opened the drawer of the kitchen table. When he saw that the tobacco tin was missing he accused Norma of using all of the crack herself. Yvonne started to speak but Jack shot her a warning glance and with a great effort she remained silent, though she went and stood behind her mother and put her arms protectively around Norma's shoulders.

Jack saw that the Prime Minister was also afraid and did the same for him.

Ali was used to the company of crackheads; a significant part of his work was taking them to and from various houses in search of the stuff. They hardly ever questioned the fare and didn't mind when he told them that he would have to leave the meter running while they conducted their business. He knew what it was like to be addicted – he used to smoke fifty Bensons a day and had once walked three miles to an all-night garage when his car was off the road. He was used to the rubbish they talked.

James said, 'You must give me what is mine; I am the Lord, the Almighty.'

When nobody moved or spoke he reached up and took down the cream-cracker tin and took out the little gun and put it to the side of the Prime Minister's head, knocking his wig off. The Prime Minister's hair seemed to have become remarkably grey in only one week.

Ali lied and said, 'I knew it was you from day one.'

Jack said to Ali, 'You've let yourself in for a lot of paper-work, Ali, the Official Secrets Act and all that.'

James was so shocked to see such a famous person he jabbed the gun against the side of the Prime Minister's head. The Prime Minister winced and James said, 'Sorry, did I hurt you?'

The Prime Minister said, 'No, not much, it's OK.'

James said in a confidential tone, 'I've got some insider information about Gibraltar, Prime Minister. Don't let those Spanish bastards get their hands on Gibraltar.' He then went on to say that the reason the Spanish government wanted Gibraltar back was because Gibraltar was entirely composed of crack. It was one big massive piece of rock; it was a geological miracle that was a gift from God to mankind. And if it were to be sympathetically mined there would be enough crack to keep every man, woman and child on earth well happy.

The Prime Minister listened as attentively as a man could with a gun pressed against his temple. He then said automatically, 'I am indebted to the honourable gentleman for that information, and I will pass it on to the relevant department.'

The Prime Minister understood for the first time the expression 'If I had a gun to my head'. It was remarkable how the gun clarified his thinking. His first thought was that the government should really do something on a huge and dramatic scale about crack-cocaine, and as the endless seconds dragged by he made his mind up about many problems that had recently been exercising him.

To attack Iraq would be madness; instead war would be declared on poverty. Centres of excellence would be built in the most deprived areas around the country. Tushinga would be taught to play jazz guitar or the violin in a music academy within walking distance of his house. The Prime Minister saw a future illustrated in the imagery used in *Watchtower* magazine, where Jehovah's Witnesses of every race walked in harmony in a verdant countryside by sparkling rivers – children could run and jump and play free from the constraints of insurance companies. He saw CCTV cameras removed and replaced by efficient street lighting; he saw state-run nurseries staffed by trained women and men where children would be taught the old art of how to play. He saw a no-fee state nursery at the end of Tushinga's road. Toyota would be free during the day to study and work. He saw glorious sports centres and more public parks and even with a gun to his head his fingers itched to sign the next election manifesto. The next generation of children and young people would be given the chance to realise their full potential.

In less than a second Jack had knocked the gun out of James's hand and James was on the floor straddled by Jack and Ali.

Norma pleaded, 'Don't hurt him, Jack, he's only a lad.'

Yvonne picked the gun up and looked at it curiously.

Norma said, 'Put it down, Yvonne, you've always been a clumsy bugger, you could have somebody's eye out with that.'

The Prime Minister once again fell back on statistics, and said that there were an estimated 740,000 unlicensed guns in Britain and that gun-related crime had risen by eight and a half disciples over the last five years.

Yvonne carried the gun carefully to the sink, threw it into the washing-up bowl and ran the tap over it. Bubbles came out of the barrel and collected on the surface like ghostly bullets.

The fight went out of James and he started to cry and said that it wasn't his fault that he'd turned out so bad. Jack cut him off. 'We don't want to hear the details. It'll be the same as everyone else's story; it'll be death, separation, disappointment, injustice and suffering, won't it?'

James nodded and Jack let him sit up. He was now weeping big jumbo-sized tears that fell off his chin on to his T-shirt. The Prime Minister turned his head away, unable to bear the sight.

Ali was unmoved. He said, 'If he started my kids on crack I'd pay somebody to blow his head off, innit. You can get it done for 250 quid in Leeds, less a seasonal discount.'

Norma said, 'Let him go, Jack, think about our Stuart.'

Jack said wearily, 'Stuart didn't buy heroin from the Co-Op, Mam, it was a bastard just like James who started him off.'

Norma tore off two pieces of kitchen towel and handed them to James, who blew his nose and wiped his eyes.

Jack asked Yvonne to go upstairs to Norma's room and find something with which to tie James's hands and feet together. James howled like a wolf throughout.

Jack said, 'You're lucky, James: you're going to prison for a long time and you'll be able to get on a degree course and you'll come out an educated man.' Then he unfastened Peter's cage from its stand and ushered everybody out of the house.

Chapter Twenty-Two

Clarke and Palmer watched the little gaggle leave the house. Their shift had finished but they were hanging around in the observation room to see how the story would end. They waited until both Ali and Yvonne's cars had left the estate before contacting the local drug squad, who, when they finally gained entry to Number Ten, assumed that James had been indulging in a bizarre sexual ritual since his hands and feet were tied together with several of Norma's lurid-coloured suspender belts and a dog collar on which hung a metal disc engraved 'Bob'.

They left Leicester and headed south on the M1 in a convoy of two. The Prime Minister sat in the back of Ali's taxi with one hand protectively on the top of the birdcage. He became more anxious with the passing of each mile. He felt fear gather around his heart. It was a familiar feeling. He was dreading returning to work the next day. There would be a thousand responsibilities waiting for him and he would be privy to many terrible secrets from around the world. He said to Jack and Ali, 'Wouldn't it be wonderful if we could drive to Dover, get on a ferry and disappear in Europe.'

Ali said, 'No, I'm missing my own bed, I can't sleep properly without Salma, she's fat and I'm thin but we fit together nice, innit.'

Jack turned in his seat to face the Prime Minister and said, 'Ed, you don't have to carry on being the Prime Minister, nobody's got a gun to your head.'

The three men laughed and Jack asked Ali to stop at the first service station, saying that he was hungry and needed to eat. Yvonne followed Ali's car as it turned into the slip road and parked in front of the main entrance. There was an air of celebration as the two parties made their way into the restaurant complex. Norma admired a display: a Horn of Plenty made of polyethylene which stood in the entrance to one of the self-service cafés; luscious plastic fruit and vegetables tumbled from its interior; sheaves of dusty corn poked from its rim; mini-boxes of Kellogg's breakfast cereal had been arranged by unseen hands to give an effect of plenitude. The Prime Minister's mouth watered. He joined Ali and Yvonne at the hot-food counter. Jack gave his mother a tray and told her to have exactly what she wanted to eat or drink, then excused himself saying he had a couple of phone calls to make.

The first was to Alexander McPherson to tell him that they would be returning to Downing Street in the early hours. McPherson said, 'I've just had an extraordinary email from the bollocking security services telling me that a man has been arrested in your mother's house who claimed that Edward Clare, the Prime Minister, tied him up with suspender belts and stole his crack. What the fuck is going on?'

Jack said, 'It'll all be in my report, McPherson. Book a room at a Travel Inn near Luton airport for my mother and sister and get them on the first flight to Malaga in the morning.'

McPherson said, 'Who the fuck do you think I am? Lunn bollocking Poly?'

Jack said, 'It's news management, McPherson. The females in my family have got big gobs.'

McPherson said, 'What's Eddy doing now?'

Jack glanced into the café. 'He's queuing up for an all-day breakfast,' he said. 'There's a truck driver behind him trying to look down the front of his dress.'

McPherson said that Jack would be required to give an initial verbal report at two o'clock the next afternoon.

Jack said he would be there. Though he couldn't guarantee the presence of the Prime Minister, who had been having serious doubts about his future in politics.

Alexander McPherson said, 'Your little holiday was meant to reinvigorate him; if he goes he takes me and you with him, Sprat.'

Jack looked into the café and saw the Prime Minister helping himself to dozens of sachets of salt, pepper and sugar and putting them into his handbag.

Jack had one more call to make. He had to talk to Pamela,

he felt like a river about to burst its banks; he had to tell her he loved her – he was afraid that unless he did he would be swept away from her by the flood of normal life. He leaned against the Horn of Plenty and pressed number one on his phone. When she answered he could tell from the noises in the background that she was in the accommodation block making her late-night checks. He became tongue-tied as soon as he heard her voice shouting, 'Hello! Hello!' above the noise of the barking dogs. She said, 'Is that you, Jack?'

'Yes,' he answered.

'Where are you?' she asked.

'Watford Gap service station,' he replied.

She laughed. 'The proverbial Watford Gap, poised between the hard north and the soft south.'

He could hear her lighting one of her cigarettes and he thought that he might take up smoking himself; he was sure that if he persevered he could grow to like it. He felt shy about telling her he loved her, knowing that his declaration would be picked up by tracking stations around the globe, but he told her anyway – why shouldn't the world know? 'I love you,' he said.

She said, surprised, 'Oh!'

There was a long silence, then he heard her saying goodnight to the dogs. It became quiet apart from the sound of her breathing. He imagined her walking up the path towards the house. He felt her absence like a physical pain and wished he was waiting in the kitchen for her with a drink and a clean ashtray. The silence was finally broken by the sound of liquid being poured into a glass. He said, 'Are you celebrating, Pamela?' He thought he would always call her Pamela and never Pam.

'As a matter of fact, I am,' she answered. 'It's many years since anybody told me they loved me, and even longer since I loved myself.'

Jack said, 'I don't believe in love at first sight.'

She said, 'Neither do I.'

'So I must have met you before,' said Jack.

'That must be it,' she agreed.

'I'll be back in London in a few hours. When are you going to come down for our Chinese meal?' said Jack.

'Very soon,' she said. 'I've been practising my chopstick technique since you left.'

Norma shouted that Jack's coffee was getting cold.

Jack said, semi-formally, 'I'll phone you again. Good-night, my love.'

He went into the gift shop and bought an absurd fluffy animal, a bear of some kind. Between its front paws the creature was holding a red satin heart on which had been embroidered in some Far Eastern factory unit, 'I love you'.

Later, in the car, when the Prime Minister asked what was in the bag, Jack showed him the bear and said, 'It's for your sister.'

The Prime Minister said, 'Pam hates anything like that. She was horribly cruel to my old toys when she was a child.'

Jack said with confidence, 'She'll like this.'

The next time the convoy of two stopped was at the motel near to Luton airport where Easy Jet would convey Yvonne and Norma through crowded skies to Malaga airport from where they would travel to Marbella.

After inspecting her room Norma came out with Yvonne to the car park to say goodbye to Peter. Peter was in his cage on the back seat of Ali's taxi, a mere smudge in the dark. The motorway thundered nearby. Norma crouched beside the car and told the dazed little bird to be a good boy and told him that she wouldn't have let James put him in the microwave. She told Peter that he was the most important person in her life. Jack and Yvonne exchanged an ironic glance and Yvonne muttered, 'Gee thanks.'

Norma stroked the bird's feathered head through the bars of his cage and said, 'Well ta-ra, then, Pete.'

The Prime Minister said, 'I'll simply say this to you, Norma: I'll do my very best to make sure that Peter becomes a fully integrated member of my family. He will be rehoused in a cage that accords with European guidelines and will receive regular veterinary care.'

'He likes to be talked to first thing in the morning,' said Norma.

Yvonne said, 'C'mon, Mam, they want to get off.'

She was right. Jack was twitching with impatience. He kissed his mother on her cheek and said, 'You've been a wonderful mother, to Pete.'

Norma nodded goodbye to the Prime Minister and Ali, then took Yvonne's arm and went into the Travel Inn. Before the door closed they heard her say to Yvonne, 'Are the fags a lot cheaper in Marbella, Vonnie?'

Jack said to the Prime Minister, 'She was a terrible mother to me, Vonnie and Stuart. She was lazy, selfish and pig-ignorant, and proud of the fact that she had never read a book. My mother put the prol into proletariat.'

The Prime Minister said, 'Well, we're all middle class now, Jack.'

Jack said, 'Don't be so fucking stupid, Ed. Can you imagine Toyota giving a dinner party and talking about house prices and the Turner Prize?'

Adele woke to find that it was dark outside and that she was alone in the small room. She lay back on the hospital pillows and touched the empty space where the end of her old nose used to be. She then felt the dressings which covered her new nose and she could tell that nobody would ever call her Concorde behind her back again.

She looked up at the white ceiling, where two small flies were dancing a jig. She felt deliciously drowsy; she had no wish to talk or give an opinion on any subject whatsoever.

There were books on the locker next to the bed, but the thought of opening them and making sense of the words inside exhausted her. She remembered that she was married to the Prime Minister of Great Britain, Edward Clare, and that she was the mother of Morgan, Estelle and Poppy, that she had written books and papers and given lectures and attended meetings and arranged dinners and receptions, that she could type, ski, dive, compute, drive, speak French, German and Italian, cook, iron, remove a stain from a carpet and juggle. For now it was enough just to lie in this high white bed and watch the flies dance. To simply exist.

Malcolm Black was sitting up in bed reading Engels' *The Condition of the Working Classes in England in 1844*. He was annotating it for Morgan Clare, as promised. Hannah came out of the adjoining bathroom wearing a short white cotton nightie and smelling of soap and toothpaste and said, 'Oh, Malc, you've got ink all over the sheets again.'

Malcolm put down the pen and nodded solemnly, registering his wife's complaint, but continued to turn the pages; he was looking for a particularly appalling passage about the rat population of Greater Manchester. She slid into bed beside him and leaned over and removed a collection of paper from his pyjama top pocket; he was in the habit of writing notes to himself before going to sleep.

She had bought him a pocket dictaphone for the bedside

table, but he had been unable to operate it successfully and it now rested unused in the bedside drawer, together with other un-mastered gadgets.

She un-scrunched one note, smoothed it flat and read:

Dear Ed,

It is with deep regret that I offer my resignation to you tonight . . .

She opened another.

Dear Ed,

It is with great regret that I have to tell you that I have been visited in your absence by a delegation of Members of Parliament and New Labour supporters requesting that I take over your duties as Prime Minister . . .

The third said:

Dear Ed,

It is with great regret that I have to tell you that I am intending to form a new political party, to be called the Old Labour Party . . .

None of them had been completed or signed.

'Listen to this,' Malcolm Black said. Then he read aloud: ' "Where there were still commons, the poor could pasture an ass, a pig, or geese, the children and young people had a place where they could play and live out of doors; but this is gradually coming to an end. The earnings of the worker are less, and the young people, deprived of their play-ground, go to the beer shops." '

'Or the crack dens,' Hannah Black muttered. Then she said, 'Malc, should you be helping Morgan with these projects? Isn't that his parents' job?'

Malcolm Black said, 'The boy is studying socialism; Ed and Adele know nothing about the subject.'

Hannah lay her head on his big chest and said, 'Which of those notes will you complete?'

'Probably all three,' he laughed.

She said, 'I'll base myself in the countryside and when you're Prime Minister you can visit me and any children we may have at the weekends, how does that sound?'

He said he thought it sounded very good indeed.

Ali's car drove through the Downing Street gates, waved on by Jack's colleagues. The door to Number Ten opened and the Prime Minister, carrying Peter's cage, Jack and Ali were ushered quickly inside. Jack had been instructed to take the Prime Minister immediately upstairs and to leave Ali in the hands of a security officer who introduced herself as Ms Pollock.

When he saw the Prime Minister, Alexander McPherson laughed and said, 'Jesus Christ, Ed, you look like a three-quid whore.'

The Prime Minister was hurt by McPherson's insult; he flounced into the bathroom and slammed the door.

Jack said, 'Go easy on him, McPherson, he's a woman on the edge of a nervous breakdown.'

The next morning when Estelle went down to the sitting room, she found her father apparently talking to himself. She overheard him say, 'I don't have to carry on, do I, Pete?'

Then she saw that he was addressing a birdcage in which sat a tatty little budgie the colour of her favourite blue pencil.

Her dad said his name was Peter.

The cage was cramped and rusting but within hours of Peter's arrival a new cage and stand had been delivered together with what a pet-shop owner in Pimlico described as 'state of the art budgie accessories'.

Later that afternoon Estelle knelt on a chair in the sitting room and observed Peter closely, wondering how old he was; according to the Internet, budgies had a lifespan of six to nine years. Estelle thought that Peter looked tired and fed up, a bit like the middle-aged people she was surrounded by in her own cage in Downing Street. She hardened her heart against being sad and prepared herself for the day when he would die. Everything died: people, flowers, birds, fish, mothers and fathers, babies and dogs, stars and trees. In the end, Estelle thought, nothing we do makes any difference.

She had once said this to her mother and Adele had said that existentialism was no excuse for not doing her homework. Mum said that Dad was a good example of somebody who had made a difference; he had already changed the face of British politics.

Morgan slept until midday, then he threw on his combats and put on his big boots and went downstairs to welcome his father back. Poor Dad was going through a stack of red boxes, but when he saw Morgan he put down his pen and held out his arms and said, 'Morgan, darling, how are you, son?'

Morgan knocked his knees against the corner of the desk in his haste to be embraced by his father.

'What was it like in the bunker, Dad?' he said. 'Was it cool?'

'I learned an awful lot about myself, Morgan,' the Prime Minister answered.

'Like what?' asked Morgan.

The Prime Minister longed to tell Morgan about the people he had met, the places he had visited and the experiences he had undergone. Instead he said, 'I simply say to you, Morgan, that Britain is prepared should the worst scenario happen.'

Morgan said, 'Dad, you're talking like a politician.'

'But I am a politician, darling,' said the Prime Minister, smiling.

'A politician without politics,' Morgan mumbled.

'Don't be absurd, Morgan; I have a very distinct political philosophy,' said the Prime Minister.

Morgan said excitedly, 'But you haven't, Dad. I've been going through your speeches searching for some kind of clear socialist vision, and I couldn't find one. You're like one of those priests who can't decide if God exists or not. If they're not sure, they should, like, leave the church and become a social worker or something.'

The Prime Minister stood up and pushed the red boxes on to the floor; they fell with a loud clatter. He said, 'I am the social worker to the nation, Morgan. I am all things to all people; I see all points of view; I try to make everybody happy. And when you are, y'know, slightly more mature, perhaps you'll understand the complexities and ambiguities of modern politics.'

Morgan picked up the red boxes from the floor and re-stacked them on the desk. 'Our family could do with a social worker,' he said.

The Prime Minister came out from behind his desk and said, 'My family is the most important thing in my life.'

'No we're not, Dad,' said Morgan passionately. 'We come somewhere between, like, Africa and the Middle East. You sacrificed us when you won the election; we could have been normal, Dad, just, like, normal!'

'I wanted to be a hero for you, Morgan.'

'All my heroes are dead apart from one,' said Morgan sadly.

'And who's that?' asked the Prime Minister.

But Morgan could not bring himself to tell his father that to him Malcolm Black was a heroic figure. Instead he said, 'The Rock, he's a wrestler.'

Edward took the children to see their mother in hospital. Poppy pulled at the dressing on Adele's nose. Adele had two black eyes but they were shining with happiness. Estelle told her mother about Peter and said she would like to own a pet shop when she grew up. Adele agreed with her that it would be a very pleasant way of making a living. Morgan gave a short speech about the iniquities of keeping a living creature in a cage and said that Peter should at least be allowed to fly around the room twice a day.

The family debated this point and agreed that the bird's cage door would be left open at certain times to be determined by Estelle.

Epilogue

Jack stood at the side of the door to Number Ten, leaning on the black railings, watching a removal van being loaded. The traditional May Day riot had passed peacefully. There had been a little light looting of a few tartan skirts from a shop window in Regent Street, and now some of the protestors were returning to their trains and buses having had a good day out.

Jack could hear in the distance the last speech of the meeting in Trafalgar Square.

Malcolm Black came out and joined Jack while he waited for his car to arrive. Jack said, 'It's a lovely evening, Prime Minister.'

Malcolm looked towards the gates of Downing Street where a large crowd had gathered. He waved his arm; the gesture was greeted by equal amounts of cheers and boos. His car drew up and Malcolm Black got in and sat beside the driver.

Jack looked up and saw a tiny scrap of cobalt blue fluttering erratically against the pale evening sky. It was Peter. Jack started to run; he followed Peter out of the street to ironic cheers from the police and the crowd at the gates.

Peter flew along Whitehall to the Cenotaph, where he rested for a while unnoticed by the crowds below. Then, with Jack helpless to stop him, he flew in a direct line towards the bigger birds in Trafalgar Square and to almost certain death.

SUE TOWNSEND

THE SECRET DIARY OF ADRIAN MOLE AGED 13¾

Wednesday June 10

Pandora and I are in love! It is official! She told Claire Nelson, who told Nigel, who told me. I told Nigel to tell Claire to tell Pandora that I return her love. I am over the moon with joy. I can overlook the fact that Pandora smokes five Benson and Hedges a day and has her own lighter. When you are in love such things cease to matter.

The Secret Diary of Adrian Mole Aged 13¾ is an unabashed, pimples-and-all glimpse into the troubled life of an adolescent. Writing candidly about his parents' marital troubles, the dog, his life as a tortured poet and 'misunderstood intellectual', teenager Adrian Mole's painfully honest diary makes hilarious and compelling reading.

THE GROWING PAINS OF ADRIAN MOLE

Monday November 29

My mother's gone right off me since Rosie was born. She was never a particularly attentive mother – I always had to clean my own shoes. But just lately I have been feeling emotionally deprived. If I turn out to be mentally deranged in adult life, it will all be my mother's fault.

Troubled teenager Adrian Mole continues to struggle valiantly against the slings and arrows of growing up and his own family's attempts to scar him for life. In between the ups and downs of his relationship with the divine Pandora and worrying that his genius is going unrecognized, Adrian Mole chronicles the pains and pleasures of a misspent adolescence.

SUE TOWNSEND

TRUE CONFESSIONS OF ADRIAN ALBERT MOLE

Monday June 13

I had a good, proper look at myself in the mirror tonight. I've always wanted to look clever, but at the age of twenty years and three months I have to admit that I look like a person who has never even *heard* of Jung or Updike.

Adrian Mole has grown up. At least that's what it says on his passport. But living at home, clinging to his threadbare cuddly rabbit 'Pinky', working as a paper pusher for the DoE and pining for the love of his life, Pandora, has proved to him that adulthood isn't quite what he hoped it would be. Still, intellectual poets can't always have things their own way...

Included here are two other less well-known diarists: Sue Townsend and Margaret Hilda Roberts, a rather ambitious grocer's daughter from Grantham.

ADRIAN MOLE: THE WILDERNESS YEARS

Wednesday April 3

I am twenty-four and one day old. *Question:* What have I done with my life? *Answer:* Nothing. Grahame Greene died today. I wrote to him four years ago, pointing out a grammatical error in his book, *The Human Factor*. He didn't reply.

Adrian Mole has at last reached physical maturity, but he can't help roaming the pages of his diary like an untamed adolescent. Finally given the heave-ho by Pandora, he seeks solace in the arms of Bianca, a qualified hydraulic engineer masquerading as a waitress. Between his dishwashing job and completing his epic novel, *Lo! The Flat Hills of My Homeland*, Adrian hopes that fame and fortune will not keep him waiting much longer.

SUE TOWNSEND

ADRIAN MOLE: THE CAPPUCCINO YEARS

He's Back. Aged 30 ¼. Twenty-first-century Mole.

Now in his thirties, Adrian's still worrying: can he be a good father? Is Viagra cheating? Why won't the BBC produce *The White Van*, his serial-killer comedy?

Will he find the fulfilment he seeks as a celebrity chef, single parent and celibate novelist? Is there a place for Adrian Mole in Blair's Brave New Britain?

THE QUEEN AND I

When a Republican party wins the General Election, their first act in power is to strip the royal family of their assets and titles and send them to live on a housing estate in the Midlands.

Exchanging Buckingham Palace for a two-bedroomed semi in Hell Close (as the locals dub it), caviar for boiled eggs, servants for a social worker named Trish, the Queen and her family learn what it means to be poor among the great unwashed. But is their breeding sufficient to allow them to rise above their changed circumstance or deep down are they really just like everyone else?